Miners' Revenge

Miners' Revenge

by
Mark R. Sneller

Published by Fresh Air Press

Visit Mark's website at
markrsneller.com

This edition was prepared for publication by
Ghost River Images
5350 East Fourth Street
Tucson, Arizona 85711
www.ghostriverimages.com

Cover images by Calistemon

ISBN 978-1-7368917-8-0
Library of Congress Control Number: 2022915784

Printed in the United States of America
September, 2022

Other books Mark R. Sneller:

A Breath of Fresh Air

Greener Cleaner Indoor Air

Greener Cleaner Indoor Air – 2nd Edition

Toxic Exposure

Dying to Read

The Mars Virus Series

 The Mars Virus

 The City Beneath the Earth

 Treasures

 Soap Opera

Strange Adventures

Rising To Eminence

Dedication

This novel is a small token of appreciation for those miners who braved the known and the unexpected worldwide over the centuries, many of whom suffered and died. They spent, and still spend, their mining years in hard labor, while their families endured. Thanks to the technology they helped bring about, their laboring efforts actually made their lives, and ours, less arduous. In the end, they brought civilization to the world and endeavor to provide every person the fruits of their labors.

Where we go with civilization is up to the rest of us.

Acknowledgments

The author wishes to extend his grateful thanks to Lionel Montana, not only for his vast international experiences and years in the mines as an explosives expert, but for the hours he spent in sharing his mining life with the author, enticing me to become captivated with the industry.

Thanks are also extended to Aubrey Lee, geologist, and Vice President of Advanced Exploration for Big River Exploration, in San Manuel, Arizona, for sharing the depth of her knowledge and mining experience, which included a detailed explanation about core sampling by demonstrating their physical characteristics going down to some 4000' in depth; and to Melanie Ginther, Site Supervisor/Drill Coordinator, for the same company, for pointing me in the directions I needed to follow in order to continue with this story.

My thanks would not be complete without acknowledging John Hernandez, former miner, Industry Liaison, newspaperman, and keeper of the archives, in both San Manuel and Oracle, Arizona, in allowing me to peruse articles going back decades. His experiences and knowledge of the archives is profound.

My grateful thanks is extended to Michael White of Ghost River Images for his infinite patience in preparing this story for publication, as I go through seemingly endless edits of this and my other manuscripts.

Introduction

The obtaining of ores from the earth originated some 4000 years ago, coal some 3000 years ago. This spring-boarded the human race into the transition stages from no metals to bronze and iron. Numerous factors contributed to the leap forward including ore availability, transportation, trade agreements, creativity, farming, and, as always, better tools for self-defense and warfare.

Mining was and still is a tough, hot, humid, laborious business fraught with danger at almost every turn. There are approximately 13,000 active ore mines in the United States alone, with perhaps 100 times that number of closures. A single relatively small city in mid-Arizona (Superior) has some 35,000 mines, both closed and open.

Mines are closed because they were played out and could no longer be cost effective; suffered an insurmountable cave-in, explosion, or fire; were flooded and lacked adequate means to remove the water; or perhaps due to legitimate environmental concerns. The arguments presented by environmental groups in many cases are profound, and the arguments for the continuation of a particular mining operation may be weak. In other instances, it's a toss-up, which frequently leads to the intervention of government arbitrators.

As an example of this, congress allocated a huge sum to develop 3000 acres of land situated an hour outside of Phoenix, Arizona. Unfortunately for the developers, it is located in the Tonto National Forest and home to the Apache Indians. Their cause is supported by various groups and state representatives. On the other side, this land is projected to become one of the world's largest underground copper mines. Known locally as Oak Flat, the project is on hold. These disputes commonly occur across the nation, if not the world.

Yes, pollutants are sent aloft from the smelting process. For the most part, smoke stacks 500-800 feet in height alleviate the problem by permitting the toxic fumes, consisting of sulfur dioxide, carbon monoxide, carbon dioxide, nitrous oxide, sulfuric acid, fly ash, and heavy metals, to enter higher wind currents, arguably, in order to avoid contaminating the nearby populace. The local population, including the people of neighboring countries, would argue the effectiveness of that procedure. Technology has served to filter these gases in many cases, but different countries have different rules and regulators' hands are often tied through a maze of bureaucracies and nepotism.

The opening of a successful mine can bring great prosperity to a community as long as it is profitable. Labor unions in the U.S. have played a major role in providing good wages to mine employees, which drives prosperity. Some states have right to work laws, which provide the same benefits to miners as the unions without employees having to join the union. However, once the mine closes, the opposite occurs. Ghost towns appear, a contraction of a one-time vibrant community.

Politics, hubris, bitter feuds with labor unions, and general ineptitude in running a mining business frequently enters the closure-equation. Worker strikes and violence occasionally drew and still draw attention to mismanagement, while positive negotiations occur frequently.

One of the worst occurrences of mine mismanagement occurred in 1917 in Bisbee, Arizona, a monster open pit copper mining operation that serves as a tourist attraction today, in which some 1300 employees were summarily fired because they objected to the working conditions that were deplorable in all respects. Discrimination against Mexican-American and other immigrants was rampant by American-European owners and site managers, not only in Bisbee, but throughout the other mines operating in the state by Phelps-Dodge at the time. Workers were rounded up and bused without food and water to New Mexico. The company argued that, by protesting, American interests in WWI were being harmed. Union representation at that time lacked the strength of today's unions. No person or agency ever got charged in the case (United States vs. Wheeler, 1920).

Oddities are numerous. For example, heavily investigated in many countries is the role of salt mines for decontamination of radioactive wastes. Much of the salt is marketed, but afterward, within the caves, countless metal drums filled with radioactive waste was and is stored. These originated from the U.S., Japan, and other countries where nuclear power is generated. At first thought, the salt would cause the drums to leak. However, reportedly, like lime, the salt absorbs the waste; thus the heat and radioactivity generated by the waste is kept localized.

As recent decades wore on, civil rights enactments came to the fore. Nevertheless, few women were hired. When they were employed by the industry, it was often as truck drivers. Even then, most complaints by women centered on being propositioned. Until the time of their entrance into the mining field, their role was relegated to teaching about geology or land reclamation. Historically, however, there are many notable examples of women who served as ore prospectors, occasional coal miners, financiers, and discoverers of great ore bodies.

The role of women in mining changed radically in the United States during the 1980s and '90s. Civil rights movements and federal equal opportunity legislation enabled women to break into the United Mine Workers of America union to eventually occupy every position in the industry, albeit at only some 10% of the labor force. Becoming a hard rock or a coal miner is not a goal every schoolgirl aspires toward.

Over the past half-century, mine safety has improved significantly thanks to federal legislation, the formation of unions, civic groups, and technological improvements. Today's deaths and injuries are a small fraction of what they once were. This is true throughout the world, although the vast majority of operations still employ slave labor with no benefits and extremely poor working conditions.

There are many not-so-glamorous aspects of the industry, yet provide us with the fruits of civilization, such as sand and gravel production, absorbent zeolite for filtration and odor removal, titanium, aluminum-bauxite, and rare earths critical for electronics. The search for gemstones is another story altogether.

This is a book of fiction based on true stories of miners. Admittedly, it is highly fictionalized at times to enhance the readability. It is my intent to present the reader with a taste of the industry, perhaps to better appreciate what goes into the making of products that augment virtually every aspect of our daily lives.

The use of copper is critical, not only for the operation of windmills and solar power, but for virtually anything requiring the transport of electrons, including medical equipment. Lest we not forget, add electric cars, buses, trucks, and sea craft to the list.

This book is not about copper mining, per se. It is about those who were, and are, involved in the mining industry and the adventures they tell, with a certain poetic license exercised by the author. An honest effort is made to avoid endless detail regarding the entire mining process and at the same time, but not being overly pedantic.

An abundance of excellent literature is available written by miners themselves, who tell their own stories. Miners' Revenge is not one of them. It is about a man on a mission who must learn patience, to take things as they come, until opportunity presents itself.

The interested reader is invited to go online to research his or her favorite mining topic. They will find the rabbit hole to be deep and broad. Indeed, in today's world, some 14 American univesities offer degrees in mining/or mineral engineering with topics that delve deeply into mathematics, thermodynamics, geological sciences and chemistry. Depending on the school, the topic at hand, and the teacher, pollution cleanup may or may not be emphasized.

The author is tempted to fall into those rabbit holes. These include the history of mining, advanced inorganic chemistry, geology, gemology, hydrology, air pollution, statistical analysis, microbiology, accuracy in assays, radioisotopes, transportation, electricity, and even magnetism.

This story will not go into the extensive glossary of mining terms, of which there are hundreds, nor the great variety of signs posted throughout the worksite, nor the numerous bell ringing codes used by the workmen, nor will we elaborate on the heroes of mining that history has all but forgotten.

Thus, I am forced to work a compromise between fictional science, reality, and creative writing in an effort to create a good easy read.

Finally, if the reader thinks that events such as these can't happen, the author might suggest they might have already occurred, they just never made the news.

Prologue

When you're a miner, you're a heartbeat away from death. If you're working at an altitude of 13,000 feet and you're an explosives expert, it's less than a heartbeat. It's easy to make a mistake when the oxygen level is 40% that of sea level and you're trying to think clearly.

This story begins in Papua New Guinea, the eastern portion of New Guinea, the second longest island in the world, behind Greenland as the longest, located to the north of Australia and only a stone's throw from the 18,000 islands belonging to Indonesia. The western half of the island is considered to be part of Indonesia, while the eastern half, known as Papua New Guinea, or PNG, is an independent nation gaining its independence from Britain in 1975.

New Guinea is situated at the juncture of the Pacific Tectonic Plate and the Indo-Australian Plate. It is both green and lush, as well as volcanic. The island is basically tropical and rains some 100-300 inches a year. It, too, has an abundance of ores.

Looking at a map, it wouldn't take a geologist to see the island had split from the Australian continent eons ago by inserting the southern peg of New Guinea into the northern portion of the larger land mass.

In each of the past few years, in PNG, Groebels Mining Conglomerate recovered from PNG a good $250 million dollars in gold, silver, and copper alone, with another 24 other minerals, bringing in another 15 percent. Ostensibly, this is a lot of income for an impoverished nation. Unfortunately, in this case, little of it came back to the people. The mine workers received subsistence wages and no real communities became enriched. In addition, the extent of the pollution to the waterways from the mining operations (and those elsewhere) had been presented in numerous volumes over the decade. It caused such grievous damage to wildlife, fish, and vegetation to require national action in many cases. In too many cases, too little too late.

Once geologists discovered copper near the summit of a 16,000 foot glacier in PNG, it took years for mining permits to be obtained. Following the permits, the mining company created a good uphill road necessary for heavy equipment to bring materials and to level the land for construction of a community, which would consist of professional miners, with many Palauan villages already entrenched even higher than the new camp.

PART I

1

New Zealand lies directly to the southeast of the Australia and is abundant in ores and cash crops. The ores include gold, silver, iron, coal and limestone. The crops include oats, barley, maize, potatoes, and peas, which are grown in rotation to keep the soil fertile.

Draco Harwood grew up a New Zealander, or Kiwi, as they were called, a name their soldiers earned during WWI. The name stuck because, like the bird, they were unique, adaptable, and a little quirky.

At the age of 16, he killed a man. Because of that single act, Draco Harwood was destined to have his demons. He would always wrestle whether he did it on purpose, though a fit of rage, or by accident.

At the time of the time of the incident, Wellington, New Zealand's capitol city, authorized the operation of numerous gold and platinum mines, which employed many hundreds of employees. Their income affected many thousands of families and businesses, small and large. Harwood's adopted father had spent his career working various mines. Childless and after two miscarriages, the Harwoods made the decision to adopt. The family was not ostentatious, but lived comfortably and maintained decent values, which they taught to their new son.

As the boy grew, school counselors suggested that he was a vessel filled with rage. In their view, he had witnessed something prior to the time when the Harwood's took him in, which had affected him greatly. Try as he might, the youth couldn't recall anything of magnitude that might lead to such behavior. The parents remained mute on the subject.

One evening at the dinner table, Harwood's father, Mason, told him they would have to take it easy on money for a while. They needed to adapt to the times.

Two men in the community loaned money to poker players in debt. The debtor always found a way to pay it off, or he would be blackballed from then on forevermore. One of those men, Mason, charged a low rate of interest, while another man named Arnold charged a very high rate of interest on his loan.

One day, a man, whom Mason knew well, approached him to explain that he owed a large sum to Arnold and if the money didn't get repaid soon, Arnold promised to have him killed. Sympathetic to the cause Mason loaned him the money, but never saw it again, because, quite accidentally, the man died in a cave-in after he had repaid the debt to Arnold. However, it they lived from paycheck to paycheck, they should be all right. Mason's family had no reserve cash. Fortunately, their home was paid for and beauty lay beyond the front door where a forest of native Silver Fir Spruce was capped with 11,000' snow covered Mt. Tasman in the background.

Some months later, sixteen-year-old the dark eyed Draco made a late night walk to a nearby store and encountered a drunk man who ran into him. The man became boisterous and argumentative and tried to strike him. No stranger to fights, the growing youth countered the blow and rained punishment upon the man until he lay unconscious. Harwood looked around to see there were no witnesses and quickly returned home to tell what had happened. When he described the man he had beaten, it turned out to be Arnold. The following day, the authorities reported the beating death of Arnold. The police assumed he had been beaten by somebody who owed him money. The police had compiled a long list of suspects. Draco Harwood was not one of them.

"Honey, you didn't do it on purpose," Draco's mom, Patricia, offered. Nearing fifty, she was a little fleshy. Once a prom queen, she married her high school sweetheart, Mason, and started a family. Well kept, but conscious about her appearance, perhaps overly conscious, she preferred sack dresses at home for comfort, and more likely, to disguise her growing figure. However, she did emanate her youthful beauty when she dressed up for church on Sunday mornings.

"The thing is, Mum, I felt like I had to keep beating him. Don't ask me why," Draco replied, puzzled by his own behavior. He had been brought up in an environment of comradery, his father's world.

Mason contributed, "I don't think there's any question. The anger comes from your earlier years before we adopted you."

"Mason, you don't need to go there," Patricia admonished. "He needs to deal with the present, not the past."

"It's about time he knew," Mason threw in. "He'll need to deal with the future."

"Know what?" Draco demanded, beginning to get agitated at the back and forth between his parents, especially when he was the topic of conversation.

Patricia gave her husband a stern look. "Let it go, Mason."

Draco's curly black hair bounced as he shook his head. "Let what go? Come on. Out with it. I just killed a man. What could be worse than that?"

Mason took a deep breath and said, "The orphanage where we found you has an obligation to tell each adoptive parent what they know about the child they are adopting. If they don't know anything, then they'll say they don't know."

"And?" asked Draco.

"And, well. . ." Mason began.

"And?" Draco prompted once again, growing impatient, tired of the games.

Mason gathered himself and looked his son in eye. He spit it out. "Your father savagely beat your mother to death. He had been beating her for years. Authorities believe you witnessed the event."

Draco flopped back in his chair, looked wide-eyed from his father to his mother and back again. Running both hands through his hair, he sat straight once more, and asked, almost accusatorily, "What happened to him? How did I get to an orphanage? Why did you take me if you knew what had happened? Why . . ."

Patricia held up her hand to stop the boy. She cried, "At the time, you lived in a flat. The neighbors heard the fighting and called the police yet another time. When they arrived it was too late. Your father was arrested, convicted for a First Degree Murder stabbing death of your mother. In turn, somebody knifed him death in prison a few years later. There were no other relatives to take you, as far as the authorities could find, so the state turned you over to the shelter. We found you only months later and fell in love with you the moment we saw you. We didn't care about your past. If anybody needed love, you did."

"Enough for now. Tomorrow we can talk about your future," Mason concluded, making a move as if to stand.

"No, we'll talk about it now," Draco insisted, stubbornly, like his adoptive father. Who wanted to be lectured about themselves? Why had he even asked? Draco's growing brain did its best to process the massive amount of data input.

Seeing his obvious discomfort, Patricia offered gently, but with a note of enthusiasm, "Honey, maybe you should keep going to school. You'll get over it in time. You can work off your energy on the rugby field."

Draco shook his head. "First off, I don't see myself doing particularly well in my school, or any other school after this, so what's the point of getting a formal education? Do you think I can get my brain wrapped around normal life after this?"

"Now that is one of the dumbest things I've ever heard you say," Mason shot.

Draco hung his head a moment and mumbled, "I know, I know."

"At least your father graduated high school before he went to the mines," Patricia added, still trying her best to keep her son from leaving home, which appeared to be where she attempted to direct the conversation.

"In general, though, I can't argue against you quitting school, at least for a while," Mason agreed, settling down again. It wasn't his decision to make. "In your view, what are your options?"

After a short discussion, the three agreed to let him apply to a mining school. New mines were opening and work could be found, even for 16 year-old males. With Mason's recommendation, he could get in. Whether or not he kept the job would be up to him.

Draco's high school would miss him, in part because of his excellence in mathematics, but primarily because the school would lose the captain of their championship rugby team. He had hoped to make their national team within a few years, the second best rugby team in the world, behind South Africa. Now his dream and their dream would have to be left behind in the face of an instant reality check where the youth suddenly faced a major a crossroads in life. He had no choice but to let down this team and himself. His mother was wrong. Even if he played, his concentration would be diluted and the team would suffer. In the end, survival came first.

Thus, he began as a common laborer at a mine separate from the one his father worked at because of new openings. Every other day he worked a double shift, learning the operation of heavy equipment during the second shift, working in the mines during the first shift. On another three days he took classes. Sundays were off.

On one occasion, he was so tired on the

way home after a 16 plus hour workday, he fell asleep in the back corner of the bus. At the end of his own shift, the driver failed to notice the youth and drove the bus into the yard and exited. When Draco awoke he had no idea where he was or the time. He managed to exit the bus to find himself in a fenced in compound among other buses with no way out. He had eaten all the food in his lunch pail, which had lasted him throughout the day.

He had no prospect to obtain food for the next day and did the only thing he could do. He reentered the bus and stretched out on the rear seat to sleep until dawn.

The sound of a new driver awoke him. He announced his presence and told his tale, seemingly unperturbed. The driver sympathized with him, led him into the offices, introduced him to the other drivers as they arrived, provided him with a voluminous cup of coffee, some breakfast roles to take with him for the day, and pointed him in the direction of the bathroom.

Harwood arrived at work early that day and surprising himself, totally enjoying the classwork that related to decibel levels associated with blast dynamics.

Within a year, he had taken classes in general mining operations, tunneling, geology, and advanced explosives. He excelled in the latter because of his analytical mind and a newfound lust for diving into danger.

Draco's father's words rung in his head like a bell: "Son, don't ignore something if you feel it's working for you. Once you get over the first humps, it becomes easier. Hard work is never hard when it's what you love to do. The more you accomplish, the easier it becomes to accomplish more."

Over the course of the next several months, Harwood had a lot of time to think about 'what ifs'. What if he hadn't gone to the store? What if Arnold hadn't died, or what if he had avoided the altercation altogether?

Instead, like some space-time traveler, he found himself in an alternate universe. Almost overnight, he found himself building a career. He told himself, *Don't screw it up.*

Each morning, Draco left his small apartment in Wellington, caught a bus to a pick-up point and then boarded a second bus to the mine, a quick 20 minute ride to the worksite. He soon found himself laying track and sledge hammering spikes into rail base plates for the iron cars to pull copper ore from the deepest levels of the mines. He rarely saw his parents, except when he returned home for a visit. Each time he did, they expressed surprise at his growth, both professionally and physically.

At these times, he shied away from his friends. He couldn't come up with a satisfactory explanation for his sudden disappearance from school. His friends stopped by the house for information, but only received the reply that he had been thinking about it for some time and told them he had made the decision to become a miner. They couldn't say he moved out of the country to visit a sick aunt when somebody might see him. Then the parents would be lying, something not in their blood.

Draco soon repaid the small loan his parents had given him as a starting/parting gift and within two years, he sent serious money back home on a monthly basis. He worked the site for another 18 months and became promoted to shift supervisor until the company offered him the opportunity to work at an open pit copper mine down in Australia. Now he *would* leave the country. Mason strongly advised him to do so for the experience and would no longer accept his money, as he and his mother were now completely debt free. Not yet 20 years of age, Draco had put on 30 pounds of muscle, stood six-three and had grown a healthy beard, bathing himself in hard physical labor whenever he could.

Because of his size and great strength, Draco graduated to working alongside others shoring up timbers in any one of forty or more levels, called drifts, each measuring some 10 feet on a side, 60 feet above one another and miles in length. Whether coal, gold, silver, copper, manganese, tungsten, or any other ore, each threatened death in its own way.

2

Harwood soon found himself losing his weekly paycheck to the hard-core poker players, just trying to be one of the boys. After eating beans and potatoes for too long, he decided to either quit the game altogether and wimp out, or to use the innate skill he had always possessed paying attention to detail and his memory. He watched the other men as much as he watched his own cards.

At work, Harwood sought the most dangerous tasks and found himself associating with those who planted the explosives. One of them, named Josh Alday, an Aussie, preferred a buzz cut to his hair, but maintained a full beard, which gave his head an asymmetrical appearance. Two years older than Harwood, he was not quite as tall, but just as broad at the shoulder. The men bonded quickly and vowed to stay together if at all possible throughout their careers.

Over the next several years, the friends found himself being offered jobs in Queensland, Asia,

Mexico, and Canada. They accepted them all, because experience is everything.

Then, the opening of the gold fields in PNG brought in a new era to the republic. Endless riches awaited the owners of Groebels Industries, a company operating in a dozen countries and growing. Mikael Nordstrom, the Site Manager/ Supervisor held no scruples, preferring to covet slave labor from indigenous Papuans for the grunt work, paying them a dollar a day (more, if they had additional wives) rather than paying the outrageous wages demanded by experienced and knowledgeable men such as Harwood and Alday, and the team they had built. The whole scheme smelled from the start.

Anna Fischer founded Groebels, who had a bent for prospecting in Germany, began panning for gold in her early twenties. Following leads, she discovered enough of the ore on her own to begin a mine. She filed a claim, obtained loans, hired workers, repaid the loans, and found more gold. She married a tough cut-throat railroad tycoon named Groebels who always treated her with respect, while he built an empire for them. With no children to inherit the business, their chief operating officer named Nordstrom received the honors. If anything, he was even more cutthroat, in a manner of speaking, than the CEO. A century after Anna Fischer made her first strike, Groebels mined the world.

When it rained in PNG, it rained hard. Between cloudbursts, the insects would come out from cracks in the earth, followed by great black collections of dragon flies, followed by swirling murmurs of bats that emerged from their own caves each day to return each evening after insect hunting. A separate fertilizer industry could be started from the guano, if the company chose to do so. The miners, natives and otherwise, were always wary of the occasional rabies-laden bat that might have wandered into one of their shafts. Uncontaminated drinking water was always a problem in these outlying areas, no matter what the elevation, whether it be by coliform bacteria or through over-mineralization, which would require filtration before boiling.

Following geological data in PNC, Harwood's men sunk an elevator shaft down 1000' to create the beginning of passages. These would lead into the mountainside where the mining for copper ore would begin. They demarked each passage that required opening, after which they lowered equipment to remove debris, known as muck. Newly installed conveyer belts dumped the muck over the side of the mountain to be front-end loaded onto trucks and hauled to the newly constructed smelters where the various ores would be separated.

To Groebels, the installation of mesh across the roof a man-made cavern to prevent the falling of rocks could be done by anyone, whether properly used spikes were used or not. The same could be said for welding, as long as fire safety rules were followed, a big if; however, governmental intervention prevented Groebels from firing the entire Kiwi team, something they wanted to do to save money.

Harwood and his partner, Josh Alday—men always worked in teams—used two cases of dynamite to open another section of rock. Working on a 7% decline, they drilled 10-foot diameter holes into the rock, inserted the sticks in the center, sides, top and bottom, linking each of the sticks to one another in a chain. In a microsecond, the center would blow first to create a hole, followed by the sides, top, and bottom, all in order. He and Alday ran the leads to the plunger far back from the blast zone and, after one last clearance check, pushed down on the plunger.

After the dust settled, more track would be laid to move equipment forward, the pile of muck would then be hauled away to begin the sequence all over again.

A lot of natives lost their lives on other poorly supervised mining jobs when they took quickie courses on the use of dynamite, or not properly shoring up timbers and braces.

Certainly, in this operation, one didn't want to get the native Papuan people pissed off at you. The dark-skinned natives, who painted their faces yellow with arrows stuck through their noses and walked around with spears, had their own code of ethics that did not mesh well with commercial business practices. Fortunately, more literate natives had previous experiences with foreign mining operations and could follow orders. These were the ones who were hired, but were not permitted to co-mingle at the compound inhabited by the few remaining "professional" miners.

Six months after the project began, Harwood was called into the office and informed, by a man he had never seen, that because he and his entire crew could not be fired, they were strongly encouraged to leave on their own. Groebels wanted to hire locals. Therefore, the Kiwis were to ordered to publicly announce their resignation *en masse*. When Harwood protested, the messenger unabashedly told him that if they said a word about it, their families would meet with unexpected accidents, whether or not they had joined the crew to live in PNG, or still lived back in New Zealand.

Harwood had a vision of Patricia and Mason who had treated him with love and gave him the life he now enjoyed. The ominous words pushed a button in him. The hard living, hand drinking, poker-playing miner did not take well to the news. In the absence of witnesses, he calmly walked up to the man and shattered his face with a terrible single blow straight on, followed by a second to the side of his face breaking his jaw in several places. Prepared to launch a third, he halted his assault, his past remembrances holding his arm in check. The man dropped to the ground, blood gushing from his mouth and his shattered nose and teeth to spread a red pool over the floor.

Almost as though another being had taken over his mind, controlling his actions, Harwood knelt down next to the man, put his mouth close to his ear and said, simply, "You should know better than to say something like that. I'm going to find out who put you up to this and, if I can, do the same to him."

Draco, what are you saying, this isn't you, he admonished *himself. Or is it? Comes with the territory. The man didn't apologize before he said what they ordered him to say. He didn't even say he had been ordered to threaten us, as though the threat was his own dictum. It might have made a difference. Oh, well, too late now.*

The man might only be the messenger, but, even after reconstructive surgery, he would be eating mashed potatoes for the rest of this life. To some members of Groebels' hierarchy, messengers were easy to come by. To Draco, he felt vindicated and proud of himself. He had restrained from beating the man to death. He, in particular, had an issue in the way they had been fired. Threats against their families pushed him over the edge to cast a remembrance that would forever hang over him and his workmates like a curse.

Vindictively, Harwood stored the information for a later date. Groebels would pay out more than they saved. Revenge takes patience. If it were at all within his ability, he would ensure that Groebels would lose a fortune and would be reminded of why they had lost so much.

Joshua Alday also took the matter seriously. He confronted the mine superintendent, Mikael Nordstrom, whom he believed was behind the firing with the words, "If anything at all happens to a family member of any team member, I will personally come looking for you no matter where in the world you might hide."

"I'll remember what you said," Nordstrom replied, totally ignoring his own edict to the same effect.

"Oh, I want you to," Alday retorted.

Retribution can be a two way street.

3

A dozen years after the incident and the firing, many of Harwood's men had either retired or hired into management positions by other companies, of which there were numerous, while Harwood kept his eye on the activities of Groebels. In this business, many had short memories when altercations were involved. In Harwood's case, if anybody did recall the incident surrounding his dismissal, well, hey, it was just another day at the ranch.

Harwood gave serious thought about going to Alaska where Groebels had just opened a silver mine, when Australia announced the purchase of acreages they had purchased in Arizona. The entire southeastern quadrant of the state, along with large portions of New Mexico, Texas, northern Mexico, and the southern portion of the Rocky Mountains reeked of copper, silver, and gold, elements that geological forces had uplifted to where they became mineable.

Copper Mining, Inc., hired Harwood and Alday to head a team for operations in southern Arizona in what could turn out to be the largest copper mining operation in the world. The main ore body ran some 9000 feet both in length and width and 1000' deep. The body was structured like a shortened molar tooth with the ore body as the pulp. Both men accepted leadership roles, accepting their enhanced paychecks without complaint. Groebels would have to wait.

Mining of the area had actually begun in the mid-to-late 50s with the beginning of an open pit mine. Within a short time, the community of San Manuel was born. Over a short period of time, the mining company constructed hundreds of homes, five schools, a football stadium and ball fields, churches, a sewage treatment system, company store, medical facilities, two swimming pools (one Olympic size), and two shopping districts, along with a heavy-equipment repair shop. Citizens added bars and eateries.

Outside the residential portion of the community, Copper Mining, Inc. constructed a steel-framed rock crusher along with a huge smelter displaying twin 500' smokestack towers.

The Galiuro mountain range ran across the southern portion of the mine complex, the high peak of which stood at 7600', with the average of about 4000', which defined a portion of the San Pedro River Valley. The entire region had so much copper that preparations were being made to take core samples on the other side of the mountains. Arizona had so much copper it became known as The Copper State, in addition to bragging rights to the Grand Canyon, Meteor Crater, the Petrified Forest, the Apache Tears State Park and home to the infamous Glen Canyon Dam.

Many miners already lived in the large city of Tucson with a population nearing a million, some 50 miles to the southeast, most of whom carpooled to work. Hundreds of other employees took advantage of low-rent housing near the mine. Others took up residence 15 minutes up the road in the small town of Oracle, bringing prosperity to both small townships.

Many, if not most, mining wives stay at home, each day melding into the next, a routine so entrenched that escape became a word, not an eventuality. For the worker, it was different. He said hello to friends, then proceeded to drill, hammer, blast, sweat, curse, shovel, eat lunch, pick, haul, and try to stay close to a partner. Afterward, he would go home to eat, kiss the children, and maybe go out to let loose the tension, thankful for making it through another day, hoping he might have the skill level and the political savvy to move up the chain of command. If you didn't love the work, never say it couldn't be worse than this.

Back in 1955 the company had initially invested more than $100 million into the project. By the time the two men arrived, a huge green-

brown pit that been carved out of the earth 1000'
in depth. It had circular roads running around the
circumference for the bulldozers to descend and
ascend, hauling the raw ore to waiting trucks or
rail cars for delivery to the crusher and then to a
nearby newly constructed smelter for refinement
into slag. The pit narrowed at the bottom like a
wide-mouth funnel.

Mining lacked the seasonality of lobster fishing. It was usually 365 and 24/7, if not working
it, then thinking about it. Three shifts operated
around the clock, which meant the bars and poker games followed the same schedule. Harwood
and Alday did their best to supplement their income several nights a week, or depleted it, as
the case may be. They did this by playing poker
aided with rounds of whiskey, or, if one really
wanted to lose a paycheck, shots of tequila followed by beer chasers.

Cheryl Kirk had grown up in Auckland, some
400 miles from Wellington. Members of her
family were firemen, others were miners. One
brother was shot and killed in the line of duty,
her father died in a cave-in, also in the line of
duty. As such, she accepted danger, war stories,
use of strong language, and off-the-wall behavior. She filled her youth with school, working
odd jobs, and trying to figure out what she wanted to do with her life. Joining sewing circles
did not appeal to her, nor did secretarial work.

She needed a career based on her talents. These included her comfort in the presence of strong men, her tolerance for miscreant behavior, and her gift of gab.

Neither the mining nor the fire industry had much use for women (who still comprise a small percentage of the mining workforce) so she settled for bartending, beginning at the age of 17. The discomfort of her mother regarding her decision melted when she soon earned as much money in salary and tips as did a mining foreman, a full-time fireman, or full-time police officer, and had more fun doing it.

Sweet and charming, Cheryl, a diminutive firebrand, had earned a reputation: she could kick either a trouble-making man or woman between the legs in an instant, if the need for self-defense arose. She became a more tolerant person when she fell for Josh Alday, fractured face and all. She took a liking to his sense of humor and the men he hung with. She met him in a bar in her home city of Auckland some three years after the PNG fiasco finding him protective, warm, honest, and rough at the same time. After a brief engagement, they were married and she moved with him to his various job locations until they eventually ended up in Arizona with their two sons.

By appearance, no one would never know the boys were brothers. Both were big for their age, and home-schooled smart. David, 12, the older and taller, named after his grandfather, had an angular face compared with Julian, age 10, who was named after her grandfather. He had a round face, like his mother.

David had an avid interest electronics and paid attention close attention to father's skills working with explosives, claiming he wanted to become an explosives expert in the military. His parents were not amused by his decision.

Julian's interest leaned toward the geological sciences. He loved his colorful rock collection of split geodes, agates, opals, jaspers and garnets, many of which were provided by his father, who told him early on that he could collect as many as he wanted. However, he would be the one carrying the boxes, not somebody else, whenever the family moved to a new location. His brother jokingly tried to point him in the direction of stamp collecting.

Aware of Josh's nickname of All Night, she trimmed Alday's horns at home. He had told her about how Harwood (nicknamed Hardwood by some and Hardass by others) had saved his life during a rock fall when it crushed his right cheekbone and gave him a slight speech impediment by changing the shape of his mouth. After healing, his face took on an asymmetrical appearance. Had he not worn a hardhat and had Harwood not dragged him to safety, he would surely have died.

Prepared to go to Alaska, cold weather, icy

mountains, and whales, in order to mine for silver, she suddenly found herself in the heat of a great desert of prickly pear cactus, lizards, and rattlesnakes with her husband mining for copper. It's all in the paycheck.

Only Alday knew of Harwood's desire to repay Groebels, plus, he owed him his life. Not if, but when, they did their dirty work, they would do it together. They knew Groebels' publicly eschewed threats against employees. Unstated policy fell under different guidelines. Therefore, the edict must have come from the site superintendent, Mike Nordstrom, a man who had slashed and burned his way to dominance in a world full of men toughened to the ways of a hard world, now made all the worse by his edict. Neither man would forget his name, whose expertise lay in the fields of backstabbing, negotiating, and strong-arming his way through the ranks while backed by almost unlimited dollars, part of his family's muscle.

4

As rough and tough as they came, Nordstrom, now in his early-sixties, had all the money he needed. With thousands working under his command, the gray-haired man had fought his way to the top, one way or the other, with facial scars to prove it. Robotic, totally business oriented, and twice divorced, the head of the current projects in Alaska would bring success where others had failed. Poised to become the next Executive Vice President of the internationally renowned corporation based in Cologne, Germany, Nordstrom was destined to achieve a goal he had sought his entire career.

In Alaska, Nordstrom oversaw operations in Anchorage, Fairbanks, Nome, Sitka, and Delta Junction. Each required a step-by-step process. First, geologists had to discover by appearance and define areas to be core-sampled. Once these astute men ascertained the extent of the field, environmental impact statements had to be filed along with permits to ensure the local environment would be returned to its natural state. Environmental protest groups were a frequent problem, which, occasionally, caused the abandonment of a project and the loss of millions of investment dollars and years of planning. Would the deep-pit or the mine shaft method be used to extract the crude ore? Would both, or additional techniques be needed? These factors had to be addressed prior to beginning any project. Years would pass before refined ores could be obtained. Investors would have to be mollified and learn to be patient because mining was a dicey business in every regard, but when fortunes are at state, high rollers were coveted who were willing to roll the dice.

Ore mining techniques vary depending on whether the earth is sandy, loamy, hard rock, or a combination of these. Generally, open pit, tunneling, and placer (stream bed) are the most prominent methods. In the first instance, overburden (dirt and rocks) is first removed in order to access the ore body. This method has the greatest impact on the local environment.

Crew management took skill. There were occasional work stoppages due to weather, accidents, or protesting environmental groups. Harwood learned quickly from personal experience. He had the ability to accept criticism and assistance from those more experienced, as long as he wasn't insulted. His past haunted him, but he had reached a point in life where he understood that each person must overcome their own burden, many heavier than his. Still, he had difficulty separating what his father called an inner rage from what he called inner fire. He often feared what might happen should another altercation occur, not an unlikely scenario in his world.

Following the example of his father, Harwood held the poker games at his house on-site where he would be the dealer and thus receive a percentage of the action.

Although both men did not play poker in the upper ranks, in the world of the poker-playing miner, they did quite well for themselves, occasionally losing a fair sum, but gaining much more.

The two men bonded like brothers, If they played their cards right, they had big careers ahead of them. Alday was the only person Harwood had ever told about how and why he had become a miner. Alday had also grown up in a mining family. As the oldest of five children, he learned responsibility early in life. By the time he began his first mining job after completing high school, he understood the intricacies of the business. He only lacked the experience.

5

Now at end of June, the temperature had been running in the triple digits every day of the month and the hills were on fire. The backside of the Santa Catalina Mountains was aglow and the fire threatened the small town of Oracle with a population of less than 3000. Citizens were advised to prepare for evacuation. Between Oracle and Tucson, the developing community of Catalina kept growing like a weed.

In a last ditch fling, residents flocked to the Oracle Inn Steak House, crowding the large bar section. TV screens were dialed in on various games while beer, burgers, peanuts, Beer Nuts, and other finger foods adorned the tables. Occasional shouts could be heard when a team got a lead. The building was frequented by miners who were not into gambling, or who didn't have families to care for, or perhaps would return to them later full of smoke and drink.

Comfortable in the rowdy hang-loose atmosphere of the room, Harwood, Alday, and Cheryl found a table. Tired of spending an excessive amount of time washing his hair every day, Harwood had cut the black ringlets shorter and reduced the mullet to a fraction of what it had been. The married couple had left their children with neighbors, who had children of the same age. The men still wore their work overalls, which they called bibs, with T-shirts and Long Johns beneath, and steel-toed work boots. Cheryl wore jeans, sneakers and her own T-shirt, in keeping with the other women present. Exhaust fans in the building kept the cigarette smoke from becoming a nuisance.

Harwood casually went to the bar to order at the same time another woman appeared. She stood about 5'7", some eight inches shorter than he, and six inches taller than Cheryl. The woman's face and arms were adorned with varied patters of smoke smudges to complement her sweat-stained work shirt. She wore jeans and work boots. If one looked through the grime on her face, she could have been in her mid-twenties, a trace over plain in appearance, with well-muscled farms and shoulders.

When the bartender came over, Harwood said, "A pitcher of beer and three mugs, Mate. Also, give me a large pepperoni pizza."

The woman said, "Add two pitchers and two more pizzas."

Harwood asked, "You going to drink them both?"

"No, I have help," the woman said, pointing to a table where four men sat, looking as grimy as she did.

Harwood looked her up and down in an obvious manner, then grinned and said, "Hard day at the office?"

She said, "About average. Pausing, as if gathering up her nerve, she stated, "You know you talk funny."

Harwood said, "I was going to say the same thing to you."

"British or Aussie?" she asked

"New Zealand. My friend over there is from my home, too, but his wife is from Australia."

"Same thing, isn't it?" she asked, an obvious tease. "I mean, New Zealand and Australia."

Harwood laughed. "Don't tell them. Are you the same as Canada? You can tell the difference, because Aussies' accents are different from ours."

"Point taken," she said. "You look like you just came off work, too. Miner?"

"Yep. You?"

"Part time amateur smoke jumper, except for today, "she replied. "Cross-winds are too nasty, even for insertion on the margins."

"Guess we're sort of in opposite professions. You try to put out fires and I blow things up," he chuckled.

An older bearded man on crutches opened the door to the bar and hobbled in, one foot in a plaster cast. He saw Harwood and waved. Harwood returned the wave and pointed to where his group was seated. The man nodded and made it over to the table.

"Who's that?" Ally asked.

Harwood laughed. "Ronnie Donald. At birth, his parents gave him the unfortunate name of Ronald Donald. He prefers Ronnie or Donnie. Everyone calls him Big Mac, you know, the Ronald McDonald chap. He's another blaster. Got more experience than me and my buddy over there put together. Freak accident. Ducked behind a train car when he set a charge in the raise to free the debris, but his foot stuck out a little. A piece of shrapnel got him good. Nice guy. Kids are grown. Wife is dead. Instead of retiring, he likes to destroy things as perfectly as he can. He calls it 'immaculate destruction'. Until the accident, he'd get hired to blow up buildings, or blow them down, as the case may be. Hell of a poker player."

"What kind of blasting did you do?" she asked, giving the impression she would understand his answer.

"All types. Chute Blaster, Raise Blaster, Car Loaders to blast down hang-ups, wherever." He paused a moment, then asked, thoughtfully, "What was the toughest job you ever did?"

Her eyes wandered a bit until she replied, "Hard to say. They all have their degrees of difficulty. I guess I'd have to say my very first professional jump scared me the most. We were chuting down on the outskirts of a fire when the wind shifted instantly in our direction. I was at about maybe 70 feet up when a house exploded, *kaboom,* like a bomb hit it. Must have been a meth lab or something. Anyway, pieces of fiery debris flew everywhere. I'm watching this and can't do anything about it. Right? I get hit in my leg with something and pieces are raining down on me like snow. Some land on my chute and it catches fire. I go down like a rock."

Ally began laughing. "Landed in the swimming pool of the same house that blew up. Climbed out, found my crew, and went to work. Your turn," she prodded.

Harwood chastised himself. *Shit. Why did I have to open up that can of worms? I went and picked a scab off a bad wound.* Forced to reply, avoiding the truth, he said, "Like you say, 'tough' is a relative term. When we mine, we spike in steel mesh over the ceiling to prevent rock falls. One administrator in a company I used to work for in another country decided to cut corners, which is not recommended when miners' lives are at stake. He decides to hire local natives and pay them maybe one or two percent of what he paid us. They did a crappy job. When we blew out a section of a wall, the vibration caused a portion of the ceiling to collapse and several of them got killed."

This man wasn't trying to hit on her, Ally decided. Not that anyone would in her condition, but with men, you never knew. She shook her head at the sad tale, admitting, "Well, yours is bigger than mine. Tell you what, you seem interesting. Why don't you and your friends join us?"

Harwood shrugged, happy to get off the subject. He reset the time clock at zero to begin the wound-healing process again. "Sure, let me grab my friends."

The beers arrived and the pair carried the three pitchers back to the woman's table. Harwood went over to Alday and Cheryl and returned with them where he took a seat at the end next to the woman. Chairs screeched as room was made for the couple to pull up their chairs. Hardhats were already beneath the chairs.

"My name is Draco Harwood. What's yours?" He began.

"Allison Brooks," she replied. "People call me Ally. Not the street kind," she added quickly. She'd said it before. The two shook hands.

"What do you do when you're not jumping out of airplanes?" he asked.

"I'm a diesel mechanic," she replied.

"There's a match," he joked.

"In all honesty, I wanted to be a science teacher at one time, college level, but fate dictated otherwise." Lying, she added, "It didn't take much for me to discover that I like to deal with machines and inanimate objects more than with people." It sounded plausible.

"No worries," he said, her story, once again, bringing back his own recollection of why he had quit his ow education.

"What do you do when you're not mining?" she asked.

"Play poker."

"Married?" she asked.

"Nah. Only to poker. In that game, when you do something stupid, you don't have to apologize to anyone."

At the other end of the table, Cheryl had established herself with the men. As people around her quickly learned, she could go toe-to-toe with them both verbally and otherwise, if necessary.

Alday had engaged himself in a heavy conversation with the other smoke jumpers.

"You married?" Harwood asked.

"Tried it once. Didn't work. He didn't like my job." Ally answered.

"Which one, putting out fires or fixing things?"

"Neither. He wanted me to stay home and take orders," she threw in. "I bailed out two weeks later, so to speak."

"Isn't love wonderful?" he quipped.

"Not really. That happened six months ago. He's been stalking me, showing up when I least expect it, midnight phone calls, the whole bit."

Instantly she added, "Sorry, not your problem." She shook her head, apologizing to herself for her loose tongue. She took a long pull of beer. "Drink starting to talk, not me. How long you been with the mines?" she suddenly asked, hoping to get away from talking about her personal life with a total stranger. She had the odd sense that he was doing the same thing.

"Years," he replied, simply, picking up the hint to move on with the conversation. Harwood found her easy to talk to, laid back, with her human foibles, regrets, strengths. She'd might make a good friend.

"I'm curious, why do you get involved with explosives?" she asked.

"It's the most dangerous job in the business," he answered, simply, without elaboration. "My friend, Josh, feels the same way."

The pizzas arrived and everyone took time off to help themselves, dislodging slices and taking bites followed by ample swallows of cold beer.

Ally called down the table, "Hey, Freddie, this man blows things up."

"Dynamite? Like his friend here?" Freddie called back.

"One and the same," Harwood told him. "In school, we learned about plastics like C-4 and Semtex, but we haven't used the last one yet."

"When did you start mining?" she asked.

"When I was 16. Took after my father. When did you start jumping out of planes?"

"When I was 13. I didn't follow after my father. He never had the pleasure of the experience."

Harwood looked more closely at this woman. Hair short enough to fit beneath a hardhat and not catch on fire, not like the babes they showed on the telly who were firefighters and who wore their hair shoulder length begging to torch. Not too smart. This one had sparkling intelligent hazel eyes matching her auburn hair, strong jaw, great lips curling slightly upward rather than downward. Good teeth, nose more European than Asian.

Freddie began asking Harwood technical questions about explosives. It soon became apparent that Harwood's knowledge exceeded Freddie's.

"How long are you going to be working here?" Ally asked, more from a professional standpoint than a personal one.

"Depends on what the company wants. Maybe a year, could be five years," Harwood answered.

"You know, we might could use your help," she stated.

"Sorry, sky diving is not one of my strong suits," he replied.

"No, promise, not it's not jumping out of airplanes. There's a section we really need to drive into for fire clearance purposes. If we don't get to it tomorrow, the town will lose a school, guaranteed, but large boulders are blocking our way. Do you think you could blow them up or something?"

"Sure. Have to run it by my boss, though," he said.

"Come with me," Ally said, and stood up. Harwood followed her to the bar.

"Where's your phone?" she asked the bartender.

The bartender pulled out a landline from under the counter and set it on top. She dialed a number and in a moment began speaking about Harwood and Alday. A moment later she handed the receiver to Harwood and said, "Fire chief want to talk to you."

Harwood took the phone, identified himself, listened a moment, then said, "Yeah, I've got advanced degrees in explosives from three different mining schools. Hell, we've done platinum in Korea, lead in Queensland, copper, gold and silver in New Zealand, Australia, and . . . other places." He left out the mention of Papua New Guinea. "Almost got to see Alaska until the company sent us here to the desert. Tungsten is the worst, silver is the most fun. With tungsten, just to set the charges you can lose five diamond-tipped drill bits trying to go in a foot."

"Would you be able to give us a hand," the fire chief asked, satisfied with Harwood's reply.

"Absolutely," Harwood replied.

"What's your administrator's phone number, if you don't mind?" the fire chief asked. Harwood gave it to him.

"What's your phone number where you're

at?" the chief asked.

"Say, Mate, what's your number here?" Harwood asked the bartender, then repeated it into the phone.

He told Ally, "He said, he'd call us back to see if it's a go."

"No worries," she said, with a toothy smile, "All we can do is try."

She led them back to their seats for more food and drink. Ten minutes later the bartender approached the table and said to Ally, "Call for you."

Ally went over and took the call. She returned to the table within a short minute. "Time is of the essence. It's a go for 8:00 am tomorrow morning."

"Why so late?" Harwood inquired.

"Chief needs to get the drills, power, and heavy equipment organized," she said.

Harwood looked over at the wall clock. "I guess we'd better do the same. We'll give it few more minutes, then we'd better get going."

"Can I watch?" Ally asked, almost as though it were a sexual innuendo.

"Sure, if daddy gives you permission and you can take the excitement," He answered, amused at her clever response.

"We'll be here tomorrow night, same time. Maybe you can make it," she offered.

"Be happy to, if it works out," he concluded.

Harwood thought for a moment and asked,

"Where do you work when you're not here?"

"Up near Phoenix."

"Phoenix is about, what, a hundred miles north of Tucson?" Harwood tried to recall a map of Arizona.

"Correct," she replied.

"Do you know how to drive the beasties?"

"Have to see if they work after I fix them, don't I?"

"How do you start a CAT 420 F2?"

"The front end loader with the back hoe?" She told him, then elaborated on its operation and the parts that most commonly need replacement.

"If you were to work on a grade, what kind of bulldozer would you use?" he prodded, now growing more interested.

"Definitely a crawler. Wheels won't grab in slop like from heavy rain. Maybe a CAT D6, depends on the work site. They're more stable on slants, mud, and inclement weather," she replied, immediately.

Harwood continued, "I'm not trying to hit on you, but where you live? There's a reason I'm asking."

"Why? Planning to stalk me?" She shook her head, angry at herself for saying exactly what she promised herself not to say. "In an apartment in Phoenix," she managed, trying to sound casual again.

"Expensive?"

"Let's say it eats into my paycheck."

Harwood unconsciously turned down his mouth in approval of Ally's quick mind, conversational ability, experience, and forthrightness. "If I can ask, how much do they pay you there?"

She told him and he offered, "Tell you what. I hire and I fire. After you get finished with this work and give suitable notice to your employer, I'll triple your salary and give you a house with minimal rent and no utility bills. Plus, you'll be living in a very small community. You'll save a fortune on gas and out-of-pocket expenses."

"Uh, huh. Promises are also free. What's the kicker?" she asked, giving him a suspicious sideways glance.

He looked at this woman covered with smoke and grime. If she had washed her face after work, she hadn't done a very good job. "You have to put up with a bunch of men," Harwood answered, truthfully.

"I knew there had to be a catch," she laughed.

He joined her in the laugh and offered, "When you get a day off, come on by and I'll show you the lay of the land. You can decide what to do once you see what you're getting into. I need repairmen and operators, both." He found a paper napkin and wrote his cell and landline numbers on it. "In case we don't see each other for a while after tomorrow."

Now Ally looked at the wall clock and said, "Deal. Now we'd better get going. Tomorrow is going to be another scorcher. I'll be on the ground crew working right around the corner from here. See if we can save a school."

"Eight o'clock it is," Harwood confirmed. He stood and motioned to Alday and Cheryl. Time to go. Tomorrow would be an important day, a necessary one to add their small part toward saving a school and maybe a community from burning to the ground.

Ally's group paid the bill, Harwood left the tip, and she gave him directions to the area of the school, only a mile down American Way, the two-mile long main street of Oracle.

6

In the morning, Harwood and Alday drove the company's flatbed with a hydraulic-lift gate, coming up the back way into the town, as they had done the evening before. Harwood took the rig up the hill to an elevation of some 4600 feet, turned left at the sign to Oracle, and passed three churches, the steak house, a trailer park, a small market, a community library, and an auto repair shop. At the convenience store, they made a hard left and went south another half-mile to the school.

The fire had moved down the mountain to bring it much closer to the community at large, although winds had temporarily shifted to hold it at bay. Helicopters were already dropping retardant at this early hour with the use of large containers of the liquid hung at the end of 100' long cables beneath the machines. Although official orders had not been given, many members of the community had self-evacuated.

The men pulled the truck around with its

back facing the hill between a dump truck and a loader. Two fire trucks stood nearby, one of them hooked up to a curbside hydrant next to the school.

The two heavily muscled miners got out of the flatbed; Harwood from the passenger side, face more stubbled than the night before; the shorter Alday, with his full beard, emerging from the passenger side. Both men looked as though they could bench press 400 pounds with ease.

Harwood quickly noted perhaps ten people standing together, waiting, ready to work, all wearing hardhats and steel-toed boots. Shovels, and gas-powered chain saws lay on the earth along with pulaskis, single-bladed axes with a grub-hoe on the opposite side.

He recognized a couple of the people from the previous night. Ally stood among them and gave a brief nod. He smiled and nodded back. *At least she washed her face; not bad looking,* Harwood mused.

The fire chief approached to greet the men. He stood tall and proud, in his mid-fifties, with a look that bespoke of experience.

The two miners off-loaded crates of dynamite, primers, rolls of wire, and det (detonation) cord. Alday raised the lift to lower a Jack Leg drill with a water hookup and air compression hose.

The sun hung behind them clear and yellow. The smoke from the fire, however, totally obscured the skies all the way down to Tucson to the southwest of their location.

The school consisted of a single large building serving both primary and middle-school students. A once green playground was now brown with dryness. The men could see that the grassland immediately to the south of the school nearest the hillside had been cleared, but above the clearing, boulders, while acting as a firebreak themselves, were preventing crews from accessing the nearest trees, which they desperately needed to fell.

Harwood, Alday, and the fire chief walked the length of the area of concern and discussed the plan of action. Wafts of fire heat washed over them. Once the wind shifted again and the nearest trees caught fire, it would be all over for the school and the adjoining neighborhood as firebrands broke loose and went flying.

Freddie, their own explosives expert came over to join the conversation. "What can we do to help?" he asked, clearly anxious to participate.

Alday said to Freddie, "Sure. You can hook up this Jack Leg drill to a power source and connect this hose to a water feed. When we drill to place the charges, we need to run water through the drill bit" . . . Alday paused in his narrative to show the chief the hole running through the middle of the long bit . . . "so we can cool and flush the drill hole as we go in before loading it, but you probably already know that. For this big boulder, we'll need four sticks around the circumference. When we're ready, we'll ask you to spray the air to keep down the dust when we blow it. Freddie, you can give us a hand in tamping the charges."

"Couldn't you use plastic explosives in some cases here?" Freddie asked.

"Yes, but we're better with dynamite. We do use plastics underground for small three-footers, not for the big stuff like this. It would take too much."

Minutes later the men had spiked the Jack Leg into the ground nearest one of the big boulders and began the drilling process with the firemen working the pumps, power and water flow. Once the holes were drilled, the two men went to a second and third rock, working down to the smaller ones. Captivated by the spectacle in front of them, everyone watched these experts insert a single stick of dynamite into each hole and take some time tamping on a firing cap and wiring the charges to one another in a sequence. In the end, they would go off independently, but still within microseconds of one another.

The men pulled the Jack Leg and wheeled it back to the flatbed. Harwood and Alday ran the wires back to the plunger situated well behind one of the fire trucks, still some 70 feet back from the rocks.

Harwood said, "Okay, set your hose on some

kind of finer spray. Spray the rocks and the air between them and us."

The firemen did as directed and satisfied at their work thus far, Harwood yelled, "Find shelter and cover your ears."

With Alday on hold, Harwood walked back out in the open to ensure his orders had been followed, then returned to his partner and gave the nod. Alday pushed down the plunger.

Within a half second, twenty sticks of dynamite exploded almost simultaneously which covered over 100 linear feet. Rocks and debris flew upward and outward, pinging the vehicles around them.

A few moments later, Harwood stood and yelled, "Come on out. It's all done. Time to go to work."

Ally walked over to the front end loader, but paused in her climb to the driver's seat. She turned and walked back to Harwood. "Thank you," she said, and held out her hand before the fire chief could get there. "Impressive, Draco. I can see why you and Josh like your jobs so much. If the offer is still open to visit your mining operation, I'd like to take you up on it."

Harwood took her hand and held it while speaking, "Give me fair warning and you'll be my guest for the day." He wanted to say, "And for the night," but let it go.

Ally pulled away, somewhat reluctantly, and mounted the great yellow machine, pushing the power button to ignite the diesel. The engine began its rattle and she lowered the shovel, expertly moving into position to scoop the debris and load it into the waiting dump truck. Within seconds, the others had entered the forest. Now the work would begin. The fire chief, who had been directing entry into the forest by the crew, came over to thank the two men.

Between the time Harwood and Alday had left San Manuel and the time they returned, all the power to Oracle and San Manuel had been lost. The smaller power grid located in the area lacked enough energy during the ongoing heat wave to serve the local communities that totaled less than 7,000 population, not an uncommon occurrence during the season.

In the smelter, the coke furnaces continued to operate, but a good dozen electrically operated processes ceased, as did the cooling to the control rooms and the gauges necessary to keep track of the purification process. Emergency generators picked up the slack after only a brief pause.

Unfortunately, eight men were trapped at the bottom of a 3660' shaft. Backup generators supplied the men with air and water, but lacked enough power to operate the cage used to bring men and supplies to the various levels.

When Harwood and Alday returned the equipment they had borrowed for their rock-blasting episode, the man in the supply shed told them the news and Harwood asked, "Who's the crew chief down there?"

"Carter," came the reply.

Both big men laughed. Alday said, "No worries. Carter always carries a deck of cards with him, they all have their tobacco chew and cigarettes, and the backup generators will provide them with air, water, and light until the main power comes back. If they're conservative, their headlamps will help them see the cards well enough to have a good time. If I know Carter, he'll have a container of coffee beans with him. He eats them like candy. "

Harwood inserted, "Wish we were with them."

Alday said, "By the way, did you ever find out what happened to the guy you beat up back in PNG?

"Where did that come from? No, should I have?"

"Well, I did. He had 24 years into the company, so Groebels must have figured the man had enough experience to give you the bad news without crying. Turns out they fired him for getting into an altercation on company grounds. No medical, no dental, and no pension."

"Bastards," Harwood cursed.

7

The first of the heavy summer monsoon rains began and the fire issue came to a smoldering end, but Ally did not call for several days. When she did, it was shortly after dawn when his land-line rang. She sounded anxious and wanted to come down the same day; immediately, if possible.

Surprised and pleased by the call, Harwood didn't realize how much time he had spent thinking about her. Ally told him it would be a 90 minute drive from where she was down to Tucson and then another 90 minutes to reach the mine. It sounded as though she were ready to leave at the moment. Harwood gave her specific directions to find his office once she took the highway past Oracle Junction and past the town of Oracle to the short drive through a low mountain pass into San Manuel.

The mining town resembled so many others around the world. The men went to work, the majority of wives had no work but to stay home

or visit, perhaps to venture into some small business to occupy their time while the children were
at school. If a single shift operated, all the men
came home in a single flock and the flurry of activity would begin, defined by meals and televi-
sion, rivers of cold beer, and going out with the
boys. When three shifts were in operation, three
flocks would descend at different times, like
three pulse waves woven into a single fabric.

The homes, most of which were built in the
50s, were constructed of wood, insulation, and
drywall. All were set back from the street with
a yard the width of the home, many with lawns
others with rock and cactus gardens. The occasional trailer stood on its own lot, or in a driveway. Each house had a single-car garage, most
often used for storage, unless the summer heat
required their protection.

Similar to Tucson, the climate of San Manuel
is semi-arid desert, both sitting at an elevation of
ca. 2600', some 2000 feet less than Oracle's altitude. The latter is prone to winter snow storms
of short duration. Almost idyllic in a country sort
of way, a hard cold front occasionally rocks the
community when the heavy air mass prevents
the smelter fumes from escaping, not unlike
similar situations around the world. This causes
the dark, fume-laden mass to settle down over
the township, leading to complaints and hospital
visits from miners, wives, and children alike.

Between Tucson and Oracle lies the Santa

Catalina Mountains topping out at some 9200' with a ski resort and ample winter snowfall. It is also home to a forest of conifers, birch, alder, and juniper, all of which go up in smoke every few years. Unlike many mountains, there are no mines atop this one.

An office in name only, Harwood rarely visited his small 18' trailer, spending most of his time in the drifts themselves, or operating the heavy equipment blasting deeper down into the ore pit. His trailer possessed enough windows to negate the effect of the air conditioning system, although they still enabled him to see the dig on one side and the twin 500' tall smokestacks of the smelter on the other.

First he heard, then saw, an SUV drive up and surmised it belonged to Ally. He got up from the desk, where he was signing paychecks, looked at the clock for the nth time, and walked outside into the heavily overcast hot humid air to greet her. When she got out, she beamed when she saw him, albeit looking a little haggard. He resisted the impulse to hug her. For all he knew, she could file charges against him for harassment, charges that would stay with him forever. He had good vibes about her, but caution is the better part of an early affair.

"Thought I'd take you up on your offer," she said with an honest smile.

"I'm glad you did. Come on in," he offered.

"I've got lots of cold water."

He motioned for her to sit in a rolling chair in front of the desk in the dusty surrounds, and, on an impulse, pulled his out from behind the desk to sit next to her, trying to avoid being too formal. He went to the cooler and drew a full cup of water, which he handed to her.

For several minutes, the conversation centered around the fire and the weather, until she finally said, "I wanted to call you before today, but got hung up on another matter."

"You mean about giving your employer notice? No, sorry, we hadn't hired you, yet. Oh, you mean about your ex?"

"Yeah, phone calls all night . . . The usual sort of thing."

"Take the phone off the hook," he suggested.

"I did. He shows up at work just to let me see him," she said, obviously reluctant to go into it further.

Harwood offered, "Well, if you're qualified and you get hired here, then he'll be out of the picture."

"He has a way of finding things out, so, he might show up. Just saying. I wanted you to know what you're getting into with me around."

"You're not a cheap date, eh?" Harwood grinned. "Come on, let me give you the grand tour. One step at a time."

He paused and said, "If I sign you on, I can't have you gone for weeks at a time to fight fires.

You'll need to make a commitment. Understood?"

"Understood," she responded, without hesitation.

Three hours later Harwood and Ally had visited the interior of finished drifts and those in progress, the two shafts, each over 3800' in depth, the rock crushing mill, the interior of the smelter, the repair shop, the company bank, and the housing. He concluded the tour by taking her to the commissary for a light meal.

Returning to his office, Harwood checked the time and said, "I'll have to leave you pretty soon. I have to go get set up for tomorrow. I'll be back in an hour. "

"I'll take the job," Ally said, suddenly.

"Great." Harwood said, just as quickly, caught by surprise at the suddenness of her statement, but feeling good about it. "How much time do you need to move?" he asked.

"None. Everything I own is in the car."

"Don't you have furniture?"

"Nope. It's all rented. I told a friend of mine at work to take care of things for me in case I'm approved."

"What about your job?" he asked.

"It'll be all right. Things are a little slow now, anyway. I'll call them later. I'm on good terms with my boss. In fact, after I told him about this place, he wanted in. If it worked out for me, he wouldn't mind paying you a visit."

Harwood laughed out loud. "When it rains, it pours. Come on, I've got a place in mind for you to move into next to the other families. It's actually larger than my house, it's a two bedroom, my house is a single. Turns out, they back onto one another. It's already furnished. Right now, we need you to fill out some paperwork."

When Harwood returned some 90 minutes later, he led her to her new residence. She was surprised to find a phone on a nightstand. He helped carry in suitcases, boxes, and a small bookcase, then left her to settle in.

Ally actually had her own private phone number. She replaced the time-worn pictures of dogs playing poker and forest greens with her own. One of them was of an old 19th Century three-masted schooner bucking the high seas in a gale, and another of a lighthouse with waves crashing about it. She missed the ocean.

She set up the small two-foot-wide three-tiered bookcase into which she placed her wide-ranging assortment of books, most of which pertained to science and discoveries.

Ally had her quirks, which she didn't like to openly divulge, unlike many New Age thinkers who forced their opinions onto their captured prey. To her, it is in the nature of the human to seek a challenge. Therefore, a person should seek excellence in their quest for money, spirituality, intellect, education, moral values, and physical fitness. The seeking of money is a good thing, not because of the possible betterment of life itself, but because it challenged the intellect.

At least she lacked the superstitions of miners worldwide, everything from universal truths to the unimaginable. Whatever the human mind could conjure up was fair game for them. Pay attention to the date. If you go to work on Friday the 13th and something goes wrong at home, you have only yourself to blame. If you put your shirt on backwards, leave it. Turning it around can bring about bad luck somewhere down the line. The converse to this is, if you incur good fortune, stay the course because you must be doing something right.

Miners were happy to learn, especially when their lives might be affected. They found out the hard way that a canary in a cage did not always fall over dead in the presence of toxic gases, because it might die frozen on its perch as rigor mortis set in. The miners solved the problem by clipping the claws of the canary. Then it fell over. She scratched her head. If something looked alive, could it actually be dead? She decided to deep think the subject when she had the chance.

Preparing to place the charges, Harwood explained to his friend all that had transpired during the day he had spent with his new employee. Alday asked, "What are you going to do about this guy who's harassing her?"

"Me? Nothing. I'm not an enforcer or every-body's protector," Harwood answered, grimly.

Alday offered, somewhat slyly, "If you can get his address, I'll be happy to speak with him."

"Thanks for the offer, but I expect he's out of the picture. Tomorrow, she'll start at the shop and I'll give her a training lesson on our CATs and the safety precautions we take when we haul."

At 3:00 am the next morning the skies opened and two inches of rain fell, followed by a steady soaker. Harwood directed Ally to remain in the repair shop for remainder of the day to avoid possible mud slides in the pit.

On cruise ship, crew members and most of-ficers share accommodations in a small 6' x 8' cabin. This small room contains a bunk bed, small closet, small dresser, and a tiny bathroom.

Not so with Harwood and the miners. Most home occupants did not consider space to be a major issue except for those with large families. Rock bottom rent prices tended to dampen com-plaints.

Harwood's home claimed a large living room. In this area, he had a poker table set up with seating for six along with two arm chairs and a sofa, enough to accommodate as many as ten at once with an open kitchen and bar. No-body complained about the crowded conditions or the drinks.

Two weeks passed. He had forgotten about Ally, until his phone rang. He let it go. He held a winning hand. It rang again.

"Somebody take it off the hook," he ordered to no one.

Alday picked up, talked for a few seconds, talked again, and said, "Draco, it's from you-know-who."

Perturbed, without looking up, Harwood said, "I'm busy. Tell you-know-who I'll call back tomorrow. Tell them to leave a number."

Harwood heard Alday repeat his instructions and returned to the game, trying to regain his concentration.

By 9:00 am the next morning, Harwood and Alday blasted new rock and helped to shore timbers, trying to avoid men who were in the process of laying track. Driven by a motorman, the train would be pulled by an electrically operated engine at the front, tied to an electrical cable beneath the ceiling from which it would draw power. Once the cars were filled, the load would be side-dumped onto a conveyor belt leading to the surface where it would be loaded onto trucks or train cars and taken to the mill for crushing and pulverizing. From there it would go to the smelter for refinement and separation of the various elements.

Harwood preferred his own home shower to that within the mine. When he returned home at the end of another workday, he found Ally seated on the steps of this front porch. Surprised to see her he asked, simply, "Hello. What . . . I mean, how did you know where I live?"

"Your house backs onto mine, remember you said? Aside from two fences and an alley, that is."

"Right."

"Draco, I have to quit," she simply, although it took some effort to say it.

Accustomed to the events out of the ordinary, Harwood said, "Well, come on in and let's talk about it?"

"He showed up today," she mumbled. "I can't drag you into my personal problems. I love it here, it's absolutely perfect for me, but . . . "

"How did what's his name . . . "

"Doug."

"How did Doug find you?"

"My old boss didn't know about our problems. Doug went to him and said he wanted to repay a lot of money I loaned him, so my boss told him where I am. He can be quite charming if he wants to be. He's got an older brother. I think he likes to emulate him.

"Look, the guy is a magnet for bad luck," she went on. She had to get it out of her system. "He's a walking talking example of Murphy's law. He'll lose money he's supposed to repay, or we'll be making out in the car and a cop shines a light on us, or an old girlfriend will find us eating dinner and start screaming at both of us in public. I was in a bad place in my life and thought maybe I could fix a bird with a broken wing, but I was the one who needed fixing. Then we got married on a fling and I finally came to my senses."

Harwood felt torn. He'd heard nothing but rave reviews about the quality of Ally's work and her ethic of always showing up early and leaving late. Now she had decided to leave a new job because of something that had nothing to do with him. Or did it? He made up his mind. "Where does this Doug guy live?" he asked.

Deeply abashed, Ally ripped herself for getting a new acquaintance involved in her life. This man took an interest in her life, her future. He would not let it go. She faced a stronger force than she felt herself to be at the moment.

Prepared to face the gods of fate, she replied to the inquisitor, "Draco, leave it alone. His brother is bad news. They're tied in with a small crowd of bad people."

"How many in the crowd?" Harwood inquired, as though he might be asking about how many ducks swam in the pond.

"A small bunch, I guess. Nothing heavy," she said.

"Again, where does he live?"

He lives in a small town called Eloy, just outside of Casa Grande, south of Phoenix. Why?"

"Never heard of it."

"Not surprising. From what I've seen of the little place, there are a handful of scattered homes acres apart on desert land, three bars, a car repair shop, and a gun store. Basically, there's not a lot to do but to watch TV, drink beer, and polish your weapons."

"No, his address. I want to write him a polite letter," Harwood encouraged, trying to get the right answer.

She told him. He remembered it. Keeping it totally businesslike, like a call for a single card, "Okay, no worries. You should be fine. I'll let you know what he says. Plan on going back to work here tomorrow."

When Ally departed, Harwood called Alday, who had gotten home ahead of him and said, "Say, Mate, you want to have some fun tonight. You might not get home till after midnight." He described the situation to his friend.

Alday replied, "Wouldn't miss it. If I tell Cheryl the details, she might want to go along for the ride."

"Whatever, you work it out. Get something to eat and I'll pick you up in, say, an hour," Harwood said, preparing for a hot soapy shower and thinking about this woman who had managed in a short time, to find herself extremely popular in the mining community. She possessed the unheard of ability to discuss virtually any topic without rancor, prejudice, or overstated opinions, while accepting alternate viewpoints.

When not reading, she talked on the phone, or attended numerous requests for a home visit and friendly chat, avoiding invitations to join mothers' sewing circles. She began to be called "The Professor," a name she despised. Lacking a college degree, she felt very uncomfortable about being touted for something she was not. She only sought companionship and good conversation. If she could help her neighbors with friendly advice, so be it.

Ally never graduated college. She didn't need to. Some people have a degree, but are no wiser for it. She had the wisdom and the drive to self-teach, which separated her from her peers. This spring-boarded her into a balance sheet comprised of forthright honesty, political correctness, and despite her new acquaintances, realizing her drive was borne out a sense of loneliness. Wasn't there anybody she could speak with on an equal footing?

8

Somehow, a sense of satisfaction infused Harwood the next morning. He, Alday, and Cheryl, returned before midnight and had gotten several hours of solid sleep. Cheryl had remained in the vehicle while the men negotiated with Doug. On the return trip, the three went into a truck stop for coffee and pie where she insisted on hearing what had transpired. Alday explained, "If Doug were another player and knew he held a losing hand, he would drop out of the game, which he did."

Cheryl didn't bother to examine the men's knuckles for bruises. Knowing her husband, he probably concentrated on the soft targets, his preference. She wanted to hear the sordid details, but understood that the less she knew the better.

In the morning, Harwood put on fresh clothing and waited until 8:00 am before going to the repair shop. As usual, Ally lay already beneath one of the big rigs on a trolley with a wrench in a greasy hand. He kicked at the trolley and she slid out.

"What? Oh, hi. I mean, good morning, Draco," she mumbled, trying not to sound stupid.

Harwood grinned and said, "Problem solved. Your Doug buddy got an express message and you'll never see him or hear from him again."

"What? You didn't . . . "

Harwood winked and said, "There won't be any police involvement. I like to take care of my people. Again, problem solved."

When Ally slid back beneath the vehicle, she had nothing but lurid fantasies about Draco Harwood and mused about what kind of message he had given Doug. It was all so deliciously exciting, this new life she found herself into.

Three nights later, the couple sat in a corner booth of the quiet restaurant portion of the Oracle Inn Steak House. Only eight other patrons were present on this, an early Thursday night. Harwood worked on a 16-oz rib eye steak with mashed potatoes and beer, while Ally took in a bison burger, fries, and a glass of chardonnay. Country-Western music played in the background, a little too loudly to suit ether of them. They were forced to lean in to one another to speak.

Finally, tired of fighting the noise, Harwood complained to the waitress and moved across the table to sit next to Ally. She asked, "A lot of miners stay in one place their entire careers. You like to move around. Why?"

Harwood grunted. "Right. I like new experiences. I've worked in countries down under and elsewhere, including Papua New Guinea years ago."

"You know PNG?" she asked, shocked at the revelation. What are the odds? She felt like she was attending a party and ran into somebody who had the same birth date.

"Know it well, Froze my cojones at 13,000 feet, excuse my language."

"I know it too. Tough stuff," she responded, unhappily. "When I was a teenager, Mom and I and one of my older brothers lived in Port Moresby."

"Port Moresby," Harwood repeated. "That's one of the most corrupt and violent cities in the world. Gangs, break-ins, car-jackings. If a traffic light happens to be working by accident and it turns red, you don't stop. If you do, somebody will stick a gun in your face, take your money and your car."

Ally laughed, "It's not like we roamed the streets at night. We lived in a better section of the city in a walled-in compound. Besides, mom and I spent more time up at the mining camp than we did at the house. Less people, you know."

"Did you ever eat at Port Moresby Gardens?" he asked.

"The Chinese place? Sure. Just don't try their

spicy beef-broccoli," she inserted.

"Spot on. I once saw a couple of Chinese guys cooking it on the side of the volcano," Harwood quipped.

She laughed again. She had a good voice.

"What do you really want in life," she asked, testing the waters, "Don't you want to strike it rich?"

"Rich is a relative term. I have a few good friends, a decent salary, and food on the table, my health . . . a whole lot better than what most of the world's population have."

"What would you do with real money if you had it," she continued, not wanting to get too deep into her philosophy of life, not wanting to scare away another man.

"What would you do?" he turned it around.

Surprised by the question, she replied, "Flaunting it would be bad luck. But no matter what you do, you would attract both nuisance flies and stinging hornets. How many lottery winners regret having gotten involved? Absolutely everything has changed for them, including the way they think. It eats up their time. Me, I'd probably lay low, maybe buy an extra ice cream without worrying about the money."

Finally, the Country-Western music got turned down and Tanya Tucker sang more quietly. Harwood stayed by her side. Suddenly, he snapped his fingers. Pondering her name, he queried, "Wait a minute, you're James Brooks' daughter, aren't you?"

He looked at this woman in a new light. She was a cut off the old block. Brooks had told him he had served three years with the Rangers, fighting alongside Australians and British in the Middle East, before going into the family mining business.

"You know my father?" she asked, taken aback.

"You bet. I met him in PNG when James joined my team. I should have made the connection when we first talked, which means you and I were in PNG at the same time."

Harwood went on to describe the man in glowing terms. He concluded by saying, "Your father is the definition of a loyalist to the job and to his team. He's a rare man, totally trustworthy. A man of honor."

Switching the conversation to her, he asked, "Where did you grow up?"

"Wyoming. My grandfather worked lead and gold mines; a little phosphorous there too, I think."

Ally felt comfortable enough to open up more. "My mom's from South Carolina, originally. That's in the southeastern part of the country. To you, she'll have a funny accent when you hear her speak. Anyway, I never did grow up in one place. We kept moving. Spent a lot of time in your part of the world, the places you mentioned. My dad considers himself a Kiwi."

The couple ate in silence for some time, ordered dessert and coffee, and finally returned home at an early hour.

The following day, he told Alday, "On the way back I asked her to pay our regards to her father for us. She said she hadn't had a chance to tell him about the change in her life with everything happening so fast. Anyway, her parents are off in Germany. He's working a mine over there."

"Germany. Isn't Groebels headquartered there? Sounds like it could be a case of paying the fox a lot of money to guard the chicken coop," Alday suggested.

Harwood nodded his head slowly without replying, back in thought.

"The world's a small place," Alday commented. You'd better keep a sharp eye on the gal. She might or might not be up to something, but, whatever it is, I don't think she's going to bite us in the bum. Not with James Brooks as her father. Still, you never know."

"Copy that," Harwood agreed, loading another case of dynamite sticks onto a truck. Back in good spirits, Harwood added, "I'm thinking that when the time is right, we should blow up the right thing and see what's left over when the dust settles."

9

Two months passed. Between showers, the daily temperature remained dry, hot and burning, until the next storm system rolled in.

Although she occasionally went in Oracle with Harwood's group or with others who invited her, Ally preferred to remain at home either reading or decorating. She and Harwood saw little of each other because both were engrossed in their work, or with her activities and her newly contrived vegetable garden.

Surprised by Harwood's call one evening, she acceded to his request to meet him at his home the next morning. At her knock, he invited her in. As bachelor pads went, she'd seen worse. Perhaps he had pickup up expecting her arrival. The thought flashed through her mind that she might get fired if she opened a closet door. Seeing her eye his living area, he asked her to take a seat on the sofa and, sitting next to her, got to the point. "Ally, I needed to tell you in person that Bob Cargill, our new site superintendent, wants us to do some out of town work starting tomorrow. The super before him wouldn't permit something like what we're going to do, but I guess that's why our company is considered progressive."

"Okaaay," she said, slyly, cocking her head, waiting for the rest of it.

Harwood said, "Corporate wants me to trouble shoot and take somebody with me, if I choose to do so. You're it. First we're going to Mammoth about a 15 minute drive where they're working on gold and copper. We can come back to our homes in the evening. After Mammoth, we'll be gone a week, maybe two, maybe longer, troubleshooting at the Grand Canyon.

"They've got copper, silver, and gold up there. They also have uranium. As I'm sure you know, aside from basic generalities, mining for almost each type of product requires different techniques and precautions. It also depends on whether you don't care if slave labor removes radioactive elements by hand, or by machinery."

"I don't know anything about ore mining first hand, other than what I see when I'm driving a bulldozer or listening to my dad's stories," she said.

Harwood said, "Yeah, I know about stories. When I was 20, I learned a hell of a lot about explosives from my father, just like, I'll bet you heard all the sordid details about mining different ores while you were growing up. Am I right?"

Ally remarked, with a sly grin, "Did you tell your teachers in school that you knew how to blow things up?"

"Sure. How do you think I got good grades? They wanted to be on my good side," Harwood chuckled.

Accustomed to male banter, having grown up with three older brothers and working with men all her adult life, she mused at their comfortable exchange. She asked, "Seriously, what kind of trouble-shooting are we looking for and why me?"

Harwood said, "I'll answer the second question first. I implicitly trust Josh to run my arm of the operation. As for you, I'll need second opinions from a more objective observer than from somebody who is entrenched in the field; plus, you're a female and may be able to get information that might not be told to me."

"You're using me?" she asked, only half seriously.

"Let's say I'm utilizing your full potential along with your innate, natural abilities."

"Sounds like politi-speak to me," she accused.

Ignoring her, Harwood continued, "As far as the first part of the question, somebody is stealing gold ingots from Mammoth. I'll tell you the rest later."

The township of Mammoth—at first thought, a strange name for a community that encompassed only 26 square miles—was named after the Mammoth Mine. Unlike many ghost towns around the world, which Mammoth would eventually become, this one never boomed, its employees preferring to stay in San Manuel or Oracle.

Mammoth's small school district entertained a number of children of different ethnicities and a poor administrative staff lacked the skills to integrate the students properly. While this problem did not affect the mining operation directly, it did so indirectly by forcing miners to take time off in order to cope with errant children who were sent home.

Enter Allison Brooks, newly appointed ombudsman, to resolve the issues. While she expressed surprise at the new role cast upon her, Harwood tended to a more serious problem. Purified liquefied gold was being stolen from the local smelter.

The extraction and purification of ore from earth includes a number of complex processes. One method is amalgamation. Another is smelting. Among other processes, these involve rock crushing, grinding, high heat, aeration, floatation, chemical treatments, acid washing, electrolysis, filtration, magnetic separation, and possible bioleaching with bacteria. Eventually, the extracted gold is 99.99% pure metal. It is poured into molds where it will harden.

Harwood found himself uncomfortable in his new role as an investigator. He was a simple miner and a blaster, not a chemist or a professional investigator, yet he had been directed to find out where and how the ingots disappeared. It came down to the element of trust. He was not about to disappoint those who put their trust in him. His default sense of duty would never allow that to occur.

10

The Mammoth Board of Education consisted of five men, ages 32-65. They met bi-weekly in the old wooden courthouse constructed a century before, the front portion of which had been converted into a bar. The bar portion opened for business while the men met in the back room, which, in turn, had been converted to a gambling area complete with roulette, billiards, and poker, games waiting to happen. Decorum demanded that the games entertain a hiatus to enable the board to discuss the latest problems in their educational system.

Ally had a little trouble finding the building that stood among a number of other look-alikes. Sounds of a nearby gun range demarked an otherwise quiet day. Finding several cars in a cluster helped her find the place. That, and a hand-painted sign that read COURTHOUSE, with a number of bullet holes through it. She parked her company pick-up next to several others, turned off the ignition, put on a company baseball cap, took a deep breath, and walked into a bar. She passed through stares to enter a back room where she found five men standing about in a good-sized room adorned with pictures of miners and mines. A long table stood at one end with chairs behind it. The room smelled of cigar and cigarette smoke, although none of the men were smoking at the present time.

Ostensibly, these were the board members. All, but one, were active with the mine and owed their loyalties to their provider. To that end, it was imperative that they resolve the issues that presently affected the 163 children of varying ages under their care, which translated to affecting the efficiency of their fathers at work. To that end they were pleased that the corporation had delegated an expert to help them resolve their present crisis. However, all but one of them were pleased to find out that the ombudsman was a woman.

The lone exception was the 32-year-old businessman by the name of Juan Ochoa, of Mexican-American heritage. Strikingly handsome Ochoa stood a thin, but muscular, six feet in height. With a full head of jet black hair combed straight back, his face appeared to be sculpted, with large and dark, penetrating eyes. His ears stood flat against his head and the man might have served as a model in another life. When greeting her, his voice sounded smooth, silky, reeking with desire, yet businesslike at the same time. Indeed, Ochoa described himself as a simple businessman, which of course, signaled caution to Ally. She had prepared for this. She had not prepared herself for Ochoa. Harwood had apprised her of the situation. She knew men, or so she thought. Ochoa was just another sly dog, yearning for a kill.

The problem she faced revolved around the board's decision to leave things as they were, while the mothers protested that more arts and crafts needed to be integrated at the sacrifice of sports.

Because no women were present in this, a closed and private meeting, Ally sat in a single chair facing the men who sat behind the long table. She listened appreciatively and appeared thoughtful, as though weighing the situation heavily. In truth, she had already come to a conclusion prior to the meeting. She men were respectful, knowing full well where the town's money came from.

Reviewing a printout sheet of the curriculum, Ally finally grinned and said, light heartedly, "I have a number of brothers, and frankly, at more times than I like to admit, I feel closer to their activities than I do to my feminine desires. Your curriculum seems solid. I do note that you have six forty-five minute classes per day with a 30 minute lunch period. I might suggest you cut your classes to 40 minutes in length and cut five minutes from your lunch period. That will keep the school day the same length but give you an extra 35 minutes. You can have the mothers work in their own routine for arts and crafts for an extra class each day. Let them fight it out about what that extra class will be. That should keep them off your neck. Your sports will not suffer and neither will your workers. Who knows, some of the kids might even like what the mothers bring to the table, such as new hobbies to keep them occupied at home keep them out of trouble."

When the meeting ended, four of the board members migrated to the front of the house to enjoy the bar portion that had begun to fill, while Ochoa came over to speak with Ally.

Ready to return to her home in San Manuel, only a 15 minute drive from Mammoth, she felt intrigued by this man who invited her out for a drink and a light dinner of sandwiches at a lone table in the bar. Clearly, he wanted to get into her pants. Never one to say no to the combination of a handsome man and free drink, she accepted the offer. What the heck. She had nothing else going on. Cordial and striking as he might be, Harwood was out of the picture. The man had not made a single move toward her, although he had had numerous opportunities to do so. She could thank him for a lot of things, but he didn't run her social life.

Ochoa impressed her. The man had social graces. Ladies first, no elbows on the table, and no talking with food in the mouth.

Taking a sip from a frosty mug, Ally asked, "Rumor has it you're more of a businessman than an educator."

Ochoa gave a genuine laugh. He held up his own mug and toasted, "Here's to rumor and gossip. Yes, my family and I are investors in mining communities that possess growth potential. It can be very lucrative if they grow, but it's a roll of the dice if they die, if, say, the mine gets played out."

None of that made sense to Ally. Invest is a funny word. Did he invest in buildings or perhaps ore stock? If so, why hang out in a small town like this? About to ask him about it further, he asked questions about her life, instead.

She got home later than she intended, but with thoughts of the next night. She had accomplished her assignment and would continue to work at the San Manuel mine until Harwood had finished his work in Mammoth. In the meantime, the evenings belonged to her.

11

On their second date, Ally met Ochoa at his home in Mammoth, considering the lack of options for activities in these small communities and her need to work the next day. He lived in a large three bedroom brick and mortar in a limited upscale portion of the township. Apparently, he lived alone, although a maid's quarters occupied one portion of the neatly appointed house.

He prepared spaghetti, meatballs, a spicy meat sauce, and salad for dinner, and afterward, drove her to Oracle where they ate popcorn and watched a three-act play performed by children in a small playhouse. Ally figured Ochoa would want her to stay at his home for the night, but anticipating his request, told him that she'd better get back once she returned to her car. She didn't feel quite ready for intimacy with him, especially when she had to work the next day. When they did return, she and Ochoa stood among the ocotillo and Saguaro cactus to kiss good night.

At last, back home and preparing for bed, Ally's phone rang.

"I've been trying to reach you," Harwood said.

"I was out on a date," she replied, unabashedly.

After a slight hesitation, uncertain how to respond, Harwood said, "Well, pack up. We're heading north to the Grand Canyon in the morning. I'll pick you up at 8:00 am."

Ally hesitated. Damn. Just when things were getting interesting, she thought, disappointedly. In a way, she felt relieved. She had forgotten her cell at home, possibly on purpose. Harwood's call might have spoiled the evening. She needed to call Ochoa, then realized that neither had the other's number. She would have to apologize when she returned from their trip, whenever that was.

She asked, "You mentioned the Grand Canyon before. Why do you need me?"

"I don't," Harwood replied.

"Thanks," Ally said, somewhat put off by his reply.

Harwood laughed, "It's not like that. I'll explain what I mean on the trip up." He planned to take 77 north for the short hour-long drive to the City of Superior, located to the west of Phoenix, cut west to I-10 then 93 northwest to eventually arrive at the south rim of the canyon.

He picked up Ally in the morning in a new, but battered, white Ford 150 with COPPER

MINING, INC. emblazoned in turquoise on each of the doors.

Passing through Mammoth, Ally bit her tongue, resisting the urge to ask Harwood to stop at Ochoa's house for a minute. Soon, she felt as though a weight had been lifted from her shoulders. She hadn't realized how cloistered she had been hung up between the triad of small communities. She had begun to think of Oracle as a big city. With open skies and desert surrounded by low mountain ranges soaking into her, she reflected on the man who sat to her left, who she decided, was married to his work, plain and simple. Still, she wouldn't mind a little occasional intimacy. Then she thought of her mother's old admonition "Mixing work with pleasure can ruin both."

Harwood broke her out of her thoughts by asking, "How did your meeting go with the education folks?"

"That was three days ago, Draco, but thanks for asking," Ally replied, a little more snippy than she intended. She took a breath and told him about her proposal and their acceptance of it, leaving out any mention of Juan Ochoa. What he didn't know wouldn't hurt him.

It was her turn to ask about his project. Harwood set the truck on cruise and said, "When gold comes out of the smelter, it's 80% pure. Then it goes to the nearby refinery. When it comes out, it is in liquid form and cast into ingots at 99.9% purity. From there, it goes by armored car to what's called a bullion bank in Phoenix.

"Two long-time guards thought they would get cute and make fake ingots. All they needed was a good acetylene torch, lots of lead, which is dirt cheap, a face shield, heavy gloves, an ingot mold, and an exhaust fan. After melting the equivalent of two ingots of lead, they painted them the same color as the gold and substituted them for the ingots while in the truck. They made a quick stop on the way to the bank and transferred the real ingots into a waiting car."

Ally looked surprised. "Sounds primitive. The way you tell it, you must have caught them?"

Harwood laughed. "Yes. The men made a mistake by thinking the ingots would remain on the pallet in the bank for weeks, if not months. By that time, they would be long gone. They didn't consider that each ingot is weighed upon receipt. An ingot of gold weighs about 27-32 pounds, an ingot of lead weighs about 19 pounds. Once the weight differential was confirmed, the inspectors scraped the paint off the suspected ingots to find the lead. You can't make it up. Good thing they weren't dumb enough to use aluminum which weighs 10% that of lead."

Ally began to relax in Harwood's presence, until he asked, "So who was your date?"

"Huh?"

"When I called you at home last night you said you were on a date. Can I ask who it was?" Harwood queried.

"Just some guy I met at the board meeting. No big deal," she said.

"Is he a miner, too?" Seeing the not so well hidden look of annoyance on her face, he added, "Just making conversation."

"He's a businessman," she said.

"What kind of business?" Harwood continued, asking innocently.

Starting to get piqued by the questioning, Ally replied with a trace of sarcasm, "He invests in the development of mining communities."

Harwood shook his head slowly back and forth and grunted, "Oh, boy." He kept both hands on the wheel. The winding mountain pass leading north to the mining community of Globe loomed ahead.

"What?" she wanted to know, eager to end the subject. Harwood had begun to irritate her. She didn't need any more negativity in her life.

Keeping his eyes glued ahead, Harwood replied, "Let me guess. He's fairly tall, and if you're going to date him, he's going to be good looking. This close to the border, my guess is that he's Hispanic. Since he's not a miner, he's fairly well dressed and lives in a better home than most. How am I doing so far?" Harwood asked.

"Did you have me followed?" Ally accused.

"I guess I hit that nail on the head by your response." he chuckled.

He continued, "This is more than you need to know, but I'm going to tell you anyway. Some miners smoke marijuana during working hours. It takes the pressure off. They need a supplier. Your new friend . . . what's his name . . . "

"Juan Ochoa," she said, suddenly concerned.

"Juan Ochoa," Harwood repeated. "He's probably that supplier. I'm not saying for certain and frankly, it's not that big a deal to me. Unfortunately, we've had reports out of Mammoth that hard drugs were getting into the mines, drugs like opioids and meth. Using those can lead to mistakes and deaths. With me so far? Be careful that you're not one of his victims, if that's what he's up to."

Ally remained silent. Her first impulse was to confront Juan and ask him directly. Then what? If he said "yes," she would have to bail out. If he denied it and she found out later, she'd have to bail out, but she'd have already slept with him and would feel badly. And if he said "no" and tried to convince her otherwise, how could she believe him? Where exactly did his money come from? Perhaps the best thing to do would be to drop him from her life. She had a lot to think about.

"Instead of talking about my private life, why don't you tell me about why we're going where we're going?" she finally asked, desperately needing to take the conversation in a different direction.

"All right," he began. "From what I'm told, there are some half-million abandoned mines in the U.S, tens of thousands in this state alone. The vast majority are abandoned. One of the hot issues surrounding the industry is land reclamation after a company gets through scraping, blasting, digging, and dredging. Environmental groups around the world, well, in most countries, put pressure on companies and governments to return the land to a semblance of its former self. Copper Mining, Inc. is one of the good guys, at least the present management purports to be.

"As far as the Grand Canyon, some of the richest uranium finds in the country are found in that region. A lot of mining companies are after that ore. Environmental groups say that we have plenty of enriched uranium and less than half a percent of our uranium comes from the Grand Canyon so why even mess with it.

"Plus, the way it's recovered threatens contamination of the aquifer and the wildlife in the area."

"How is it mined?" she asked.

"Deep drilling down deep naturally formed tubes, where it accumulates," he replied, leaving it at that.

"It's an eight hour drive and we're in no rush to get there, so we'll stop over in a town called Wickenburg, just northwest of Phoenix and finish up tomorrow morning. We can do some reading in the meantime."

"Reading?"

"In my briefcase, you'll find a lot of literature about the issues. We're going to look it over carefully to make sure we know what we're talking about. Once we arrive at the south rim and find a place to stay, we'll take a day or two to drive around to review the sites in question. Some are closed, but various companies are vying to get them open again."

Ally frowned, "I still don't get it. What are we supposed to do?"

"Like most ores, uranium is mined in different ways," Harwood explained. "At the Grand Canyon, geological factors resulted in large holes in the earth hundreds of feet deep where water had flowed downward over the centuries and which resulted in the concentration of uranium and other ores. It has to be mined from the top down which could cause a rift in the hole. If that happens, radioactive uranium will flood the water aquiver, Colorado River, and its tributaries. Do you know how many millions of people would be affected from this if it were allowed to go without the strictest of regulations?

"Most of this state's land is occupied by Indians. The loudest voices belong to the Navajos, along with another dozen Indian nations. We're going into Navajo country. Just like mining companies pay politicians to issue permits, our employer is on the side of the good guys, but doesn't want to go on record paying off politicians to deny permits, so they'd rather pay environmental groups under the table to protest and stay out of it.

"Remember, a lot of the legislations come from the federal government including the Bureau of Land Management and the U.S. Geological Survey. The tourist businesses say they do quite well, as long as the area isn't contaminated through excessive mining. That could cost the state hundreds of millions. We're going to listen to their concerns and ensure they receive a lot of money for their cause. In short, no uranium mining at or near the Grand Canyon, other than, say, what is grandfathered in, or is safe and properly approved.

"Oh, slight addition, some of these groups are spearheaded by women. You're going to make friends with them."

Checking into the Wickenburg Hotel, Harwood ordered a room with two queen beds. On the elevator up to the room, Ally asked, "Are you trying to save company money by getting one room?"

Harwood stopped and made as if to push a button, saying, "Okay, I'll go back and change it to two rooms."

Enough of this passivity nonsense. Ally grabbed his arm and said, slyly, "Better not, or I'll file a complaint against you for failure to sexually harass me."

"I can take a hint," Harwood put his arm around her and, to her great pleasure, kissed her on the lips. She did not pull away.

12

After meeting with three separate groups on both the north and south rims of the Grand Canyon, the couple spent time touring the northern portion of the state, including Jerome, Prescott, and colorful red rock Sedona, three must see cities proximal to one another and must see tourist sites for anyone visiting the Western states.

Business had concluded. The couple made plans to enjoy a good vacation. At odds with herself, Ally knew she possessed a cold heart. Raw intimacy, if there is such a thing, does not require the breaching of emotional walls. Spending long hours with Harwood frightened her because of her resolve stemming from her abortion during the last semester in college. She had been devastated by the discovery of her pregnancy. Worse, she went against her own values that she associated with the goodness of environmental protection movements as a whole, but was unable to step up enough to give birth.

Majoring in geology, she did not consider herself to be an environmental over-the-top wacco. She wasn't about to cost a thousand men their jobs to save a single frog species inhabiting a small pond. She believed that she might get more mileage out her fight to change laws and influence people by taking a more reasonable stance. Her old boyfriend, whom she thought she loved, had disappeared after hearing the bad news, ostensibly to join another school somewhere. Ally suspected her father had something to do with his exit, in part because of his vehement denials.

Leaving the decision to her, Ally's parents did not lecture her, nor ascribe value judgments to their daughter, accepting her decision, whatever it might be. Like the man she wanted to fall in love with, she, too, felt uncomfortable with school in her own way. You don't need a formal education for a job or to continue to learn, she philosophized, turning to one of her many strengths—mechanics—telling no one of her past.

What her father had told her, and what really made her crazy, was that the vast majority of mines in the United States are foreign owned, including uranium, gold, and copper, and whatever else comes out of the ground. With no serious intention to cleanup afterward. The countries currently mining in the United States included Australia, Canada, Chile, Argentina, Peru, Russia, and a dozen others. No royalties are paid to the U.S. government, the profits going to the foreign governments with no obligations for cleanup afterward.

Ally's real problem had always been her high intelligence. When others read fiction novels for enjoyment, she read history, geography, science, technology, world news—in fact, anything but fiction. As she grew into womanhood, she tried to dial down her intellect, not wanting to appear as a know-it-all, welcoming a chance to exchange intellectual conversation with anybody, only to find that, other than her mother, few people she met were diverse enough in their knowledge base to stimulate her.

That is, until she discovered Harwood and began to understood that there are different kinds of smart. Did 'wise' fit into that category? From what he had told her, another name for a blaster was Explosive Ordnance Handler or Blast Setter. He had to complete his GED and take classes in first aid and safety procedures, how to choose the proper explosive, its placement, dealing with hang fire issues, and blast designs. The latter involved extensive lectures and the reading of manuals that contained formulas, graphics and physics equations. He had even taken extra courses on taking down a building with the use of explosives. But nothing beats experience, which he had. The man was bursting with knowledge in a field she knew nothing about. That excited her.

She tried her best to take pleasure in every moment with him, day and night, feeling her resolve to never love again, melting. Along with that melt, came the need for honesty. Almost every person holds secrets they would take to the grave with them. Others want to build on a relationship. They feel an inner pressure to begin that relationship with honesty, because without trust, there is nothing but a house of cards. She would tell him when the time was right—perhaps.

Ally liked to research a site before visiting it. She did this by reading about it online, or by picking up literature at a local hotel or chamber of commerce. She could take charge, show Harwood her leadership capabilities.

Unlike the dozen states belonging to the Great Plains of the Midwest, the several Western states are quite mountainous. Arizona alone has over 200 mountain ranges, with the bulk of them in the northern half of the state, as exemplified by the small hilltop town of Jerome.

Now, a national historic district, population 450, Jerome once entertained a population of 15,000. It bragged the largest copper mine in Arizona earlier in the early 20th Century producing 3 million pounds a month, serving as a major supplier of copper during WW II. It is also home to the Gold King Mine, begun in 1890, when prospectors were looking for copper, but found gold instead. Over time, miners, bootleggers, gamblers, and prostitutes gave way to tourists, artists, musicians, and gift shop proprietors selling CBD oil.

Only 35 miles southwest of Jerome lies Prescott where Whiskey Row graces a central park downtown. On that street can be found a saloon that once saw the likes of Virgil Earp and Doc Holliday. The saloon is filled with firearms and mining accoutrements from that era.

Leading Harwood by the arm down a crowded sidewalk filled with tourists, she explained, "Honey, you know that back in those days, when gold and silver miners came in frequent contact with local Indian tribes, it usually did not lead the great satisfaction of either group. No surprise there. By the way, there's a century old gold mine for sale nearby. Want to go home with a gold mine?"

"Something tells me it's played out. Anyway, I already have one," Harwood said, squeezing her shoulder, surprising Ally with the statement.

Feeling warm and protected, she continued, "Do you know that the city also holds the world's oldest Rodeo, continuous since 1888. This small downtown area is stuffed with antique stores and great restaurants. Let's try them all."

"I'll pass on that," Harwood chimed, as they walked across the grassy central park area, dodging flying Frisbees.

"You didn't research any of this, did you?" she accused.

"No, my manhood lies in other areas," he bragged.

"Well, I've got some mines for us to visit, then we're going over to spectacular Sedona Valley which is world-renowned for its incredible red rocks and spires covered with iron oxide and sandstone. For the gemologist, jasper and the rare fire agate can be found for the looking. The fire agate is unique to this region."

He drove, she talked. "Sedona is the place to purchase Indian turquoise set into belts, bracelets, knives, and pendants. The city also serves as a hub for the healing arts. If one needs to be purified for anything, healers can be easily found to supply the right crystal to hang in your home, or car, or to carry with you to serve your needs."

Harwood shook his head back and forth intrigued by the depth of her knowledge, starting to wonder what she was doing with a simple man like him. It was more than that, though. She wanted to express herself, not to show off, but to please him, a very nice gesture. She titillated his imagination with her almost encyclopedic knowledge and her ability to accept challenges.

No tour of Arizona would be complete without a visit to Tombstone, Arizona, home of the famous 1881 shootout at the OK Corral. This event occurred two years after the founding of the city.

Mid-afternoon, the couple walked down the boardwalk of the hard dirt-packed street belonging to the popular tourist attraction in the sunlit morning, having walked Boot Hill Cemetery, where some 250 men were buried with their boots on. As one gravestone proclaimed, Here lies Lester Moore, 4 slugs from a .44, no Les no More.

The couple walked from shop to shop, crossing the street, visiting any business that might draw the tourist, from candy stores to leather stores. Men and women dressed as they might have dressed well over a years before, sauntered the streets main hard-pack street, many wearing low slung side arms. Women wore fluffy pink and red dresses, their hair made up in the style of the day, the men dressed and sauntered as the movies depicted. A stagecoach rumbled down the street, drawn by four horses, passengers waving.

Ally and Harwood had heard of Tombstone from their mining to their gunfight. Who hadn't? From the mining standpoint, it produced more silver than any other mine in the district and at one time had boasted a population of 50,000 thanks to ample work. A high percentage of the citizenry that time consisted of Chinese, the highest population outside of San Francisco.

She read from a pamphlet, trying to get the attention of her companion, who examined every feature of the gun-toting Westerners. "Honey, it says here that the Earp brothers and Doc Holliday-by the way, he was a real medical doctor and a real gunslinger faced the McLaury brothers and Billy Clanton. Get this, they used .45 caliber 1879 6-shot Colt Peacemakers that weighed about 2.4 pounds fully loaded. No quick draws here. The guys stood six-feet apart because they were usually drunk and their guns weren't that accurate. Their ammo was questionable, anyway. It also says that circling-the-wagons was a Hollywood concept. It didn't occurred in reality. Are you listening?" she asked.

"I heard you, every word," Harwood answered, giving her a reassuring smile. Checking the clock on a tower, he saw the hour approached 3:00 pm. The time for the gunfight reenactment had arrived. Watching men shoot at each other didn't interest him so much as what she said about distance from the opponent. To overcome the problem, one would need an extremely accurate weapon that had some kick to it. Nordstrom still walked the earth, eight time zones away. Thoughts cycled through his mind regarding which weapon to use and how to employ it. One way or another, there would be a shootout.

13

After spending a week, leisurely visiting forested northern Arizona, along with more of the open lower desert with its buttes and mesas, the couple reluctantly returned home, full of the wonder of it all.

Ten days later after returning to work and playing catch-up, Ally and Harwood made the escape to Oracle. To her, it felt good to get out again with the gang. Pitchers of beer, pizza, and chit-chat with Cheryl put Ally in a good mood. The two had become close friends. Alday told ribald stories and three other miners from Mammoth walked in to join them. Football played on the tubes and watchers sang their curses or cheers, as the case may be.

Thoroughly enjoying herself next to Harwood, Ally glanced up at the screen above the bar to see what had ignited the yelling when she saw a familiar face. Her stomach churned instantly. Her face lost color. She tried to turn before Juan saw her. A buxom blond and another couple accompanied him. The second man looked big and rough with long hair and shaggy beard, weighing over 300 pounds. His date looked like she could have been is twin sister. A matched set.

Ochoa wore designer jeans and a white silk shirt open at the collar with a gold chain around his neck, an unusual manner of dress for a small town resident. Ochoa said something to his date, left her behind, and came over to their table. She didn't need this. She had basically forgotten about him and feared a confrontation. She had absolutely no idea what she would say.

"Well, Ally, it's been a while. I thought we had a good thing going. I wondered what happened to you. Why don't you introduce me to your friends," Ochoa said, pleasantly, with open candor.

A few at her table continued with their conversation, while Harwood watched the interchange. It didn't take him long to figure out the man's identity.

Ally began, uncomfortably, "Uh, I got caught up in work." She announced to those who were looking their way, keeping it simple, "This is Juan Ochoa."

Harwood inserted, "I know who he is."

With calm diplomacy, Ochoa looked at Harwood and said, "Do you? Who am I?"

"You're the drug dealer in Mammoth. We arrested the guy you sent into San Manuel, or hadn't you heard."

"That's quite an accusation. I hope you have proof of that statement," Ochoa replied, smoothly, without concern.

"We have a couple of sick children who got into their father's stash." Harwood threw out.

Ally wanted to crawl under a rock. Through no fault of her own, she had brought this on. She felt responsible for whatever might happen. Ochoa had done her no harm. The evening would be ruined, possibly the night, as well. She had dismissed the thought of Ochoa's connection with drugs when Harwood had first mentioned it, yet the issue had recycled.

Harwood slid his chair back and stood to his full height to look down on Ochoa. He had changed into jeans and T-shirt and still wore a leather jacket he had come in with, which gave him even greater girth. He said, "No more hard drugs to my men. Anywhere. It stops as of this moment. If I hear that you're still selling them, you'll hear from me."

At those words, Alday also stood, his disfigured face, full beard, and large frame lent more muscle to the confrontation. If all else failed, they could always rely on Cheryl for backup.

Ochoa quickly glanced at Alday, assessing the situation, and turned back to Harwood. "Assuming I am involved in some way, or what?" he asked, calmly, almost cheerily, as though he were ordering a round of beer.

The man must think he's invincible, thought Harwood. For added emphasis, Harwood placed a possessive hand on Ally's shoulder and said, "You'll will regret that day and re-evaluate your life. You'll also have trouble wiping yourself with both hands in casts, assuming you are involved. We know where you live. If not, then I guess there's no problem. So, excuse us while we continue enjoying ourselves. Go watch football or something."

At that, Ochoa chuckled and shrugged. Looking at Ally, he offered, "Sorry, Ally, your friend here seems to have the wrong idea about me. Maybe you should talk to him." He turned to casually amble back to the bar. In a moment, his large friend apparently asked him what was going on. Ochoa could be seen explaining, laughing, almost mockingly pointing back at the table with obvious gestures, throwing coals onto the fire.

Cheryl leaned in front of Ally and asked, "Draco, how did you know he's the guy?"

Seating himself, Harwood replied, "Because his man put a couple of my people in the hospital from overdoses. We told them they wouldn't be fired if they told us who sold them the drugs, which they did. That man fingered Ochoa."

"Why don't you go after him legally," Alday asked.

"Because my men will continue to buy marijuana. With him, they already have a supplier.

With him gone, another more hard-core dealer will move in to take his place. Before we go to another level, let's see how this works first," Harwood said, pouring himself another glass of beer, as though the single minute of verbal exchange with Ochoa had never occurred.

The big man who arrived with Ochoa walked over to the table where everyone had regained their seats. "He leaned down and said into Harwood's left ear, "You the asshole who's giving my friend grief? Maybe you should take it up with me?"

Harwood jerked his head to the right to clear the space, pivoted to the left and hooked his right fist, like a block of iron, into the man's nose and upper teeth, followed by a second one to the eye to ensure he would get a good shiner, then quickly stepped to the side while the man grasped his face with both hands, trying to staunch the gush of blood running through his fingers and down the front of his shirt. Harwood finished by driving another hard fist deep into the man's solar plexus watching him drop to his knees. At that, his date came over to take up where her boyfriend had left off, when diminutive Cheryl stood and launched a well-practiced kick to catch her hard in the crotch. The act reminded her of the time years ago when she had ridden a brother's bike, hit a hard bump, flew from the seat to land on the steel bar of the frame. The big woman gave a scream and she, too, went down, maintaining their matched set appearance. Both might need to hold off from having sex for some time.

Still on his knees, the man reached behind him. Alday was all over him, He grabbed the man's wrist and pulled it up sharply into a hard hammer lock. The man yelled in pain, letting go of his nose with his left hand to grasp his ruined shoulder while Alday took the razor-sharp blade from his hand. Alday grabbed the man's right thumb and twisted it back hard enough to break it.

Ochoa and his date had left. Minutes later, the other two made it to the door followed by Alday to ensure they drove away, following their car with his eyes until it disappeared out of sight.

When he returned, a janitor had a bucket and mop working on the floor to remove the blood. A few moments later he placed a sign at the area that read: Caution—Wet Floor.

"Sorry, baby," Harwood said, "something got a hold of me."

Ally felt relieved when she realized that Ochoa would never set foot in that bar again and confident he would never try to find her, not with Draco Harwood in her life—the man that she had made up her mind to keep.

14

Two weeks later, the general alarm went off at 2:13 am. The coded sequence indicated a fire in one of the tunnels. Because shifts were working around the clock, everybody knew what that meant. Miners were trapped. The exit to their drift might be blocked. This was a copper mine, not a coal mine. The only way for that to occur is with a failure in the electrical system, or through a welding incident, which would mean toxic gases would be emitted into the airways, which could easily disable or kill the workers. That might also suggest a cave-in.

Ten seconds after the general alarm sounded Harwood's phone rang as did Alday's. Seven minutes after that both men were in the elevator with another 10 men, all carrying tools, fire extinguishers, and gas masks, descending down to level 12, far below the surface. The smoke was palpable. Burned plastic wiring has a distinct flavor of its own. Twelve men were at risk.

The collection of men found the opening to

the level clear of debris with the miners waiting to be rescued. Apparently, an electrical short had disable the send-call from their end to call for the elevator. One man's hand had second degree burns, the others suffered from smoke inhalation. The crews shifted places, with the miners taking the elevator to the surface and Harwood, Alday, and the others extinguished the fires and exhausted the drift through the use of fans that were wired to surface power.

Harwood and Alday followed the injured man to the San Manuel clinic, where, on a hunch, Harwood asked the staff to run a blood test on him.

"What happened, Jim," Harwood asked.

"Yesterday, we blew out another five feet and cleaned out the muck to lay the tracks for the generator to be rolled in. We just finished wiring the lights to the new section and I reversed the polarities on the generator plug-ins. That caused a short, which resulted in a fire. I did a dumb thing. I've never done anything even close to that in all my years."

Later that day, the results came back on the blood test to reveal a high concentration of opioids. Harwood and Alday returned to the hospital for another visit to find Jim with both hands bandaged. At the least, he would be out for a month. His children were at school, but his wife was present.

Harwood told him what the blood work disclosed. Jim looked sheepishly at his wife, who didn't appear to be surprised and said, "Some of us started on this stuff maybe three months ago, then that guy got disappeared and this new guy suddenly shows up dressed like one of us, trying to be a good old boy. He says everything is the same until I tried it and realized that it was much stronger. That's how I made my mistake. Am I going to lose my job?"

Neither man answered, until Alday said, "We'll be in touch."

The men had heard enough. With Cheryl insisting she be part of it this time, the three drove to Ochoa's house, deciding not to involve Ally in their activities.

Well after dark, Ochoa received a knock on his door. Dressed in a robe and drink in hand, curious as to who might be visiting him at this hour, unless, of course, it were a forlorn lover, he opened it. His eyes widened in surprise as the three entered.

Harwood said, "You remember what I told you. Still, you ignored it. Why?"

Ochoa glared at him and spat, "Because nobody tells me what to do. Now get the fuck out of my house, you losers, before I call the police." At that he glared at Cheryl, looked her up and down, and shook his head sadly.

Ochoa's in-your-face attitude and his sense of invincibility infuriated them all. Cheryl was the first to respond. She kicked him in the nuts so hard she sprained a couple of her toes. She would be bobbling for a week and would proclaim it as a household accident. If his pecker got caught in there somewhere, so much the better. Nobody had ever seen her use a follow-up move.

Then the men went to work on him, punching and stomping. When they were finished, and with Cheryl standing guard over the writhing, bloody body, the men ransacked the home to find thousands of dollars in cash, all in small bills. They stuffed the money into a pillowcase to distribute among a number of families who could use it, including Jim's, and found Ochoa's large drug stash. Returning to the victim, Harwood forced several tablets down his throat, not caring what they were, washed them down with the rest of the bourbon Ochoa was working on, and flushed the rest down the toilet.

They gagged and dragged the man out to the pickup and loaded him into the back, erasing the drag marks his bare and broken feet left in the dirt. Minutes later, the three dropped him off in the desert five miles away. When they did so, Harwood said, "Ochoa, this is only the beginning. We'll find you if there are any recriminations, or if our names are mentioned. We know where you live."

Ally sought internal peace and harmony to all things, but to these three, law had nothing to do with their actions. Nor did they consider themselves to be above the law. Right now, the bad guys ruled the world and somebody had to step up to take on what nefarious forces they could. A vote among their peers might likely result in a majority in disapproval of their actions this evening. If the wives, were excluded, the vote in their favor might increase, if it meant more safety for them all.

The three acted in concert, alone, not seeking a vote, on a mission a lot larger than that of Ochoa's actions. He was an early-on designated warmup for a game yet to be played.

As for Ochoa himself, no amount of plastic surgery would ever make his face and hands right again.

15

A pair of tunnels bore through the south side of the mountain where it curved around the valley, one above the other. Each of the tunnels possessed four drifts, two going the right and two going to the left, none symmetrical with the others. They weren't supposed to be. The miners followed the richness of the ore bodies. The foreman of the track-laying crew felt satisfied in that the men under his charge had done a good job, ensuring that conveyer belts were operational.

The upper level was complete with a chute (raise) about a quarter mile into the mountainside into which rocks and debris would be pushed through the funnel-shaped hole into a rail car located 60' below on the lower, or haulage level. The raises were situated 40' apart with walk-boards over them.

Completely satisfied with the work on the new project thus far, the site supervisor, Bob Cargill, known for his cough, respected for his years of coal mining experience, announced that all workers could take a full week of vacation. The smelter would operate with a skeleton crew.

The departure of the miners left only Harwood and Alday to oversee the "Open to the Public Day" twice annual open house activity along with a residual staff of rescue members, until the entire operation shut down in a few hours. While many closed mines offered regular public tours to bring income to the local community, an active mine could not engage in such a luxury.

Following the open house, the extended family would depart for Phoenix to see the zoo, various museums, scary movies, and browse the car dealerships on Scottsdale Boulevard, home to Porsche, Ferrari, Rolls Royce, Lamborghini, and Cadillac, along with more commonly shopped makes.

Curiously, despite their colorful family backgrounds, neither woman had ever been inside a mine. Now that open house loomed ahead, they announced their intent to bring the boys along for the public's tour inside the new tunnel.

As members of the mine rescue team, Harwood and Alday instructed 30 passengers to take their seats on the narrow-gauge train for the ride into the darkness, ensuring that each headlamp was operational. Called a Mantrip, the train is used to transport miners from the vertical shaft deep into the haulage level.

On this second tour of the day, five children, ages 12 and younger, rode with one or both parents. Their orders were clear: No drinking, follow all instructions, remain together as a group, and closely watch any minors in their charge.

After a double-check head count, Alday rode at the front of the train with Harwood at the rear, opposite of the first tour. As the electric train began to move, Alday began his lecture.

"The train you're on is the one the miners use to travel farther back into the work area. Like any railroad, we can switch tracks to take us to side drifts. The tunnel, or level, we're in is part of a pair because they're are made together. We call this one the haulage level because we haul out ore from it. We use train cars like the one you're on, but they carry the ore from above. How do they get that ore? The level 60' above us is called the production level. It gets made by the use of a tunnel boring machine, or TBM. It took a half-century of failures, innovation, power, inventiveness, and electronics, to get it to work. It drills smooth round holes 15' in diameter. This makes for regular particle sizes and more efficient cooling. The TBM saves money, time, and cuts down on injury because of basic all around efficiency.

"As you can imagine, the amount of dust generated by explosions, welding, drilling, ore dumping, diesel machine operations, walking, and the various activities within the mine can be terribly high. We try to keep it down by various methods such as flooding fresh air into the mine to flush out the dust. My partner and I worked jobs overseas where none of that existed and still doesn't. You become what you breathe."

Alday continued, "If you look up, you will see holes some 12' across every 40'. Those holes lead to the top production level where the dirt, or muck as we call it, is sent down a chute into the waiting train cars. Most of time, however, we don't have the TBM and have to do everything by hand using axes, shovels, jackhammers, and tools you never heard of. If big rocks plug up the hole, we need to stick some dynamite up in there to break it loose."

After a minute the train stopped at a great pillard room. Off to the left stood a cavern hollowed out of the earth. It stood 10' in height and 70 yards on a side with pillars of dirt left standing every eight feet or so to hold up the ceiling. Alday permitted the group to leave the train for a closer inspection, a few remaining behind, fearful of what they might find, regretting ever having signed up for the tour. Lights created ghostly shadows from the six-foot-wide pillars of dirt. The room smelled of hot dampness. In a moment of silence, the occasional drip drip of water came from somewhere, like something out of an Edgar Allan Poe or H.P. Lovecraft story.

"Our first stop is the changing room where we put on our 'diggers' or 'bibs' overalls, steel-toed boots, and safety equipment. This includes the hats, battery packs, and lights you're all wearing, safety glasses, respirator for dust control, and emergency breathing device. Then we clock in. The lunch room is air conditioned. It's just down the way. No fresh air today. No water pumps in operation. It's going to get hot and humid soon. Modern conveniences provide us with good air flow, unlike the vast majority of mines around the world. And yes, we do have toilets that need to be cleaned on a regular basis.

"This particular mine pulled out some 70,000 tons of raw ore a day. However you measure it, a lot of miners put in a lot of hard work. If this were a coal mine, how would you like to be breathing in oily coal dust and wind up with black lung, or inhale particles of uranium, radon, mercury, cadmium, and who knows what else all day every day? My partner and I have worked jobs where there are no modern conveniences such as exhaust fans and sprayers to keep down the dust level. Someday, we may come to pay for it."

Ally thought about what Alday had said. The level of PM10s must be extremely high, especially those particles in the 2.5 micron range, the same size particles that big cities such as Delhi, Beijing, and Los Angeles endure, which annually serves to shock the asthmatic population into reality.

"Here are some copper questions for you.

Some copper is green and some is orange-red. What's the difference?"

One boy about ten raised his hand. "When air gets to the copper, it turns it color."

"Correct, young man. Copper oxide is what you're looking at. When we first blast into new rock, we see the red. Which explains why the Statue of Liberty is green. When the United States received it from France, it first arrived in its natural state. But if that's the case," he went on, "why isn't a copper penny green?"

One man in front answered, "Because it's not all copper. It has a coating of some type."

"Almost correct," Alday confirmed. "It's mostly zinc coated with copper. There's so little of it that it won't turn green. Older pennies were made entirely of copper and would turn green in time.

"The nickel coin is mostly made with that same element. In fact, without metals, no country in the world would have coins." He then revealed that one local mine alone had produced $8 billion in copper, gold, silver, and zinc.

The train moved on to the entrance of a new drift, then to the air-conditioned lunch room and shower area. Passengers grouped around for the lecture, regaining their seats, sometimes at random, after Alday went into generalities about each mining process.

To Ally, as the nearly silent train moved deeper into the darkness, she slowly came to the realization of what these men went through day after day, night after night, years on end, with only headlamps to see by. They were like subterranean termites that created chambers and tubes around themselves tunneling though a mountain, eating their way through miles of earth, never to stop until the food ran out. All told, the men spent more time in the dark than they did in the light.

She smelled the dampness. She could feel the darkness eating away at the light on her headlamp like a living thing feasting on the glow. More than that, it ate away at her sanity. She couldn't imagine would how she would react if all the lights went out at once, not able to see the teeth or the whites of the person's eyes standing inches from you, only smelling their breath in the absence of speech to know of their presence.

Feeling the warm squeeze of Cheryl's hand on hers Ally squeezed back. She looked at the faces of others nearby, all in awe, perhaps as fearful as she, that this would not be a one way journey where monsters lurked at the terminal—a perfect oxymoron. If airlines regaled their arrival and departures point as terminals, would this be their end?

The train stopped. Alday asked everyone to join him at the entrance to a drift. Harwood took the rear of the group. Alday explained that, more than a century ago, miners used acetylene and water to produce a flame by which they could see. "Before that, they used candles in their hats. You couldn't use either of those in a coal mine, could you? Why not?"

Various answers would come forth. One man in front guessed that the presence of methane gas could lead to an explosion, to which Alday would reply, "Correct. The miners learned that the hard way." Or, "Can you imagine not having enough electricity to heat the shower water to adequately wash off the coal dust?"

Harwood's mind began to wander back two decades when he had returned home for a visit from his night classes only to find out that his father wanted to have him transferred. His mother had implored, "Mason, he's only been hard rock mining a year and you want him to work in a coal mine? That's one of the most dangerous of them all what with breathing coal dust, black lung disease, coal dust and methane gas explosions, and cave-ins. I did learn a few things living with you. Come on. I'm not that stupid."

"That's exactly why I'm having him work there. I want him to have a taste for it. You don't appreciate what you have until you live in worse shoes than yours. It's called an education," Mason argued. "Mum, no worries. Men work in pairs. They watch out for each other."

Mason had no intention of bringing harm to his son. The state owned the operation. Since he had worked there years before, New Zealand had invested a lot of money to bring the operation up to speed with the intent of making it a super-efficient producer of anthracite coal, not the bituminous variety that has four times the mercury content of the other varieties, but the highly dense, high energy, low pollution type found in Northeastern Pennsylvania where the largest reserves in the world could be found.

The word "coal" had received a black eye and in the States, all varieties were cast under the same shadow. Well, fine, New Zealand would sell anthracite to Europe and Australia and Brazil. They need clean coal to make steam energy to power smelters to make metals for civilization to exist. China didn't appear to care one way or another. And damn it, New Zealand had coal and New Zealand would sell. If the Harwoods could play a small part in the venture, so be it.

Draco's mother chimed on, "Where are you going to put him, driving one of those four-foot high cars chasing after a drilling machine creating clouds of dust, or carving out huge chambers, or learning how to blast into the coal seam trapped underground?"

"Hopefully, a little of everything," Mason stated, looking at Harwood, who had gotten lost in the technicalities.

The 17 year-old was met at the new jobsite by a clean-shaven man who called himself Wes. He wore a hard hat and stood even larger than the growing youth. The site was situated in what was once a lush valley surrounded by mid-range mountains covered with forest.

Wes greeted him cordially by name. "Draco, is it? Let me show you our operation. By the way, you came highly recommended by your father. Despite what you may have heard or read, we run a modern operation here."

Wes patiently explained, "There are some 7 million coal miners directly employed in the industry. The vast majority of them are in China where they just won't stop mining the stuff, burning it like there's no tomorrow with no ecological concerns."

Harwood tried to imagine a country without any concern whatsoever about pollution, whether it be water, soil, air, or human health. It made his head swim.

Wes continued with the youth's education. "There's good coal and bad coal. They use the bad stuff loaded with mercury, iron and manganese that gets into their waterways. I've never been there, but from what I've heard there's not a lot of unpolluted water in that country."

Wes drove them in his pickup to a short distance to a denuded area were strips of overburden had been removed, perhaps a quarter-mile in width. Down some 50 feet glared a black streak of ancient dead compressed plant material, the coal seam that ran for miles in each direction. Pointing, he said, "That's one of the ways we mine it here. We remove the coal by blasting, gouging, scraping and hauling. Another way we do it is underground because there is another seam several hundred feet down where we have created pillard rooms and small tunnels. That's the fun one. You're going to be working the tunnels."

The following morning Harwood took a company bus from his studio apartment to the once picturesque valley, now partially denuded. He checked in, walked a quarter mile, then boarded a two man train that took him and a seasoned partner by rail a full seven miles deep into a mountain. The headlamps on the front of the train and on their heads provided sufficient light to enable Harwood to become shocked at what he saw. The walls were white, although the train traveled through the middle of a coal seam.

Racking his brain for an explanation, he could come up with no good answer. Above the track ran tubes that carried fresh air inward and stale air outward. He could see why men could die from lack of oxygen this deep into the tunnel. On the trip inward, they passed great pillard rooms where men had left pillars of coal to hold up the ceiling, while high and wide vaults were carved from the coal that comprised this section of the mountain, formed some 300 million years ago when marshlands covered much of the planet. When that section had been mined to their satisfaction, the coal support pillars would be dropped and harvested, one by one, allowing the ceiling to collapse behind them.

An hour later, the train arrived at the workface. The super had told him, "You're going to be trained on the use of a remote control device that operates a 600 horsepower Continuous Miner—a large machine that grinds the coal with large sharp teeth. In a single minute, it can go through the same amount of coal it used to take miners a week to harvest, perhaps still do, in certain countries and in outlying areas. During the grinding process, it also loads the coal onto a conveyer belt at the same time. No picks, shovels, and mules here, my friend."

His partner picked up the hand-held remote control unit adorned with toggles and switches, as though he were preparing to play a video game. He explained, "The super wants me to educate you. Without coal, my friend, some 80% of the electric utility companies and most of the paper, glass, textiles, aluminum, and concrete production companies would be out of business. We wouldn't have steel. We wouldn't have metals. The burning of coal makes steam, which drives turbines, which generates heat and electricity. See, it's a fuel that is reliable, inexpensive, and independent of weather. There're over a trillion tons of it available."

Harwood had heard arguments on both sides of the fence. At the moment, he wasn't about to get into a pollution argument with a man who had spent a career in the industry, because he knew what Wes's reply would be. It would be the same his father kept repeating: "If governments spent a fraction of the money they pissed away on pay raises for themselves and put it toward new technology to recycle the air that is emitted from the smelters, we could have limitless energy. The sad part is that if we had really wanted to do it, if could have been done by now. The brain of man came up with the atom bomb from scratch the better part of a century ago, but too many people don't want to invest in giving us almost free energy. Instead, they want to make a hundred million batteries that will end up in landfills. Go figure. I'd love to see a country run by scientists and engineers."

One catch. These folks weren't above pranking a newbee. It took him nearly three hours to return to the entrance after his partner took the train by himself at the end of the workday. Their joke would reach its climax when the crew saw his reaction upon emergence from the tunnel, or the angry words he spoke the next day.

His first thoughts were of despair. These morphed into rage. He had a lot of time to think. In the end he came up with a game plan. Praying his headlamp wouldn't go out, Harwood followed the narrow gauge track back the only way he could go. At least he could stand to his full height. Some of the tunnels he had been shown were only four feet in height. He'd never make seven miles hunched over, or without adequate ventilation.

To everyone's great disappointment, Harwood said absolutely nothing about his return walk, as though the event never occurred.

He did, however, ask about the white walls. Surprised by the trainee's lack of anger or frustration over his ordeal, his partner wasn't surprised by the question, having been forewarned about the inquisitive nature of the youth. "We spray the ceiling and walls with a lime solution to keep down the dust. The treatment also helps reduce the outgassing of methane, carbon monoxide, and hydrogen sulfide trapped in the coal seams. You can't smell the first two. The last one smells like rotten eggs. The first and last ones are explosive," his partner explained.

Harwood thanked the man for the education. Two days later he returned the favor by taking the train back by himself.

16

Alday snapped Harwood out of his reflections by requesting everyone return to their seats on the train, which continued for two more stops, now a good mile from the entrance. In the absence of the headlamps, the sunlight at the entrance would shrink to a tiny dot like a single star in a pitch black sky devoid of other stars. One man enjoyed being the first to guess the right answer, to be the one who could speak for everyone.

At last, the slow-moving train came to the welcome glare of sanctity, sanity— the entrance. Many pulled out their sunglasses. Thankfully, most passenger had gained faith and confidence in these men who watched over them, who provided shelter, transportation, and civilization.

Time for another head count while people remained seated. It was easier that way. The count came up one short. A second count came up with the same result. A smaller, clean-cut man dressed in expensive jeans and a polo shirt stood, walked the fifty feet to the end of the train that contained only a single row of passengers, and announced, "My son, I don't see him."

All but the man who made the announcement were dismissed to drop off their helmets and battery packs with Harwood, free to go except for Ally, Cheryl and their sons, who, as a family, felt compelled to stay. Harwood asked for the boy's name and description for the record, not that there would be a lot of children people wandering the drifts. "Stay here at the entrance," Harwood ordered the father.

He placed a call to the head of the mine rescue team to explain the situation. The team consisted of 40 experienced miners, half of whom had taken leave for the long week. As part of the group, the tour guides felt obliged to begin the search before the bulk of the team arrived.

The episode threw Harwood back to his youth, to the mining visits with his father, to his fascination with it all. He remembered taking off his helmet and playing with the headlamp, causing it to go off by disconnecting it from the battery pack, to the admonition of his father never to do that. Had this 5-year old boy, named Billy, done the same thing, somehow wandering off to explore on his own, while the group stood around discussing history with Alday on one of their several stops? If he hadn't been under the strict supervision of his father, that's what he would do. Guaranteed.

Billy stood at the rear of the group, his father leaving him to move to the front where one man did the talking while the other one stood toward the rear. He couldn't see the man talking with all the people in front of him and his father stood at the front. The man standing to the side moved into the group to calm a little girl who began crying.

Billy began to play with his headlamp, placing a hand in front of it, removing the hand, and placing it back again to cover the light. He turned around and, with his hand over the light, wandered into a side drift near where the train had stopped. The instant he removed his hand from the light, he ran into an outcropping. The lamp shattered and his helmet fell to the floor. He groped around and managed to find the helmet and replace it, but became disoriented in the presence of total blackness. This was new. Even at home he slept with a little light on.

Thinking he would soon rejoin the group, he wandered further into the dark of the drift. Occasionally stumbling on the rails, he touched the wall with one hand for guidance. The first signs of panic began to set in when visions of unspeakable monsters occurred, monsters that would tear him to shreds or eat him alive. These were the monsters his father told him about at night, the ones that would eat him if he misbehaved. He had to pee badly and did.

He was not alone in his terror. Miners throughout history believed in the terror of goblins in the absolute pitch blackness of a deep mine where no moonlight, flashlight, candlelight, reflection, or glow existed. Even outer space has stars. The thick soup of the absolute darkest of the dark, not even imagined, took big chomps at the minds of the most stable of men, in time, turning them into vegetables, sometimes after they had been rescued. When alone, one fears the ghouls. The stories had to come from somewhere, didn't they?

Something told Billy he might be headed in the wrong direction. Shrinking low to keep his head from getting bitten off, he lost track of time and had no idea how long he'd been wandering. Turning around, he returned the way he had come, thought he saw an opening, wandered away from the wall, and fell into a raise.

"You lost my son!" the man screamed, poking a finger into Harwood's chest. "I don't care how big you are, if anything happens to him, I'll hang you both. Do you know who I am?" A Chihuahua barking at a pit-bull.

He wore cut-offs and hiking boots, like he was climbing Mt. Everest, but wasn't prepared for the cold—heat in this case. Farmer stood nearly 6' in height with a fleshy face and the wisp of a mustache he might have been cultivating since his teen years. His once well-groomed dark brown hair stuck up after removing the hard hat. Overall, though, the man's facial features were well proportioned. Ally found him not unattractive. She did notice a pale circle around his ring finger suggesting a recent divorce.

"No, but we're starting to get a pretty good idea," Harwood grinned broadly. "Poke me one more time and I'll break your hand. Scout's honor."

"You're new on the job, aren't you? Trying to spread your wings?" Cheryl asked. She normally didn't butt in, however she must have found something she didn't like about the man.

"Well . . . "

"I'll take that as a 'yes' to both questions," she threw out. "Are we having anger management issues today?"

Harwood gave her a stern 'not appropriate' look, as did the man. Returning his glare to Harwood and Alday, he spit out, "Whatever. I'm an assistant district attorney and I'll have you both up on charges if you don't find him fast."

"What's you point?" Alday inquired. "We've got a lost kid and you lost him. Why wasn't he next to you on the train?"

"What! You're putting this on me?" the man yelled, staring hard into Alday's eyes, feeling fearless, self-absorbed, reeking with power. Another Ochoa. "I'll have you know . . . "

Harwood told the women and the boys, "You guys go on home. There is nothing you can do here. We'll let you know what happens." Reluctant to leave the scene in the middle of a heated argument, they departed for home to finish packing for their upcoming vacation.

Once they had left, Harwood asked, "What's your name?"

"Jerry Farmer," the man announced, proudly, squaring his shoulders.

"Hang on a second, Jerr." Harwood held up his hand to silence the attorney and pulled out his cell phone. Keeping it formal, he said, "Sheriff, this is Draco Harwood. We have an unruly citizen who refused to follow the explicit instructions we gave on watching their children and now we have a lost child in the mines. The mine rescue squad is on their way. He is hindering our search by continuing to be argumentative and unruly. He made physical contact with me. I want to file assault charges. In our view, the man needs to be taken into custody. I think child neglect charges might not be ruled out. Yes, we're at the entrance to the new tunnel. We just completed the tour. Thank you, he will stay here to meet you. We need to go find that child."

Alday said to the man, "We strongly recommend you remain here until the sheriff arrives. We will be filing charges against you. By 'we', I mean Copper Mining, Inc. If you decide to leave, you could be leaving the scene of a crime, if the law sees it as such. A little time behind bars for various charges, including child neglect, should go well on your résumé."

Belligerence did not set well with the men, especially when they were charged with the well-being of others. Families took care of one another.

In spite of Farmer's continued protests, the two miners had turned to re-enter the shaft in search of a lost 5-year-old. The threats against Farmer weren't hollow, although they needn't have occurred had Farmer not attempted to be so domineering. Alday grabbed two spotlights from a storage compartment on the train and started the electric motor. Both men sat at the front, playing the lights to the front and sides.

Each time a drift came up to the right or the left, one man left the train to explore it. The drifts dead-ended well into the mountain. Checking into the raises along the way, they saw a cache of rocks and debris from completely empty to completely full. Walk boards covered them, incompletely in some cases.

Small amounts of water accumulated on the floors that would have to be pumped out once power resumed at the return of the crew in a week hence. Various pieces of machinery and ore cars lay dormant on rails in each drift that ran a good quarter-to- half-mile till the drift ended into a wall or rock. The men called out Billy's name, but only heard echoes. They saw no lights.

Keeping in touch by radio, the two sweating

men merged into the main corridor at about the same time to see numerous headlamps coming their way, led by a man named Scott. In his late 50s, Scott could only be described as a heavily bearded, tobacco chewing, grizzled old coot who looked as comfortable in a tunnel as most did in front of a TV. Of all the men there, he might be the sole person to remain sane if the lights ever went out for a period of time. Several members headed off to recheck the drifts, others stayed with the train awaiting instructions. .

Scott asked, "Find anything?"

"No, we still have the far drift to go. That was next on the list, until we saw your beautiful ass," Harwood commented.

"You'll see it again the next time I take your money at the next game with your girlfriend draped all over me," Scott retorted, leading a number of men. The remaining men took the train another half-mile back into the shaft where the last lecture had been given and went into the drift to the right. They found the first raise to be full, and the second cut at a downward angle to reach the haulage level below. The boards across the top were separated. If any raise were empty, or partially full, he could have fallen to his death. Several men leaned over the edge, securing their hardhats and headlamps as they did so, to find the raise to be relatively full, only 10' feet from the top.

This particular raise was of medium diameter measuring some 12' across. A boy lay unconscious on top of the rocky debris. When he fell, every observer surmised that he must have fallen in the opening between one plank and the edge, to slide down several feet where he now lay toward the middle of the pile of rubble.

Scott contacted the men by radio to announce the find. He took a length rope handed to him by one of the men who wore it coiled over one shoulder. A harness was tied to one end. He looped his head and arms through the harness and lowered himself to the surface of the dirt pile, while the men held the rope. He tried not to put undue pressure on the pile, which might cause tons of rocks to give way. Even though the raise was closed at the bottom, he didn't feel like being the straw that broke the camel's back. At that point, it would all collapse, taking him and the child downward another 50' feet into an ore car and to their deaths.

The men gave Scott enough slack for him to move to the boy, prepared at any instant to haul him free should a collapse occur. He carefully examined the unconscious child to find bruising on one side of his rib cage and the right leg broken at the femur. Blood oozed from a gash on the side of the child's head. He would have to be checked for concussion and internal injuries. Scott yelled up the few feet to the men waiting to hear his report, then two men lowered a backboard and neck brace.

Scott needed more slack to strap the child in. He also needed to put his entire weight on the debris to do so. Holding his breathe, he completed the tasks and signaled for the crew to haul up the strapped-in youth. Once the package had reached the surface, the others assisted Scott in his ascent.

The crowd of men climbed onto the waiting train, which brought them to the entrance in the waning daylight at the mouth of the tunnel, the falling sun directly in their eyes. The men dispersed, leaving the rest to authorities. Sheriff Jennings, a deputy, and Farmer waited for Harwood and Alday to emerge. One of the rescue team members had already called for an ambulance.

"My son, is he all right? It's about time you found him. Where was he?" the man cried.

"He fell down a raise. He's going to the hospital," Scott said, listing the problems he found on first inspection.

"I want to see him," insisted the man, making a move toward the unconscious child.

"I think you'd better come with me, at least until we straighten this out," said Jennings, with great protestations from the father, trying to avoid the handcuffs the deputy presented. The officers slammed the man against the patrol car, pulling his hands behind his back to lock him in the cuffs. The man yelled, insisting that the small town hick sheriff would hear about his actions, thus earning charges against him for "resisting arrest," "intimidating an officer," and "disorderly conduct," in addition to those Harwood had mentioned initially. Knowing the sheriff, Harwood and Alday believed he would not take kindly to the moniker 'small town hick'.

"You guys are probably all union jerks, aren't you? Why don't you go work for a living?" Farmer yelled over his shoulder at the same time a deputy shoved him into the back seat.

A mining town is never a dull place for law enforcement. Like any profession, the unexpected can lend color to an occasionally dull day. The arrest of a My-Dick-is Bigger-than-Yours self-absorbed public official can go a long way toward assisting law enforcement personnel in obtaining a good night's sleep.

"I define a vacation as doing the same thing in a different place," Alday said, watching the patrol car leave the same time the ambulance arrived.

"If that's the case, I am past ready to drive all the way to Phoenix for their brand of pizza and beer," Harwood quipped.

"One reason why I love Cheryl is that she has class, especially because it's all low. Once I tell her about the final chapter, she's going to want to make an anonymous call to the newspapers once she finds out who exactly this guy is," Alday commented.

Harwood suggested, "Before she does that,

it might be best to wait a day or so to see what charges are filed. Keeps the good guys on our side. I have a feeling this is not the end of it."

"I don't like hush-hush when assholes are stinking up the place," Alday snorted.

Harwood clapped his friend on the shoulder. "Don't worry, Jennings is as much a company man as we are. It's all good. Here's more good news. When we were inside, I spoke to Cargill and let him know the situation. He has no problem prosecuting this guy with the full weight of the company behind him. They don't need this shit. By the time we're finished with him, he won't even get approved for unemployment."

The men returned home to pick up the others. During the telling of the tale, the boys kept interrupting by asking questions about the location and exact dimensions of the hole and the injuries sustained to the child, while the women expressed their concerns about the father. .

"What's his name?" Ally asked. "I mean, we don't even know if he's from in state or out of state. "

What county is this?" Cheryl asked.

"Pinal," Ally replied.

She went online and looked up Assistant DAs for Pinal County, but could find no hits.

"What county is Tucson in?"

"Pima," Ally said. A moment later, she added, "No hits there either. I know Phoenix is in Maricopa County."

"Why don't you just look up his name?" Alday asked

"There he is." Ally enlarged the photo.

"One and the same," both men said in unison.

"Says here his daddy is a superior court judge. Bet he's wired in," Ally offered.

"He's going to try to shut it down fast, pull strings, threaten, cajole, whatever takes. We need to give Cargill and Jennings a heads up," Harwood stood up straight after leaning over the computer, tired of looking at Farmer's face.

"Heads up won't stop Farmer Senior from getting him off," Cheryl shot.

Harwood directed, "Ally, you're the educated one here. Why don't you compose a letter to a couple of newspapers and TV stations that we can send out? If you don't want to do it, I'll write my own damn letter. Once charges are filed, I expect the jerk will be let out of jail soon enough. Maybe we can cause the family a little embarrassment."

Cheryl held up a finger. "Hold on. Who's your union rep here?"

Alday answered, "Scott Ferrell, the same man who saved the boy. Why"?

"Was he there when this Farmer cussed out the union?" Cheryl inquired.

"No, he left with the ambulance. What's your point?" Harwood asked.

Cheryl continued, "You guys are talking about heading them off at the pass. Well, I say get the letter out. If we blow this thing up, the press will only report it as an anonymous source, which they will verify. The judge will go nuts and want to come down hard on somebody. Guess who little Jerr is going to point the finger at?

"If you let Scott know, he may want to get organized to take on the judge. Wanna guess who's going to win the fight and who's going to get slammed in the newspapers? First clue, it won't be you."

Alday broke out laughing. "I told you she had class."

Ally contributed "The press doesn't like day old news. They like to move fast. Call it the nature of the beast. Let's do this now."

"It's better to ask for forgiveness than to ask for permission," Harwood said.

"You could get canned either way. We all could," Alday added.

"And?" Cheryl added.

Cheryl wasn't finished. "Who appoints a superior court judge in this country?"

Ally replied, "The governor."

"I rest my case," Cheryl announced.

Alday stated, "Scott's going to take on the governor? Probably not, but I'll bet the Mine Workers of America might be willing to get in the fight."

Harwood threw out. "Ally, you write the letter, if you don't mind. I'm going to make a couple of calls just in case there's a valid reason why we shouldn't do it. Just saying."

Half-an hour later, Ally completed writing and emailing the story. Neither Cargill, Jennings, nor Scott Ferrell had any qualms with it. At that, the family took off for a week in the land of the sun for some well needed relaxation.

17

To Harwood's way of thinking, the entire concept of martial arts was deeply flawed. He'd spent a few years off and on studying the arts when he was younger, as did most kids in New Zealand and Australia, or around the world for that matter. It didn't matter what style, whether it be Japanese, Korean, Chinese, Philippino, Brazilian, or another system. Hard linear, soft circular, kicking first, blocking first, whatever. Virtually all taught strength through defense. Remain passive but strong, refrain from violent behavior; meet the first attack with equal, but not excessive force.

Really? That's bullshit. To Harwood, it made no sense. What does made sense is that if somebody clearly and deliberately insults you or your family, you make the first move. Becoming concerned with the fallout weakens the punch. Call it revenge, call it retribution, call it fun and games, one way or another, you make it happen. He had read that in the last century, two things could get a man hung: horse stealing and bringing harm to another in the presence of witnesses.

Arnold, the man he had killed some two decades in the past, had gotten his, Doug and Ochoa had gotten what they deserved, others had gotten theirs before them, and Farmer would get his. To him, it didn't matter what they knew or professed to know. He who fucks first fucks best.

Draco Harwood was a man who had clearly defined his personal boundaries, a man who enjoyed the dangerous, often absurd adventure, all without apparent fear. Those who knew him would trust him implicitly in a firefight.

For Ally, this part of him truly excited her. She reconciled his bent toward violence with her desire for unity with nature by deciding that the universe is a violent place and let it go at that for the moment.

18

If statistics were correct in that one-third of metropolitan cities in the U.S. were devoted to transportation, Phoenix would be a representative. It bragged two million miles of freeways, boulevards, streets and alleys, along with driveways, home garages, parking lots, RV and auto sales, repair shops, parts stores, drive-thru eateries, auto detail facilities, and whatever else got under the fence. Blasters though they might be, and their children, all experienced fear of driving on the freeway during the day as traffic casually sped by them at 90 mph. Ally soon became the designated driver.

Despite the tens of thousands of miles traveled by the family over their lifetimes and the fact that Ally had lived in an apartment at the outskirts of Phoenix, except for Cheryl who grew up in Auckland, none had ever spent time in the midst of a city of millions. They were basically small town folks who felt comfortable in mining camps among their own. If thrown into the stew pot, perhaps Ally with her school teacher's attitude, might make a go of it, even range far and wide if need be. If not, she could satisfy herself by reading about the wonders of the world. Of course, a little love and attention never hurt.

A two-hour drive brought the car to the Glendale Holiday Inn Hotel on the southern outskirts of Phoenix at 8:00 pm. Traffic was heavy. Cheryl called ahead to inform the hotel that their parties would be arriving late and while doing so, ensured that the hotel restaurant would still be open. By 10:00 pm everyone was in bed.

Habitually early risers, the party showered and made it down to the breakfast bar by 8:00 am. The boys were anxious to hit the pool immediately afterward when Cheryl Okayed them to do so. "Don't swim too much after you eat, boys," she admonished.

"Mom, there's a volleyball net in the pool. We couldn't swim if we wanted to," David argued.

Not expecting to see anything of interest, Ally picked up the local Phoenix paper from the hotel desk, planning to read it immediately after breakfast. To her great surprise, she saw the story: Asst. DA arrested for child endangerment.

All the gory details were listed, including an interview with the sheriff and the mention of anonymous sources. The article even mentioned the attorney's father.

"Can we safely assume you're pleased with this article, Draco?" Ally asked, cheerily.

"So far so good," he replied, with a toothy grin.

The four adults went upstairs to change into swimwear and met back down in the pool area. A number of other patrons appeared, with several carrying non-descript containers filled with wine to set them at ease before the desert sun took its toll.

Harwood hadn't seen Ally in a swimsuit before. To him, she looked great. She also looked great without anything on too.

Cheryl showed a slight bump in the middle, but she had a cute face that went well with a two-piece. As for Josh, Harwood hadn't seen him shirtless for some time and felt self-conscious, looking at his friend who had more muscle definition than he, although Harwood could brag a broader chest, bigger deltoids, thicker neck and more muscular legs. Two big men who held the same values.

There is not a lot of need for ornate jewelry and expensive clothing in a mining community, so the women settled for looking, but not buying, in a local mall while the four males made the rounds of sporting goods stores and men's wear stores. A great way to come out financially ahead is not to buy what you don't need. The group stuck to a routine of going out three hours in the morning, eating a leisurely lunch, and going out again three hours in the afternoon. After dinner hours were occupied by going to a movie or lounging poolside.

The township of San Manuel has a handful of streets, signals, and stop signs. Phoenix, one of the largest and most sprawling cities in the country, boasts a heck of a lot of street and freeway miles, which include some 20,000 stop signs and signals. For the country folk, negotiating the freeways and the city in general quickly became stressful, a consideration that brought them to a strategy: stick to the downtown sports arenas, museums, and restaurants, except for outlying areas such as the zoo.

Enjoy it while you can, Harwood told himself. Except that he didn't enjoy it as much as he thought he would. He couldn't let go. The wound refused to heal. If childhood trauma were ignored, a big if, it all began with Nordstrom's crony in PNG, then Ally asking him about his worst moments, then having to deal with this Doug ex-husband, then Ochoa, then the ongoing saga with Farmer. He saw threat as the common denominator, one that constantly picked at the old scab. To anybody else, they were independent events to be dealt with independently. Harwood viewed the events as linked. Did the chain have an end to it?

And if it did all begin before he could remember? Did his true father threaten his mother? How many times had he done so? Importantly, had he been a witness to it as Mason had postulated. In the end, did any of it matter? Everyone has their baggage to deal with. I'm no different, he thought, trying to console himself, disturbed by his self-analysis.

The group had left on a Friday evening and returned mid-day Saturday, eight days later. Ally, the designated driver, dropped off the Aldays at their home, then drove to Harwood's to take him up on his offer for a steak dinner. Two hours later, he walked outside to check on a steak he had set on the backyard picnic table to thaw when his cell phone rang. He listened, grunted, and hung up.

She asked, "Who was that, honey?"

He replied, almost cheerily, "Bob Cargill. Seems there is one angry pissed off superior court judge who wants to know why his son is charged with a couple of felonies and a half-dozen misdemeanors."

"He's out of jail isn't he?"

"On his own recognizance," Harwood answered. "The judge is coming down tomorrow with a couple of people. Bob wants me and Josh to be there along with Scott to take him on the tour. If they expected to ride the tour train, he says to tell them it's down for servicing, so he and his friends get to walk along the tracks wearing a headlamp and can sweat their asses off. We'll take a couple of miles back and forth through the drifts, like we had to do, and show them the stops the train made. We'll tell them where the kid disappeared and show them the pit his grandson fell into though his own son's negligence."

"You're bad," Ally shook her finger at him. "You know, baby, it might be nice if you had a reporter or two along for the ride."

Harwood nodded thoughtfully, then kissed her for the suggestion.

"Let me check on something," Ally said, wiping her hands. Harwood followed her inside to find her on the computer. He waited patiently for his in-house librarian to finish her project.

After several minutes, she looked up at him and said, "The boy had a concussion, a head laceration that needed stitches, two cracked ribs and a broken femur. Whether or not he regains full cognitive abilities remains to be seen.

"Jerry Farmer is a Harvard grad. His mother and older brothers are also attorneys. A few years ago he got charged with spousal abuse. The case was dropped."

"Some of that doesn't sound like it's public record," Harwood muttered, almost to himself.

"Sweetheart, in today's world, the information is available. All you have to know is where to look to get your hands on it," she replied, sweetly.

At 11:00 am, Scott Ferrell, Josh Alday, and Draco Harwood stood at the opening to the top shaft of the dual tunnels. They were joined by a reporter from the largest newspaper in Phoenix, The Arizona Republic; the same reporter who had written the story. All wore work clothes and work boots. The tour train stood on the tracks, like dark snake at rest. It was not operational because it was under repairs, or so it would be reported to the visitors. Within the drifts would be found other railed machinery such as a generator, welding equipment, a Jack Leg Drill, water hoses, air compressors, misting equipment, axes, and shovels.

On schedule, Cargill drove his white company truck up the dirt road past the first shaft to a cleared area where the four men stood, some 200 yards up the mountain followed by a black Mercedes. Once the Mercedes came to a stop, Cargill made a U-turn to disappear, leaving the rest up to the men he trusted, including the reporter.

Three men, all wearing expensive suits, ties, and dress shoes, emerged from the car and walked over to the men standing at the entrance. The one in the middle turned to look behind him at the open pit mine hundreds of feet deep, the surrounding desert and the community of San Manuel from his elevated vantage point. Turning back, he said, "I'm Lawrence Farmer. Shall we get on with it?"

Harwood and Alday exchanged eyeball glances. That was it. No greetings, no handshakes. Harwood introduced himself and the other three men, paying special attention to Scott, their union representative, head of the mine rescue team, and the one who had saved the boy.

The two men accompanying the judge did not get introduced, looking like cardboard cut-outs of one another, looking around as though, when not at home, they had never seen the outside of an office or a bar other than to drive between them.

Harwood began explaining about the ride and their standard instructions to the passengers, displaying a pamphlet that all passengers received saying the same thing. He gave the judge a copy.

Alday handed each man a hardhat with a lantern on it along with a battery pack to attach to their belt. The gray-haired judge was about to object when Alday announced, "Everybody wears one, absolutely no exceptions. Let's go."

He began leading the group into the mine tunnel. Because the mine had been closed, the pumps were not operational. Water had accumulated in the gutters next to the rails. The floor shined wet. The fans were off, the air was dead, the humidity had risen to an almost suffocating level, with the temperature nearing 100°F in the deeper spaces. An occasional curse came from one of the visitors when he stumbled, or fell to one knee. Alday led his disgruntled followers on the outside of the tracks to avoid various pieces of equipment remaining. After 15 minutes, he stopped and remarked that this was the first tour stop.

Harwood took over, leading them into a drift, all the while explaining how the two stayed in contact by radio while they searched, noting the sweat running down the men's faces, soaking their shirts, their loosened ties, ruining their expensive shoes. The reporter remained stoic, basically invisible, doing his job, closely eyeing the guests, perhaps enjoying his job.

Despite protestations, Harwood, Alday, and Ferrell ensured the men spent a good 90 minutes inside the tunnels, at one point having everyone turn off their lights at the battery pack to experience pitch blackness, trying to walk forward, explaining that this is what a lost boy must have felt.

Scott took over, asked the guests to turn on the lamps again, finally leading them to the raise that, by this time tomorrow, would be emptied into the ore cars below. He explained the process of the rescue, emphasizing the father's negligence in trying to impress the crowd, rather than staying with his son as instructed. When he could, he inserted the word 'grandson' to emphasize a point, to cement the connection between the judge and the youngster.

No questions were asked. The only sounds from the visitors were grunts and complaints.

Another half mile to go to reach the exit.

The reporter had taken before and after photographs, his voice-activated recorder had been in operation.

"That's the tour, gentlemen," Harwood told the men, once they reached the glaring sun of the early afternoon. As one, the guests reached into their suit pockets for their sunglasses.

The judge turned to his hosts and said, stoically, exhibiting a great deal of class, "Thank you, gentlemen, you are both very instructive." He reached out a sweaty hand to shake theirs.

"I want copies of those 'befores' and 'afters' for my wall," Alday told the reporter, watching the men get into their car.

"Make that three sets," Scott threw out.

"My treat," said the reporter. "Very instructive," he repeated.

The four watched the driver start the car and play with some switches, doubtless to set the air conditioning on high. The temperature in the sun-baked car exceeded that of the mines by some 20 degrees.

The reporter checked to ensure the recorder had operated correctly and commented, "Thanks for letting me keep a record of your tour lecture. I can use it to run a promo for your next visitor's day. If you have a place I can relax and write this story, I can send it in before I drive back and get it into tomorrow's edition."

Harwood clapped him on the back and announced, "My house. Beer's on me."

"What do you think's going to happen to Mr. Farmer?" the reporter asked. "Get a slap on the wrist?"

Harwood laughed. "The way daddy looked, I'd say he's going to dismember Jerry. I've seen that pursed lips look before. After after your story comes out, I wouldn't be surprised to see Jerry resign."

The reporter concluded, "There's a clear line between subjective and objective writing, but I'll see what I can do to help things along, maybe if I can get away with throwing a little color into the story."

19

This drift reflected the high extreme. Not only was copper abundantly visible, but veins of silver and gold permeated the walls and ceiling. To Harwood, this particular drift not only smelled differently, it echoed differently. In addition, although metals themselves do not have an odor, a complex mixture of earthen chemicals and dirt combined with heat and humid air imparted a musty odor peculiar to the mixture.

There were exceptions. The sense of smell doesn't operate without the presence of moisture, either inside or outside of the nose. When water comes in contact with sulfurous compounds, a rotten-egg smell is imparted. Arsenic will have the odor of almonds when exposed to moisture.

In the typical mine, one can expect to encounter smells of dynamite powder, cigarette smoke, welding, decay of old timbers, diesel engines and power generators, combined with body odor to-all add a certain unique fragrance to the air. But this differed. It possessed a subtle, but strangely different smell that Harwood couldn't quite identify.

His father had taken him to visit a mine as a special present for his 4th birthday. Children could work in mines at the age of 16 in many places in the world. No young children at the age of four were allowed. Nobody needed an un-tethered child to break free of a father's grasp to cause mayhem, or more likely, to become injured. The repercussions would be enormous, not only for the father, but for the company as a whole.

Although Harwood's father, Mason, had been shift supervisor at the time, he still had the foresight to ask permission from the foreman, a close friend. In reply, his friend admonished, "I'll permit it only under the conditions that you go into a main corridor and not as far as a drift; that you go into a corridor that is not in operation at the time; and I never gave you permission, because you never spoke to me."

His father had explained that the top dog of a mining operation is the Mine Superintendent. Under him is a supervisor for each shift, and numerous foremen for each of the more than half-dozen specialized operations.

He explained that by the time this particular project was completed, the interior of the mountain would look like a three-dimensional spider web woven by a drunken spider.

Harwood remembered in detail the short time he had spent late that day with his father. To his great discomfort, Mason had tethered him to a harness immediately prior to entering the mouth of the tunnel. From there, they walked along the tracks, each wearing a head lamp on their helmet. He looked at the tracks, the drainage, the shoring, and the blue-green surrounds that would yield everything from copper ore to turquoise and malachite gems to be worn in jewelry. He didn't comprehend the magnitude of what was being produced, but he remembered the sights and smells, as though he were a reader who had found an ancient out-of-the-way book store and enwrapped himself in the musty smells surrounding him, or, as if one encountered a fragrance their mother had worn when they were an infant.

Each year Mason would take him into a new corridor and eventually into the drifts, and of course, where new smells presented themselves.

According to science, the sense of smell is the longest lasting memory we have, compared with sight, hearing, and touch. Harwood sensed that something might be amiss and said so.

"Josh, I don't feel right about this."

Alday lacked the youthful experiences of his friend and had learned to trust Harwood's judgment over the many hard years they had spent together. Not knowing what to say, he quipped, "Why, too much color?"

Harwood remained silent, almost as though he were sending out sensory feelers, then said, "Yes and no. There's something else."

His concerns became reality when he and Alday blew out a section of drift deeper into the mountain and hit the water table that had migrated upward into a large cavity.

At first, the water trickled in from the new blast area. Always wary, the men backed up in the presence of a bad omen. Water commonly enters mine drifts during operations from mountains or underground rivers. Water can be expected after closures because the pumps are off. Normal mining operations call for a drainage ditch on either side of the track for any incoming water to migrate outward where it is pumped to the surface. It then goes into a collecting pond.

Harwood needed to sound the alarm bell to send down the elevator cage, but that remained at the entrance to the main corridor, a good mile back and another half-mile to its entrance. It should still be in place, because they were the only crew operating at that time.

The two men kept a close eye on the water eating away at the six-foot-diameter hole they had created, increasing its flow rate by the second. Suddenly, Harwood yelled at the top of his voice for all to hear, "The water's red!" It was actually orange and red, but why mince words in an emergency.

The pair began to run back, yelling at the

same time. Men hurried to the exit, seemingly a thousand miles away. The first one pushed the button to call the cage down.

Every man there knew what red water meant. Iron sulfide lined a water cavern. That cavern had been breached. In the presence of oxygen and carbon dioxide, sulfuric acid is formed along with red-colored iron oxide, the same iron oxide that covers the hills of Sedona.

In their case, copper mines also have zinc, iron, gold, and sulfides present in the walls, ceiling and floor in extremely rich abundance. When exposed to water and air, more sulfuric acid is formed at 10-100 times the concentration found in car batteries. In short, if the wall burst, they would be in deep trouble.

Running for their lives and looking behind them at the same time, Harwood and Alday saw the rock swell, preparing to burst, and flood acid water into the drift.

"Go, go, go," Harwood yelled in front of him to the crew. "Get out. We're okay."

But they weren't.

They heard the elevator ascend, which meant the men had reached safety while the flood would soon reach the end of the corridor. There was a small saving grace. The drifts were cut at a seven degree down-slope so that thankful seconds would be gained as the lower portion filled. The men moved as quickly as they dared backtracking on the drift to where it curved into the main corridor up to the muck train. They climbed aboard the first ore car they came to as the wall burst and an ever-building current ran past them. It would continue to flow until it reached the opening to the tunnel and then fall into the vertical shaft that had been carved into the earth another 500 hundred feet down. No pumps would help their situation.

In addition to the ground water, the air had become acidic and toxic. The sulfides commonly present in the dry earth had been converted to a chemical soup of sulfide compounds, including vaporous sulfuric acid along with poisonous hydrogen sulfide gas. The air smelled like sour rotten eggs. At first the men felt a tickle in their throats, but as the concentration of poisons in the air increased, they began to cough.

As seasoned veterans, the men turned off their headlamps to preserve their battery packs, with no reason to keep them on for now. But for the flow of the torrent and their coughs, silence reigned supreme in the pitch blackness of the drift.

Sitting atop a mine car filled with copper muck, Alday said, "Got a cigar? I'm fresh out."

"No, worries, Mate," Harwood said, pulling out a small cigar from a box of Swisher Sweets in one of his bib pockets.

The men lit up and sat in silence, using the cigar smoke to offset the sour taste in their mouths, trying to breathe shallowly.

"So what's going on with you and the stunner?" Alday asked.

"The babe? Oh, she's all right, I guess."

"You got the hots for her. Right? Cheryl says she's got her hooks in you. She seemed to smile a lot more when you returned from your trip up north," Alday persisted.

"You're closer to that side. What's the water level at?" Harwood asked, taking a hit off his cigar. He coughed, put out the cigar, and wrapped a bandana around his nose and mouth.

"Why me? I'm too comfortable sitting on these sharp rocks." Alday remarked. A moment later he relented and turned on his headlamp. "About a foot below the rim of the car we're on, and don't skirt the issue. You didn't answer my question."

"It's going well. Thanks for asking," Harwood replied.

"Which tells me you're madly in love. Am I right?" Alday asserted.

"Yeah, I'm getting there. She's pretty special," Harwood replied, simply, which told his friend that the man next to him could, indeed, be in love.

A short minute later in the black silence, Alday checked the level of the water and reported, "About five inches below the rim of the car we're on. How about if we move to the start of the line?"

"Works for me," Harwood said. Both men

turned on their headlamps to carefully step over rocks and debris in the car they were on, taking a long step to the next car, trying not to break a leg or fall in a river of red. They continued the trek, at last climbing into the last car in line filled with rocks and dirt.

"They can't send the cage down until the water stops flowing," Harwood said.

Alday responded by saying, "Nope. I don't think they need it filled with this rot." At that, he, too, wrapped his face in a bandana. Their eyes were beginning to burn, as though they were in a city of heavy smog.

"Shame what happened to Ochoa," Harwood commented, reflecting on past events.

Alday said, "Cheryl told me that when you and I were finished with him and you put her in charge of watching the bastard while we ransacked his house, she worked him over on her own."

This piqued Harwood's interest enough to ask, "Did she say what she did to him?"

"Nope. She grunted and told me that I'm not old enough to understand," Alday replied.

Harwood tried to laugh, but coughed instead.

A few minutes later, Alday checked the water level and announced, "Going down. Only a foot high. When the elevator dings, I would not recommended that either of us takes a header in his mess. It won't hurt my face, but you won't be so cute anymore. On the other hand, that might be a true test of Ally's love for you, I mean, with your beautiful face cosmetically altered and your curly locks blistered off."

"When it does ding, we have, what, another 200 yards to go to get to it?" Harwood guessed, ignoring Alday's comments.

"At least."

"We'd better change boots when we get to the surface," Alday contributed.

"Yep. After that, I might get a fresh supply of cigars," Harwood muttered.

The men paid the price for being heroes. An hour later, they found themselves in the San Manuel hospital stripped to their skivvies, in bed, wearing hospital gowns, and on oxygen. They would spend a week under rehab for respiratory distress and burned lungs. Neither man would be running marathons or smoking cigars anytime soon.

20

When miners were tired of not getting better safety measures and having to pay their own hospital bills, they grumbled and then went on strike. In these cases, Groebels sent in strong-arms to break up a collection of miners who wanted to join a union, their standard practice wherever the firm operated, whether it be in PNG, Australia, Europe or Asia. The company had enough money and power to come out ahead. Not always, but enough to make it very profitable for their shareholders.

In the case of Copper Mining, Inc., a strike was ended when experienced federal negotiators combined efforts with astute company businessmen, along with a state governor who did not take sides, in order to come up with an acceptable plan of action. Both sides would work together. Choke points were cleared and production increased significantly for the benefit of everyone.

The name of Groebels came up as an example of what not to do, Harwood's hatred flared. He had been too long without a plan of action to take them down without costing some 50,000 jobs worldwide. He began to formulate a strategy. It might not even cost that much. His old partner, Ally's father, James, would be involved. He would hardly say "no" once he heard that Mike Nordstrom would be the first target.

When Harwood explained what he had in mind to Alday and Cheryl, they toasted the plan and came up with additional suggestions. If they got caught, the backlash could be devastating for all of them, a thought that added an element of excitement to the project and seemed especially luscious to Ally who had become a great fan of danger, especially when she could become involved and not evaluate the behavior of others.

Ally wanted to make the first call to her father. Once she did, Harwood went on the line and spoke with Brooks for ten minutes, explaining his idea. Brooks became enthusiastic and said he'd start working on it.

Three days later, he called back. "Draco, there are enough American tourists and military personnel here in Germany to warrant attorneys who are bilingual. It took some looking, but I found one agency that has a lawyer who specializes in investigative work. He's a native German, but got his law degree from New York University. He wanted $2000 up front to get started, which I paid. No worries. Consider it my contribution. Anything over that and I'll let you know. Ciao."

One week later, Brooks called back and said, "Sorry, my guy needs another 2K. He's not a rip-off, I can tell you that. He's got two men plus himself working on it. He's the real deal. I say invest in a winner."

Harwood and Alday left the girls out of it. They were well apprised of the situation. As such, they were totally supportive, and volunteered to contribute, but the men insisted that it was they who had been wronged, not the women. Harwood explained, unnecessarily, that what occurred happened way before their time, but if it ever worked out, the girls could pay for the drinks.

"Shit, that could cost more than the attorney's fees, the way you guys go at it," Cheryl quipped.

Three weeks later Harwood got home late to find that Ally at his house. She had been spending more time there than at her own. Now, she had signed for a certified envelope in the mail from a legal firm in Germany. She waited for him so they could open it together.

Harwood kicked off his boots, and opened two bottles of beer. They sat on the sofa to examine to documents on letterhead paper which read:

Dear Mr. Harwood:
This report regards the matter for which you engaged myself and

my firm. To wit, to investigate the background of a Mr. Mikael Helmut Nordstrom, presently Executive Vice President of Groebels Mining, Inc., Cologne, Germany.

Please find enclosed copies of several official documents, which we have obtained. The first dates back to when Mikael Nordstrom administered mining operations in PNG. As you may know, he comes from a family of great wealth which may exceed $100 million dollars. He was charged with drunken hit and run of a native woman, but the judge in the case gave him 30 days and let him go on his own recognizance. The document is the judge's release form along with a single story that appeared on the back page of a newspaper regarding the incident.

The second document is from the government of Papua New Guinea and dates to the years 1982-1986, the same time period the first offense occurred. During that period, Mr. Nordstrom headed a mining operation in which you and a Mr. James Brooks were party to.

The document is the equivalent to a warrant for his arrest for murder issued by the Papua New Guinea government for abuse and death of a number of native workers who were in his employ. Our sources confirm that he left the country immediately after the deaths occurred, ostensibly to avoid prosecution. Unfortunately, the resources of the PNG government are limited and there are many such cases on their books, thus nobody pursued Mr. Nordstrom.

The third document occurred some 10 years ago and involves charges of death of an unborn child. In that incident, he consorted with a mistress here in Germany who became pregnant and who threatened to sue. He struck her numerous times, which resulted in the loss of the child. The judge assigned to the case is close friends with his father. No penalty was assessed to Mr. Nordstrom.

Please contact us if you have any further questions regarding these matters.

Sincerely,
Wilhelm Schmidt
Attorney at Law
Schmidt and Associates.
Xc: James Brooks

"This guy seems like just your all around well-balanced nice person. Makes me feel all cozy," Ally remarked, giving a shudder.

Harwood said nothing, deep in thought. He

checked the time and went to the phone to call Josh and Cheryl. Alday said they'd be over in an hour, as soon as they finished dinner and could get their next door baby sitter to come over for a short while.

Harwood had taken a shower and changed after dinner to find that Ally had just cleared the dining room table when their friends arrived. They all took a seat and Harwood handed over the documents for them to read.

Cheryl suggested, "Let's lead from behind."

Alday nodded vigorously, "Absolutely. We'll stay out of the line of fire. James can hire the attorneys to write to the PNG government that they're located Nordstrom. If we're lucky, the German's can begin extradition proceedings."

"And we make sure it blows up in the press. This is too big to stay in Germany," Harwood said.

"We need more money," Ally said.

Harwood laughed, "I know about a dozen guys who will throw in their life savings toward the cause, myself included. The first step is to get enough money to work with. I don't want to run out when we need it the most."

Ally contributed, "I'm curious about the relationship between the two countries. I can't imagine that PNG is too happy with the German firm, after the mess they left when the mining operation played out, from what you guy have told me. The Brits might want to get involved, too, in part because PNG was a former colony."

"Which means they might jump at the chance to hang Nordstrom, so to speak," Cheryl added.

Harwood said, "Wasn't Nordstrom's father CEO of Groebels during the time period the hit-and-run occurred? Perhaps he's the one who got him off. Exposing the issues would certainly put the heat on him too. The press might have a field day. Maybe he'll even lose a night's sleep.

"Ally, I'm going to call your father and tell him what we're thinking. I'm going to ask him if he has any ideas on how to proceed."

"He's probably thinking along the same lines," she said.

Alday offered, "I'll contact our old buddies and let them know we've uncovered something hard about Nordstrom without going into specifics. We don't need any leaks, but their contributions would go a long way toward hiring good legal counsel."

Harwood said, "Good. Let's sleep on it, because there may be a more we can do to cause them pain and suffering."

"That's sick," Cheryl quipped.

"Thanks. I thought you'd never notice," Harwood concluded, sardonically.

Two weeks later, Harwood established a new bank account with several thousand dollars deposited, earmarked for their project. As far as anybody in Germany knew, James Brooks was just another mine worker, although he did make occasional visits to a certain legal firm on his days off.

As Harwood had suspected, PNG and Germany appeared friendly on the surface for the sake of international trade. Groebels did still operate several mines there and it kept a lot of people employed, albeit at base-level wages. Beneath the surface, the political scene remained ugly. Striking workers had closed down one mine and strike-breaking strong-arms hired by Groebels had beaten some of the strike leaders to the point of hospitalization. Nothing had changed. Apparently, that held true for Nordstrom, as well. From what James could glean, the man was still pompous, overbearing, and dictatorial.

Rapid advances in computer capabilities, communications, the Internet, and technology in general, made it a lot easier to follow international news than it had been only a few years earlier. Normally, an outlying area like San Manuel, is way down the list when it came to improvements of this nature, but, after some rough patches, Copper Mining, Inc. had become a model company revered for its good salaries, employee care, and "keeping up with the times." In a state that produced some 68% of the nation's copper, the company could not afford to backslide, although circumstances forced it to raise the price of its refined ores somewhat to compensate for its increased employee benefits.

Legal processes frequently take time to develop for a variety of reasons. However, with a green light to proceed and cash money paid to seal the deal, Schmidt and Associates went to work. According to James, Schmidt told him they'd been hired to file suits against Groebels a number of times over the years, but no case had ever gone to court. In these matters, the suit is frequently dropped because of settlements with the complainant, a normal business tactic used by insurance companies and corporations to make the problem go away. In other instances, the suits had been dropped for unknown reasons.

However, this case differed. Now, nations were involved, as was an executive with the largest mining company in the world. It was all too juicy. Even Wilhelm Schmidt smiled with glee when James wire-transferred the money to the agency's account. This wasn't because of the money itself, they had plenty of that, but because it would bring great notoriety to his company while they attempted to expose a bad guy at the same time.

Like a tumor surgeon preparing to excise the troubling mass, Schmidt became almost gleeful when James suggested that there may be more than one bad guy.

21

The government of PNG is a constitutional monarchy and falls under the authority of the United Kingdom. In short, even though the country and its surrounding islands are tremendously diverse in terms of ethnicities and ecosystems, the rule of law generally mirrors English law. Thus, England was brought into play once the PNG government had been officially notified that Mikael Helmut Nordstrom had been located working in Germany and still with Groebels.

The phone lines blew up and rumors started from somewhere that Nordstrom had wantonly murdered and tortured defenseless Papuan citizens, who were under the protection of the Monarch of England, no less, and perhaps had stolen a great deal of money from his own company—who knows, it could be in the millions of dollars—and that he had deliberately killed a mother and child but got away with it—maybe the judge got paid off—somebody needed to check the judge's bank account, and so forth.

Casting bread upon still waters still requires bread. Once the old loaf had been cast, the ripples became large.

Nordstrom relaxed on his 75 foot-long two-deck yacht. He had just left the port of Marseille, France, when a gunship raced behind the boat with sirens blaring, pulled alongside, and ordered the ship via megaphone to return to port. A display of weapons helped convince the yacht's steersman and the girls onboard that it might be a good idea to follow orders.

Once parked, gendarmes handcuffed the confused and now somewhat portly businessman. He would be told the charges when the time was right to do so. For now, he would be placed behind bars.

Hours later, a representative of the German embassy came to visit him along with an attorney who explained the charges and how the extradition process would proceed.

"This is all such bullshit," Nordstrom declared in English, as well as its equivalents in German and French. He desperately tried to make sense of what they were telling him. He had done nothing wrong. But the PNG government saw differently and convinced the English authorities that it might be best for relations if Nordstrom did not get off this time, but paid some kind of penalty. For openers, they suggested a lifetime in prison.

Through it all, Wilhelm Schmidt spoke daily with a representative of the PNG government and with British authorities. He had explained that, quite by accident. He personally had stumbled upon the location of Nordstrom through a number of coincidences. How he had found him didn't matter. What to do with the man would be the issue. This story was becoming international and the press couldn't wait for the next bit of gossip and innuendo, but it wouldn't come from Nordstrom. His attorney, hired by Groebels, had ordered him to keep his mouth shut.

This same attorney visited the prisoner a second time several hours after he had been arrested and said he was working on something and would return in a few days. When he did appear, his briefcase and his person having been thoroughly checked, he found his client laying on the cot, hands behind his head. The supine man quickly came to his feet when the jailer permitted the visitor to enter.

"Please sit, Mikael," said the attorney, who took up a seat next to him. He looked around as though he thought there might be spy cameras or recording devices in the cell. One could never be too certain. He leaned close to his client and said, "Your current wife filed charges against you for sexual abuse and hired Schmidt and Associates to represent her. She also claimed that the abuse she had suffered in Germany over the years negated the prenuptial agreement she had signed. Therefore, she was entitled to all of your assets. Schmidt agreed with her. It will be a fight."

"That's what you came here to tell me?" Nordstrom inquired.

"No, that was the good news. Your father is quite upset about the situation. His blood pressure is acting up again. The shareholders are voicing their concerns. Company stock is taking a beating."

"Keep going," Nordstrom asked, sarcastically. Despite what people might think about him, he did have feelings. He loved and respected his father. He had always done his best to emulate the man, but, in perspective, he was beginning to believe that perhaps that was not the wisest thing he could have done.

The attorney leaned even closer and hung his head down, as did Nordstrom. "There's talk by the German government of freezing your assets. The only good thing about that action is that your wife won't be able to get her hands on it. So, unless she's saved some money, she could be financially strapped."

In an even softer voice, the attorney said, "I know Schmidt. We go back a long way. The man doesn't happen onto a piece of information by accident, or by lucky coincidence, meaning the finding of your whereabouts. So I checked with one of my former employees who now works for Schmidt's outfit."

The attorney shifted gears. "Did you, or do

you, know a James Brooks?"

Nordstrom shook his head.

"Don't be so quick to say 'no'. Think," demanded the attorney.

Nordstrom replied, "The name sounds a little familiar. Why? Is he some guy my wife's been seeing on the side? I wouldn't put it past her."

The attorney said, "No, it's not about her. My guy over at Schmidt's said that this James Brooks came in and gave you up. So I checked a list of your employees and Brooks' name appeared. He's shift supervisor at your gold mine outside of Frankfurt."

Nordstrom threw his hands in the air halfway to indicate that he still remained clueless, then said, "How does any of that tie in with this PNG mess I'm charged with?"

"Because, my friend, Brooks used to work for you for a short time back in the day."

"Back in what day?" Nordstrom insisted, growing tired of the word games.

"Back in the PNG days. He's an American. Does that help?" asked the attorney.

Of a sudden it all clicked. "That fucking American Brooks and the Kiwis. Yeah, I laid them off. So what?"

The attorney had been on the payroll of Nordstrom's family a long time and knew his client could be obstinate. This was not the right time for that. "Come on, if there's more to the story, I need to hear it," the attorney coaxed. "Those guys can get other jobs and probably did. Why is Brooks involved?"

"I wanted to save money and told them that . . . well, if they didn't all quit under their own volition, their families would be killed."

"You did what?" the attorney said out loud, sitting up straight for a moment before hunkering down again.

"Yeah, I remember now. I told my man to tell Alday and their bunch and this fucking hardass named Harwood who turned my man into a vegetable when he got the news. Brooks was part of the bunch."

"There's your motive," the attorney, unnecessarily. "I'd keep an eye on Harwood, too. He probably had a hand in this."

"I try to watch my back," Nordstrom said.

"Really? How's that working out for you at the moment?" the attorney said, making a motion to include the surrounds. A moment later, he added, "Brooks has a daughter working out in Arizona in the southwestern United States. My contacts over at Copper Mining, Inc. tell me she got hired there not long ago and works along with Harwood and their close friends, Alday and his freaky wife."

"Well, you certainly have done your homework," Nordstrom said, turning down his mouth in a show of appreciation.

"That's why it took so long to get back to you," the attorney confessed. "What do you want to do with Brooks?"

"Don't touch him for now. If we transfer him or fire him or promote him, he'll get suspicious. Anyway, that's all interesting information you're giving me, but it doesn't get me off the PNG hook," Nordstrom said.

"Nope, but Groebels is willing to fight your case to the limit. Even if you were extradited, it could take months. Now, in case you wanted to return some favors . . . ," the attorney suggested.

Nordstrom smiled, "I know that you're not suggesting retribution or revenge. I mean, it's illegal. Something like that would require careful thought and a lot of time and patience to plan."

Nordstrom figured he had plenty of both, until the attorney suggested, "Perhaps not as much time as you might think."

Nordstrom looked at him and smiled. "I'm not saying 'yes'."

"No, you never said it," came the reply.

22

"Come on, kids, Uncle Draco wants to take us out to dinner and a movie in the big city tonight. Now get ready. I told you that before. Aunt Ally's coming with us too," Cheryl yelled.

"But mom, we want to watch our new TV," the boys, ages 8 and 10, yelled back, almost in unison.

"Sorry for the noise, Draco," Cheryl said into the receiver. "Josh will be out of the shower in a few minutes and we'll be right over."

"Okay, but expect to be home late," Harwood replied.

"I know, but at least there's no work or school tomorrow," Cheryl said, hanging up.

Ninety minutes later, the extended family ate barbeque ribs and fries, then walked across the street to the theater. A sign on the door read, "All phones off and no texting permitted. Thank you. Signed, The Management."

By 10:30, the carload of family and friends was on their way home, well past the boys' bedtime. Both were asleep in the back seat, one head on each of Cheryl's legs with Ally seated next to Harwood and Alday to her right.

As they made the turn into their community, a curious glow appeared in the sky. Driving closer, the glow grew brighter until the unpleasant sight of fire trucks and firemen appeared in front of Cheryl and Josh's home. Fire hoses were in play.

Cheryl woke the children and the six exited the car, staring at the ruins of the Alday household. "Mom, Dad, this is our house," Julian cried.

"You mean was our house," David corrected, softly, thinking about his possessions and where they would sleep tonight.

A hot wind blew smoke in their direction. "Stay here," Cheryl directed the children. The four adults approached a fireman reading pressure gauges on the fire trick to identify themselves, flabbergasted, almost speechless at the sight. "How, I mean what . . . ," Alday stammered.

"I'm really sorry, sir, we think it might have been an electrical fire," replied the fireman who had BATTALION CHIEF emblazoned on the back of his fire jacket.

The implications of that statement struck them all. If they had been home, they could have all been dead, or severely burned. By sheer chance they had gone to the movies on this, of all nights. At least their cars had escaped destruction. Cheryl had parked hers in the driveway, which enabled it to get a good washing, while Alday had parked in front of the house. The cars were unlocked because few people locked them in the community, which made it easier for the firemen to push his to the next house down in order to access the fire. Most citizens didn't lock their homes, either. Ally did because she had lived in a big city. Old habits die hard.

Harwood had a suspicious mind. He needed more information before he could come to a rational conclusion. "What time do you think it started?" he asked.

"We'll know more about it later, but the first call came in about an hour ago," replied the chief.

Harwood looked at his watch. It read 11:30. The fire started sometime between 10:00-10:30, when everybody would be asleep.

"Everything's gone," Alday moaned. "Our home, our pictures, our clothes and furniture, the kids' toys, their new TV . . ."

Ally put her arm around each of the boys. The neighbors on either side had been told to leave for their own safety and stood watching from across the street. Other neighbors had joined them. If it happened to a good family like the Aldays, it could happen to them.

Ally offered, "Look, guys, you have to stay someplace tonight, so spend the night with me.

The company loaned me a nice futon couch that folds down to sleep two. I also have enough sheets and blankets for the boys. We'll sort it out tomorrow. There's nothing we can do here."

Harwood overheard and agreed. Pulling her aside, he said, "Honey, why don't you move in with me for the time being and let them have your house? It's all company property anyway. It'll take them time to reconstruct another home for them. I know for a fact there are no more houses available, unless they want to move down to Mammoth or in Oracle. Josh doesn't like Mammoth and the company won't pay for them to live in Oracle."

Ally's head spun. Her first impulse was to ask Draco to move in with her, instead of the opposite, except that she kept her home neat, clean, and simple, while his bespoke of a failing attempt at all three. Besides, she did have a two-bedroom.

"One thing at a time," she said. "I'm off Saturday this week. That's tomorrow. I'm taking them back down to Tucson to buy clothes for them all." She thought for a second and came up with a compromise.

"Okay, I'll do it for tonight to give them more room." At that she relayed their decision to the Aldays and gave them her house key. She kept the spare to enable her to grab a few personal items for the night and the next day before going over to Harwood's.

"That's really generous of you to take them," Harwood agreed. "The company will reimburse you. Be sure to save the receipts."

"You can come along if you want," Ally offered, feeling they all needed to be together at this time.

Harwood hesitated. He had always disliked shopping. Besides, he knew his friends were in good hands. Thinking quickly, he said, "Thanks for the invitation, but what I really want to do is to find out more about this fire and talk to some people, including Cheryl. I also want to spend time with the establishment and see what they can do for them."

At 8:45 am, Harwood called Ally's home. Cheryl picked up. He asked, "You were home pretty much this week, right? Did anything unusual happen last week, or this week or did anybody come into your life or Josh's that you can think of?" he asked.

Cheryl thought for a moment before replying, "Hmmm, I wouldn't call it unusual, but a telephone repairman came by in a telephone company truck a couple days ago. I was heading out to the corner market when I saw him going house to house. I waited until he came to us. He said they had received complaints from customers and he got sent to check the exterior connections to the phone boxes on this block. When he told me he wouldn't have to come into the house, I said he could do what he needed to do.

I decided to go pee before I went out and went back into the house. When I left, I saw him continue on down the street."

Harwood wanted to follow any slim lead he could to attempt to grasp onto niggling feeling. He didn't trust Groebels an inch. Nor did he trust Nordstrom. He didn't believe in coincidences. He believed in cause and effect. "By any chance, you didn't take his picture, like I suggested we all do if any strangers come around?" he asked, slyly, as if afraid of the answer.

Cheryl wondered if he was stupid or was pretending to be. "Sure. I got a good shot of him with my Polaroid. His truck, too. He tried to look casual, but I could tell he was a little put-out with me doing that."

Harwood rubbed his forehead. Groaning, he conjectured, "No doubt the pictures got lost in the fire."

"Actually, no. I stuck them in my purse, I have them right here. Why, do you want them?" Cheryl teased.

"Did Josh see them?" Harwood asked.

"No. I forgot all about it until you mentioned it," she replied.

"Would you mind dropping them off on your way out of town, please," Harwood suggested.

"Will do."

A short while later, Harwood opened the door to see Cheryl. Beyond them, Ally sat in the second row with the boys in a white long bed company van. Alday sat behind the wheel. Cheryl grinned and handed him the photo. One depicted a man wearing a hard hat. His ears stuck out somewhat and his facial features suggested mixed races. The truck stood in the background. The second photo depicted a clear shot of the truck majestic and proud, heavily tattooed with the lettering and telephone number of a phone company based in Tucson.

Harwood looked her in the eye, bobbed his head up and down a couple of times and gave a know-it-all-thanks smile. She grinned back and left him to his own devices, without a single word spoken. Considering them all brothers and sisters, he knew none of them would discuss the matter with the kids in the car, but would wait until they got together in the evening after the boys went out to play with their friends.

Hours later, after a successful day of shopping, the group returned and dropped off boxes and bags of clothing and toys at the new Alday residence. Ally had made the decision to let them have her house once she spent a little time transferring her personal belongings to Harwood's home. Each of the boys received a new bicycle.

An hour later, the four adults sat on Harwood's front porch drinking from a cooler of beer, keeping an eye on the boys who were in the playground across the street.

Harwood said, "The phone company is missing a truck from their lot. It's still out there somewhere."

Alday replied, "I'm wondering what his boss, or bosses, will say if Ears tells them that Cheryl took his picture."

Cheryl checked her fingernails and asked, "What now? From what you've told me, I'm starting to think that Nordstrom is not the leader. It may go above him."

Harwood contributed, "True. Maybe it's his father, he's CEO. But you're right, we can't keep on keeping on."

He directed, "Ally, you need to call your father and tell him what happened and to watch his ass."

Alday remarked, "Remember what Nordstrom said when I told him I'd come after him if anything happened to any of us? That was after the blowup in PNG."

Harwood looked off and said, grimly, "Yes. He said he'd remember it. I guess he has a long memory. Well, so do I."

Allowing for the nine hour time difference between Arizona and Germany, the couple made the call to Ally's parents at a time they knew her father should be home from work.

Harwood caught James up to speed on the current situation, to which James replied, "Draco, I only spoke to Wilhelm Schmidt about this, nobody else."

To which Harwood replied, "Somebody found out. The attorney isn't going to open his mouth. Maybe somebody saw you there."

"I guess, but who?" James replied.

Harwood answered, "Talk to Schmidt again and tell him everything that's going on from our end. This time, call him on the phone, don't go there, and be careful."

"So far, so good over here. Haven't heard a word from anybody," James said.

"I don't know what bothers me more; nothing happening, or you being connected to this at some point," Harwood concluded. He handed the phone back to Ally to let her speak with her parents about lighter matters, while he brooded over the situation.

23

"What are you doing tomorrow?" Harwood asked.

"Probably helping you clean up after to-night's game. Why?" Ally asked.

"Tomorrow, a geological crew is finishing pulling up copper core samples from backside of the Galiuro mountains. This single sample took several weeks to drill."

"How far down did they go?" she ask, now quite interested, excited to hear about anything geological.

"Something like 4000 feet. Most of what you'll see is gray granite. Hopefully they found indications of copper at some depth," Harwood explained.

"Which means that's it or not it?" she asked.

"Neither. It means more samples have to be drilled to find out which direction the ore body is headed," he explained.

"Heck, yes, I'm all in," she stated, enthusi-astically. Finally, she would get back to her first true love.

"Great. It should take us some time to get to the site. You'll see the rig and the work crew when we start to come down from the mountain. And bring some rain gear."

The mountainous region did not regale in forested acreage with stands of alder, birch, pine, and spruce with deep loamy soil. Instead, scrub oak, cactus, and small rocks to large boulders covered the surrounding desert mountains. The hour-long drive was not straight, but involved numerous switchbacks wide enough for broad-based trucks to pass through.

Finally, after using the four-wheel drive throughout, Harwood descended the dirt road that had been constructed over the mountain. Before them lay endless plains of prickly pear and Saguaro cacti, creosote, and endless sand, a huge Arizona industry unto itself. The scene presented awesome beauty in its own way, with black billowing clouds moving over rolling hills that changed in hue every few minutes. Lightning flashes pulsed behind the clouds in some areas, or ran vertical and horizontal streaks through others. No swimming today. For some dark reason, she envisioned an open pit copper mine in that plain, a great man-made gouge out of the earth a thousand feet deep — a disturbing thought.

Within minutes of their descent, they had arrived at a big rig resembling a water well drilling rig rising to some 40' in height. Even from half-mile away, with the windows up and the car's air conditioning running, the sounds of a diesel engine could be heard insulting the tranquility of nature. The self-contained rig had been driven foot-by-painful-foot over the mountain. A work crew had demarked the area by poles five-feet high with a yellow banner atop each to define the periphery of the worksite. Pickup trucks were parked away from the work area with blue COPPER CORE INC., SAN MANUEL, painted on their doors in blue-green lettering.

Seven orange-vested men wearing hardhats, gloves, boots, and eye protectors were hard at work, two operating the rig that brought up half-inch thick steel pipe and its inner casing that housed the core sample. In this method, the samples were collected on an angle approximating 45 degrees. Each of the geologists present possessed a different specialty.

Every three feet the water-cooled pipe would be unscrewed with a huge wrench, laid on the ground, and the cores removed to be washed free of mud, each labeled as to location, time, date, and depth. Other men loaded the pipes into core boxes which were transferred onto two flatbeds. When the crew left, the rig would stay in place. No sense hauling it back and forth over a mountain.

By the time the visitors arrived, the cores from some 3500 feet had been brought up. Numerous gray sections of 2.5" granite cores lay on the ground slotted into core trays some 5' long. Harwood reached behind the seat and pulled out a couple of hardhats, handing one to Ally along with a pair of eye protectors. "It's dangerous work," he said. "Don't take a single thing for granted."

Recognizing the lead geologist on the project named Art Cromwell, he walked over to him to shake hands. The two spoke for a few moments, with Harwood occasionally pointing back to Ally. Art nodded and the men came back to her.

Art introduced himself and said, "I hear good things about you, Ally. For one, I hear you're good luck."

She laughed. "Somebody forgot to tell me."

Art said, "Let me give you the quickie tour. When the rig pulls up the last section, you'll see the drill bit. It looks like the screw cap lid to a container half-inch in thickness inlaid with diamond encrusted tungsten. We're not seeing any greenish-yellow shine on these samples until about 1200 feet. See, it's in small patches," Art knelt down and pointed to the area. She knelt, as well. She'd seen it before in the old days.

Art continued, "That sample is broken in half and the middle is shiny with copper. Believe it or not, that's not what we want. The rest is up to other specialists to tell us which direction we need to go in order to define the thickness and direction of this ore body. This sample is probably at 0.3 percent copper. We want 3 percent or greater, if possible."

"How high does the percentage go?" she inquired, playing innocent.

"Up to 12% and even more in some countries," Art instructed. "You'll always find other elements mixed in with it."

Leading her to other samples, he pointed to another gray tube and explained, "See the shiny chunks? That's what we like. When we lay them out in sequence at home, we examine them in detail, sometimes with a magnifying glass or even a microscope in the lab."

Ally cheerfully added, "Because when the planets were formed from an exploding star, all the heavy metals congealed together from the superheat during the early eons of the planet's formation and were pushed upward later when the mountains lifted."

"How do you know that?" Art looked at her, curiously.

"I read a lot," she replied.

"Which means that other worlds will have ores too," Harwood conjectured.

"The way we're going, we may never get a chance to mine them," she concluded, philosophically.

In love with the detail, Ally pretended to know little of the subject. Walking between the lengthy rows of cores, she soon pointed and declared, "To me, it looks like it stops at around

3200 feet, so the copper is 900 feet in thickness in this area." At that moment, she saw something that surprised her, saying nothing about it.

"Let's have a look," Art answered. He walked over to where she stood bending over at the waist, prepared to augment her statement, when he looked at the sample from a distance, leaned closer, cleaned remaining dirt from the surface, picked up the fractured core, examined it and yelled, "Hey, Jack, come here a second."

The man named Jack came over and Art handed him the piece. "Tell me that's not silver," requested Art.

"That's not silver," Jack answered.

"But it is, isn't it?" Art said.

"A fucking shitload of it," Jack replied, not caring about the presence of a lady. He went down the line and hand-scraped much of the remaining sediment from the other lengths of core tubes, which were spotted with silver and copper going down hundreds of feet.

Jack turned and yelled, "Hey, Wyatt, come here."

The bearded man named Wyatt came over. Jack handed him the sample. "Tell me that's not silver," Jack requested.

Wyatt spit on the sample, rubbed it with his hand, took out a magnifying glass, and peered closer, "That's not silver," he replied. Shaking his head back and forth, he looked at the growing crowd and continued in a more polite manner than Art, "It's a fucking boatload."

He went down the line to confirm what they all saw. A more critical examination of the core samples would occur once they were all returned to the lab.

"Obviously, silver is worth a lot more than copper," Ally recited, innocently.

"Today, about 50 times," Jack replied, surprised at the find, as were they all.

Art said, "Ally, you're my new best friend."

The couple stayed for another three hours to assist with labeling and loading until the skies opened up and the great deluge began. "Be happy it's wet and we were late to the party. Depending on terrain, when it's dry and drilling begins, there's so much dust you can't see your hand in front of your face."

Nobody was going back over the mountain anytime soon.

Safely ensconced in their vehicle with the engine on and the A/C running, Harwood asked, "Do you know how to play poker?"

"No, should I?" she inquired, wondering what the heck this had to do with the geophysical exploitation of the earth.

"Yes, you should. There should be a couple of decks of cards in the glove box. Why don't you grab one?"

Three hours later, the caravan began its muddy voyage over the mountain. The rain had ceased for the moment. If it began again, they all might be stranded overnight. In an adventurous mood, Harwood asked Ally to drive back. If she can spend all day driving a big hog on an angle in a pit, this should be child's play, he thought. Closing his eyes, he attempted to take a nap in a bouncing, swaying car.

24

Work returned to normal for the next three weeks until Harwood received another envelope in the mail from Wilhelm Schmidt. As a matter of open record, Ernst Nordstrom's life was an open book with some pluses and some minuses, but as longtime CEO of Groebels, he had brought the firm to the top of the food chain. However, there were other aspects of the business not part of the open record.

Ernst Nordstrom was, and is, a very proud German. His country became a country a 1000 years ago and began to harvest coal two centuries later. He knew his mining. A direct descendant of those first mining ancestors, they had basically owned the coal and steel industry of Germany for centuries, which, for the previous two centuries, mined coal and steel in virtually all of Europe and which supplied his country the energy and steel it required to fight two world wars. He considered himself to be part of the exactitude German scientists and investigators had exhibited to the world throughout the history of the nation.

Nordstrom did have a problem. Times had changed. In today's world, the German coal industry essentially died. Wars and grievances were always there, but the new world bragged of raging technology, rapid transportation, instantaneous communication, changing attitudes. He felt out of touch. He found himself relying on his only son, Mikael, to set thing back to where he wanted them to be, using the old ways, if necessary. And damn it to hell, if Mikael couldn't make it happen, he would show him how to do it.

Early on, his own father had taught him to dogfight, his mother even more dogmatic than his father. Here is how you get to the top. Those who follow rules get ruled. Those who operate outside the rules make the rules, then do whatever they want to do. Here is how you cover your tracks. Here is how you control people who operate inside the box. Be wary of people who are at our level of stature. You have only a single son. Train him well. Overstep him when necessary. It's business as usual.

With arson suspected as the cause of the fire, given the information provided by Cheryl, the neighbors, and the telephone company, the "repairman" remained a person of interest. This held especially true in light of the fact that the fire marshal found a small time-delay explosive device inside the exterior electrical box. Somebody clearly intended to murder the Alday family. This smacked of a stern warning that the survivors, meaning Harwood, Ally, and James Brooks, should cease their probing. Neither miner would provide the investigators any possible motive for the attack, keeping it to themselves for the moment.

This act also suggested to Harwood that retribution might not be the only motive. There might be more to uncover in the Nordstrom's family can of worms.

Ally worked late hours in the repair shop. When she returned home one evening, she found Harwood sitting on the outside porch drinking a beer reading the contents of the envelope sent from Germany.

She pulled out a large bag of groceries she had purchased from the company store and carried them up the three steps to the porch. Ignoring her, Harwood muttered, "Holy shit. Can you believe that?" He looked directly at her as though she wasn't there and flipped a page. She left him alone, but stood watching. He rubbed the stubble on his chin, scratched his head, and said. "I don't fucking believe it. What a mess."

He pulled out a final single sheet of paper, looked at it and repeated, "Holy shit," once again.

Harwood retrieved the cell from his pocket, punched a speed dial number and said to whomever answered, "I need you both over here." At that, he recognized Ally's presence.

Gathering himself, he asked, "How's your geography?"

"Probably a lot better than yours," she responded. "Do you want to keep this a secret, or let me know if we won the lottery, or do you want to let the ice cream melt? You tell me."

"No sense saying it twice," Harwood responded. "Let's put away the groceries till they get here."

Ten minutes later Josh and Cheryl arrived to take their usual seats. Helping themselves to a beer out of the cooler freshly packed with ice, the group awaited the opening salvo from Harwood. A refreshing evening breeze blew out of the north to lend a gentle air to a somber meeting, adding dust, loose candy and cigarette wrappers, to the front stairs of the home.

"Does everybody know where Unimak Island is?" Harwood asked.

"Never heard of it," Cheryl admitted.

As if in school, only Ally raised her hand. She could withhold herself no longer. Letting go in a rush, she explained, "The Aleutians were named by Captain James Cook back in 1785. They're the chain of islands that belong to Alaska. Back a couple hundred years ago, Cook and a Russian named Baranov separately discovered the islands. Baranov also discovered an island along the west coast of North America that is named after him. Sitka is located on that island which became the center of Russian activity in North America.

"After that the Russians moved in. Things got ugly between the Russians, who were seeking seal and otter pelts, and the natives, most of whom were slaughtered. The Russians laid claim to Alaska until the U.S. bought it from them in 1867 for something like 7.2 million dollars, the equivalent of 144 million today

"Abraham Lincoln's Secretary of State, William Seward, made the deal and was ostracized for it. Things got dark for decades there with absolutely no government. Even the Americans didn't want to admit they owned the place. Now, Alaska and the Aleutians are mined for all sorts of ores, not to mention the state's resources in oil, fish, and tourism."

Ally came up for air, then submerged again. "I wouldn't want to pay for a block of ice, either, the way people thought, back then. Back to point, Unimak Island belongs to the Aleutian chain, first occupied from around 10,000 years ago by Tlingit people, originally from Asia." The professor had spoken.

Harwood interrupted. "You're getting into my territory. According to this report, on that island, the mines produce about everything you can name, from copper to gold, titanium, zinc, silver, sulfur, mercury, nickel, and so forth. What Schmidt is telling us, and I'll let you read it for yourselves, is that Groebels discovered uranium on Unimak."

Cheryl said, "Let me guess. The company is selling it to the Russians across the street."

Harwood shook his head. "Worse. It's like the U.S. selling a portion of its strategic oil reserves to China during an American oil shortage. They're selling uranium, all right, but not to the Russians. They already have thousands of nukes and plenty for power plants.

"Let me back up. In this country, you don't go out and mine uranium and that's that. You need serious permits and must follow countless regulations. What Groebels is planning to do is to ship the ore to one of several crushers located on Baranof Island outside of Sitka, one earmarked for uranium. But they're already receiving the ore from other sources, so when it all goes through the crusher and then the smelter to produce a higher quality ore, a certain amount will get diverted."

An environmentalist by nature, a trait inherited by her parents and recalling a class she had taken on Regulations Pertaining to the Mining Industry, Ally had to add, "The Bureau of Land Management, U.S. Forest service, U.S. Geological Survey, (and a host of other agencies) oversee mining operations on federal lands in the United States regarding hard rock mining. Not only must a foreign concern satisfy our regulations, but must ensure that state requirements are also met. Sometimes, it takes decades of work by highly trained and well-paid mining engineers, contractors, geologists, negotiators, and politicians to bring a contract to fruition, which, as you know, can all end if the locals won't allow operations to proceed.

"One question frequently asked, is: What does the host country, or state, get out of it? For the United States, the answer is nothing. Back in 1872, when the General Mining Act was created, local laws ran the regulations. If aquifers are poisoned in the process, so be it. This is unlike oil and gas companies that pay nearly 13% royalties to the Feds. In fact, the government lacks data on how much ore is actually removed."

Harwood inserted, "Right. Something like 30 tons of waste rock is removed in order to recover a single ounce of gold. And that's under conditions of professional mining."

Ally continued, totally in her element, "In the case of Unimak, what I see is heavy island rainfall washing uranium-laden ore down the mountainside to dissolve in water courses that flow into the ocean. Typically, fisheries may check for the presence of mercury in seafood, not whether the product is radioactive.

"Again, what does the U.S. get out of it? Employment for a few miners which, in this case, amounts to nothing."

Cheryl and Harwood stared at this self-educated woman wondering whether she needed to be fact-checked, or to take her at her word. What she said made sense.

Alday read and listened at the same time, until he suddenly declared, "You have to be kidding me. They plan to send their products to North Korea and Iran."

"Bingo," declared Harwood.

Several minutes passed in silence, while the other three read Schmidt's report, occasionally popping open another beer, like a bunch of jocks watching a football game on TV rather than the world they know coming to an end.

"Gee, I can't imagine why they'd want us dead," Cheryl spat.

Ally asked, "How does a law firm come up with information like that?"

Harwood said, "My guess is that that don't specialize in divorce cases. They probably do a lot of international work and probably work closely with an investigative agency. The agency follows rumors until they hit pay dirt by finding somebody who knows something. In this case, they might slip a few dollars to somebody who has worked for Groebels, maybe got laid off by them and is happy to assist. From that point, you try to prove your case with hard evidence."

Ally pulled out the last sheet of paper in the envelope and looked at it. "Oh, is that all?" she said, looking at a bill for $28,350.

"Guess he had to pay off some people," Cheryl said.

"Must be lowlifes in the know. Big boys want big money," Harwood said. "Look at the bright side. It could have been for ten times that much."

"Wouldn't he have to ask us first before he ran up that kind of money?" Alday threw out.

"Maybe they do things differently in Germany. What do I know?" Ally said. "Or maybe my father told Schmidt to do whatever it took to expose any dirt he could get on the company. Like you said, I should think all that uranium business would be highly regulated by the government."

Harwood grunted in reply, "Regulations are made by governments, which are made up of people, who can be bought to look the other way. It's called Business 101."

The four sat in silence. The sun began to set. Finally, Cheryl stood and announced, "It's been fun, but we have to get our kids home for dinner. Let us know when you want to go fund raising. We might be busy that weekend."

When she told the news to her father and mentioned the bill, he told her that they had guessed it right in that he had instructed Schmidt to do anything necessary to expose the criminals. "I guess he thought he had to make a certain profit."

She said, "Draco and Josh said they can pay it out of their savings."

James added, "No, worries, I'll do the same,

but I'm starting to think that we're in over our heads. We got to Nordstrom. Maybe we should call it quits."

Ally moaned, "Wish we could, Dad. But you know Draco. He says that sometimes a bad hand is in the eyes of the beholder. I'm inclined to go along with him."

"How's he taking it in general?" Books asked.

"He's hard to read," Ally told him. "He says he's waiting to see somebody else's hole card."

That hole card came when the forensics expert got the telephone man's prints off the hookup boxes for the neighbor's phone. The telephone man had to check them all on that street to keep up pretenses, before inserting the detonation device in the one belonging to the Aldays' where he used gloves."

A few weeks later, Harwood, Alday, and Ally were called off the job to go to the Mine Superintendent's office, normally on-site, but in this case, located in a building of its own in town, between a barber shop and a nightclub. When they arrived, they found Cheryl seated in an office chair. Two men dressed in suits, not normally seen in the township, stood nearby, as did the sheriff.

The walls of the office were adorned with black-and-white photos of various mining operations and machinery, their own open pit copper mine, and black and whites of miners from various eras. Water stains in the ceiling tiles added character to the room, like colorful Rorschach ink blots to tease every imagination.

The sheriff spoke first. He knew them all, and in truth, had played an occasional poker hand with them. Grinning, trying to lighten the mood, he said, "Josh, your wife was kind enough to let me bring her here."

"I'll bet," Alday snorted in return, without a trace of humor. He took a seat next to Cheryl and held her hand. This couldn't be good. He'd had enough run-ins with the law in his early years, enough so that his distrust remained ingrained and permanent, never to be revealed.

"What's up, Bob," Harwood asked the super.

Cargill introduced them to two men wearing suits, who identified themselves as FBI Special Agents. The men flashed credentials to citizens who wouldn't recognize a real one from fake junk. The sheriff and Cargill leaned against the office desk, while the two agents stood.

One of the suited men appeared to be in charge. He began to explain, "Relax, this isn't about any of you directly. This is about your telephone man. First, we want to thank you for the information that reached us about him. His name is Franz Braun. He's on the international watch list with the equivalent of an asterisk after his name, which means especially dangerous. Interpol picked him up in Austria. He's been in the employ of a company called Groebels—I'm sure you heard the name—since he could walk, and we've tied him to numerous crimes in Europe and South America. The man is fluent in a number of languages, although a native speaker might pick up an accent or two. Add the States to the list of recent crimes, as per your information. Upon interrogation, he admitted to working in PNG at the same time your men did. He's implicated in the deaths of natives who demanded decent wages.

"Braun has no desire to go to prison in that country claiming they would take pleasure in torturing him and keeping him alive as long as they could at the same time. He said he would prefer spending the rest of his life in a European prison where the food is better and the torturing is less intense."

The three friends bit their tongues about what Schmidt's report had told them about uranium mining and shipping refined ore to the enemy. Now did not seem like the time to go there.

Alday suddenly understood why he and his family had been targeted. Without revealing the cause of his sudden flush, he asked, "Does that mean Mikael Nordstrom gets out of jail in France and won't be extradited to PNG? Didn't he get accused of those murders along with a number of other deaths in the mines themselves?"

"Actually, I'm afraid it's beginning to look like that," responded the agent. "In fact, neither the Mikael Nordstrom in prison, nor his father,

Ernst, say they don't know the guy. Evidence says otherwise. A couple of you might be called upon to validate that point."

Alday took special note that Nordstrom would be freed, which meant that he would soon be available to receive his own brand of retribution for trying to burn his family.

As though he were reading his friend's mind, Harwood thought, Forget it, Josh. You can come after him in other ways than physically. It not like your appearance blends in with the general population.

The second agent took out a small notebook from the breast pocket of his suit jacket, made a notation, then put the notebook away.

The sheriff spoke to Cheryl and requested, "Cheryl, you told me that you had pictures of this Braun. We need them for evidence."

Cheryl's eyes darted from the sheriff to the agents to Cargill, the latter giving her a positive nod. The four guests wondered if everything was so twisted that the men they faced weren't part of the vast Groebels conspiracy.

Ally asked, "How do I fit into this?"

"Because all of you are targets," responded the second agent. "Giving us the photos will take the pressure off you."

"But not eliminate us as targets," she said.

"I'm afraid not," the agent replied.

25

"Mrs. Alday, we'll also need your written statement as to the date and the time the pictures were taken," the first agent requested, cordially.

"Except for the part about retribution," Harwood said bluntly.

The other four looked puzzled, but he wasn't ready to show all his cards, certainly not tell them the entire story about why they went after Nordstrom in the first place. That was their secret.

"Retribution by whom?" asked the first agent, "And for what?"

"I don't know. Maybe for taking this guy's picture." He'd said enough.

"I'm afraid that's always on the table. We can offer you protection, though," said the first agent. Turning to the Aldays, he said, "And we're very sorry about the loss of your home."

Harwood calculated. With Braun in custody, there was nothing to gain by keeping the two pictures. But why had he taken the fall for Nordstrom?

The sheriff said, "If any of you are wonder-ing about these two, I received a call from their Phoenix field office yesterday about them com-ing. I know the number from previous cases. They're the real deal."

"So we're out of the picture for the time be-ing. Is that right?" Harwood asked.

"So it would seem," responded the sheriff.

Cheryl opened her purse to remove a small manila envelope. She handed it to the sheriff, who took it, pulled out the two Polaroids, looked at them, and handed them to the agents. One them placed them back in the envelope and said, "Thank you for these. If you don't mind, we'd like that statement now."

The men stepped aside as Cheryl rose and went to sit at the desk. Cargill provided her with sheet of paper and she wrote what they request-ed, including the present date and time of the writing. She handed it to Cargill, who gave it to one of the agents. He read it, nodded, careful-ly folded it in half and placed into the envelope along with the photos.

"Did you make copies of these?" the first agent asked.

"No, should I have?" she asked.

"It's best you didn't," he answered.

"If that's it, Josh and I need to destroy some-thing," Harwood said, standing to leave.

Cargill smiled at the look on the faces of the

agents and explained, "They're dynamite experts and Ally there drives and repairs the big rigs. As you may know, she also jumps out of airplanes. And Cheryl is the salt of the earth. She grew up among firemen and miners. From what I hear, she can take care of herself, if any of you want to go one on one with her."

The agents grinned, giving her a knowing smile, probably based on experience with other female combatants, "No thanks," one of them said, jovially. "We'll pass on that. Thank you for your cooperation. We sincerely mean that."

The two agents watched the four leave the office to go out to their cars. They didn't drive away, though, but stood clustered, talking. The four men inside worried about the future of these colorful people, hoping they could take care of themselves.

"Cheryl said, "What just happened?"

"They caught a bad guy," Ally contributed.

Alday snorted, "Yeah, one in and one out."

Harwood said, "I'm wondering why Braun is giving up Nordstrom. He's going to jail forever, anyway."

Alday offered, "Maybe even Braun has a family somewhere that may have gotten threatened, if he didn't take the fall. I don't care so much about him. It's all on Nordstrom. If he hadn't ordered his stooge to tell us they'd kill our families, the guy would still be employed somewhere, still have his face, and we wouldn't be in this complicated deep pile of shit. Of course, we wouldn't have found out about Groebels' deals with foreign powers either."

"Well said, Josh," Harwood replied. "Only one thing you left out. I don't think Groebels wants money, I mean, money won't help you live forever. I think they want a piece of the ultimate pie, which comes down to another player in the international game of champions. In a few years, we can look forward to a diminishing United States influence in the world game. We're already sitting at the table with Russia and China. Add North Korea and Iran to the list, and, lest we forget, Groebels, the newest player and possibly even the dealer."

At that, Cheryl and Ally eyeballed each other, while Alday threw out both palms and declared, "This is getting too rich for my blood. I say we try to get some serious money. We still have to pay Schmidt. What say, Draco?"

Harwood grinned, "I don't mind taking money from miners who are willing to lose it, but I'd rather take it from someone who has it to lose. I'm thinking hardball."

Alday laughed, "Funny you should mention that. I have a line on some serious money passing hands in the basement of at least one resort hotel in Tucson. They play every Friday night, but it's by invitation only.

"Can we get invited?" Harwood asked.

"I'll make sure we do," Alday responded.

"What's it going to take to sit down at the table?" Harwood asked.

"A thousand dollars minimum with $50 antes," Alday answered.

"Beats $20 bucks and a dollar at my house," Harwood said, hearing what he wanted to hear.

Alday added, "I'll make sure we get introduced as miners from San Manuel who saved up to join them. No doubt they'd love to play with somebody other than corporate executives."

The two women looked at each other and thought the same thing: Men.

Ten days later, Cheryl's blue Nissan Sentra pulled into the parking lot of the Crown Regency Hotel, located at the margin of an 18-hole golf course designed by one of the pros who frequented the hotel.

Alday eschewed valet parking and found a spot farther back to the rear of the lot, checked his face in the mirror to make sure he had wiped Cheryl's lipstick off his cheek, and both men got out. One minute later they climbed the 12 stairs of the hotel to the lobby. Guided by instructions given Alday by his friend, he and Harwood took the elevator to the bottom floor.

Both men had purchased designer jeans the week before, washed them twice, and had worn them around the house after work. They had also purchased medium quality short-sleeved shirts without any flash to them. Neither man wore a watch. Alday maintained his full beard and Harwood had let his stubble grow for the past week. The men walked a fine line between trying to look like miners out on a fling, without appearing to be sleeping giants waiting to pounce for the kill, which, in fact, they were. Still, in this game, things could go south very fast.

Harwood knocked on the door at 8:30 pm. In a moment a red-haired man invited them in after they identified themselves. The smoky room was large and adorned with pictures of golf legends and overhead pictures of the various holes of the course. A wet-bar stood in one corner with a bartender behind it. Two men leaned against it talking, both with drinks in hand. A room they took to be the bathroom was set into one side. This was confirmed when one man emerged, zipping up his fly. Several comfortable chairs and sofas sat against the walls, some of them occupied. Reportedly, the room rented for $3000 a night for special events such as these.

Both men noticed the lack of a clock on the wall. They also noted which men wore watches and which didn't. Typically, the house does not want players to know the time, because that would indicate they were expecting to leave the game at some point. Everybody should stay as long as possible because the house receives a percentage of the action. To the miners, they followed their own general rules: Drink no alcohol. Stay hydrated. Those who wore watches might over-bet to speed things up.

Two poker tables constituted the main feature of the room. Each held five players. A sixth man served as the dealer. Players bought and sold chips through him. Games were in progress. Many men had tumblers of ice and liquor in front of them.

"You'll have to wait your turn," the red-haired man informed the newcomers. "It could be 20 or 30 minutes."

"No problem," Harwood said. The time would give them a chance to examine the players at the tables and those who were seated.

Within a quarter-hour, one man said, "I'm done," and stood up from the table.

"Already?" said another.

"Can't concentrate tonight," returned the first.

"He's got wife problems," inserted a third.

"You need to take care of your wife better, Ernie," the second man said.

"Word is, you already did that," the third man jibbed to the second.

Another well-dressed man, replaced Ernie at the table.

Yet another man left. "You're first one through the door so you're up," red-hair told Alday.

"What about them?" Harwood motioned to take in the seated men and those at the bar.

The man laughed. "Those guys sitting there

are groupies. They don't play. They get their thrills watching others. The two at the bar are getting some liquid courage to get back into it."

Alday bought $1000 worth of chips and took a seat. Fortunately, when Harwood got called several minutes later, it was at the second table. The two wouldn't have to play against each other. Five card stud appeared to be the game of the evening.

Harwood saw the man who had the most chips. He would be the mark. Doubtless, the other man considered him in the same light. Harwood put on his robot face: no smiles, no quips, no comments about somebody's wife; total concentration. He was there to win, not to think about life's problems.

Poker is a game of reading the opponents first and the way their cards are played. Arguably, the cards they hold come in second place, and if nothing else, Harwood could read men. He watched the aggressive behavior of his main opponent, who frequently caused players to fold. With one or two players left, he would high-stake. Harwood guessed that half of the time the man lacked anything serious.

Occasionally, someone would leave one of the tables to take a break or take a leak. He might be replaced by another,

Neither Harwood nor Alday needed a clock. Almost three hours later, they were getting warmed up.

By 1:00 am only Harwood and his main opponent remained at their table. Each had a pile of chips in front of him, Harwood had a larger pile. Alday's table had emptied and now he stood by the bar nursing a cold beer, having cashed in his chips.

The man raised Harwood and Harwood raised him back. Tired of it all, Harwood went all in and pushed in the large pile of multi-colored chips in front of him for the bet. The man counted what he had, saw what he needed to match the bet, and bought more from the dealer to raise the bet again. Now Harwood was in the hole, although he saw it as a bluff. Alday came to his rescue and staked his friend for the difference. Now Harwood called the man. Time to show.

The man showed three kings.

Harwood laid down his cards one by one to show an Ace high flush, not a straight flush, but a flush nonetheless. He had won.

The man reached his hand across the table to shake hands with Harwood, who took it, still stone-faced. "Maybe I'll see you again," the man said.

"Maybe," Harwood replied, without sincerity. He got up and retrieved his money in cash from the banker, paid him the required percentage, stuffed the rest into two pockets and walked out with Alday in the middle of the night. Once in the car, he pulled out one of the rolls and repaid Alday what he had fronted him. They finally arrived home by 2:45 am.

Ally let him sleep in. When he did get up after 10:00 am, she had a full brunch waiting for him, including oatmeal topped with strawberries, ham and eggs, and a full pot of coffee. Slow jazz played softly on the stereo.

Sitting down next to him, she half teased, "Well, did Josh have to sell Cheryl's car to buy cab fare for you guys to get home?"

Between mouthfuls, he replied, "Pretty close." He reached into one bulging pocket to pull out a large rolled wad of 100s, and reached into the other to pull out an equally large role of 20s and 50s.

Ally picked up the money, examined the rolls, and said, "Damn, Honey. How much is here?"

Harwood spooned oatmeal into his mouth followed by a swallow of coffee. He said simply, "I don't know. I haven't had time to count it, but it should get us even and a lot more."

Ally began to unroll the money and started laying it out on the table to count, working to smooth out the bills. She had never seen so much money in one place at one time.

"How did Josh do? Did he win?"

Harwood replied, "Yes, but less than me. He had a single roll of bills. The table he played at didn't' have as much money to start with."

He wiped his mouth, leaned back in his chair,

and said in a more serious vein,

"I know your father can well afford what he paid to the law firm. I know he made that investment for all of us. Between Josh and me, I should think we made up our own investments and enough to pay Schmidt a lot more, if and when we decide to get serious."

Ally loved this man, but damn it, she couldn't figure him. She asked, "Which means?"

"I'm thinking" he said, and went back to work on his breakfast.

Ally threw her hands in the air in reply to his non-answer. Leaving the money on the table, she returned to the armchair to continue reading Cervantes', Don Quixote. She definitely needed a laugh.

26

Alday's headaches were getting worse. They began after the rock fall that had crushed part of his face. At first they occurred sporadically. Now, years later, they occurred almost daily. Loath to tell Cheryl about them, he had no choice, especially when they woke him in the middle of the night and would last for a lengthy period of time, causing him to wake up groggy, not a good place to be for a man in his profession.

"Okay, time off tomorrow," she dictated. "You're going to the medical center."

The MRI revealed that he had a small particle in the midst of a swelling in his brain, near where the most severe part of the injury had occurred.

The somewhat portly and bearded old doctor maintained a jovial mood, empathizing with his patients' sufferings. As a youth, he had worked the mines a half-century before, prior to the advent of better technology that increased efficiency of the mining operations to save lives. He had climbed out and became what he wanted to be: a doctor who specialized in mining injuries. Decades later, he addressed Alday, who sat in a hospital gown on the end of an examination table.

The doctor explained what they had found, then reported, "Josh, I think at the time of the accident, a tiny fragment of heavy metal got into your head. It could be lead, or zinc, or whatever. It's there. Imagine getting shot in the stomach with a .22 caliber bullet. As long it doesn't hit anything vital, it will remain in place, but the lead will leach out over time to affect your entire body. Swelling will occur around the injured area. Eventually, you will die from the wound.

"You have something like that in your head. It's on the right side. Swelling around it has been increasing over time and will continue to increase. If you haven't by now, you will soon notice a lack of attention, reasoning, and problem solving."

Alday shook his head. "Not a single one, doc. Only the headaches. Hell, man, I kicked ass in a poker game recently."

The doctor laughed. "Next time invite me. Back to the topic at hand, you will need a little brain surgery. If you don't get that piece out of there, you will crash hard very soon. The alarm bells are ringing."

"Okay, doc, but while you're in there, could

you adjust a couple of other things like some personality issues I have, and improve my game-playing skills and maybe work in the sex part too?"

"I'll do my best. I might even give you some super powers for a little extra charge," the doctor jibed in return. "Josh, we need to get that particle out of there. I expect the swelling to reduce after the surgery. We'll follow up, of course. The operation should be a no-brainer, which in your case, should go smoothly."

Alday laughed and said, "A no-brainer it is. But if you screw this up, you'll be dealing with Cheryl after that."

"Talk about pressure," laughed the doctor.

Unfortunately, pre-surgery did not go as planned. With more advanced equipment at Tucson General Hospital, more micro-fragments were identified in a semi-circular pattern around the original particle. Josh got sent home to contemplate the choices given him. The doctor told him, "The bad news is that after all the particles are removed, it might not be a good idea to play poker again and expect to win. Also, expect some memory loss and a shortened ability to concentrate. Beyond that, all should be normal."

To Alday, one thing he noticed the doctor didn't say was that his motivations and drive would disappear after the surgery. Keeping an eye on his avowed target, Josh Alday consented to the procedure.

The surgeon explained that first a biopsy would have to be obtained to determine if the brain tissue in question might be cancerous. After shaving a portion of his head, a local anesthetic would be applied and a small drill would be used to cut a hole through his skull while he remained awake. He wouldn't feel it.

The surgeon scheduled the procedure and Josh went back to work for a few days until the procedure. The doctor was right. He didn't feel a thing. He returned to his hospital bed to await the findings and given a meal of ice chips. His wife and friends remained at the hospital until the results came back three hours later. No cancer. The operation could proceed as planned. To do so would involve cutting an access port—a circular area of bone would have to be removed.

Through the use of thermal imaging cameras and other electronic aids, the surgeon removed the small troublesome metallic particles in question and several hours later, the patient slept peacefully back in his room.

Subsequent MRIs and x-rays failed to find any other particles. After a week of observation, Cheryl drove the patient home carrying a simplified sheet of instructions on how to take care of the head after brain surgery, as though he had gone in for removal of a hangnail. When she saw his shaved and stitched head, she remarked that she didn't know he was so handsome, which now gave his original injuries more prominence.

She gushed that it turned her on.

"You should have told them to shave the other side, too, for balance," she suggested.

Josh remained out of work for two weeks until the local swelling subsided. After that he was to keep it protected for another month. He didn't need any more dirt to infect the wound. The stitches would dissolve on their own in time.

Although his headaches disappeared, Alday soon found his short term memory was indeed affected, which extended to his card-playing skills, as tested by Harwood. The doctors were correct. He could lose at cards all he wanted, but he wouldn't winning any more money with that particular skill. In his manner, he used the problem to his advantage by accidentally forgetting to take out the trash at home. Cheryl could prove him neither right nor wrong.

PART II

1

Unimak Island is the first (or the last—depending on perspective) island belonging to the Aleutian chain in the Bering Strait off Alaska. It is one of the most inhospitable places on planet Earth for humans, and even vegetative matter, to live. There are no native trees on Unimak, although the interior grizzlies and larger coastal brown bears do well there, relying on scrub grass and salmon for their diets. The richer diet enables the brown bear to reach a height of 11' feet when standing on its hind legs and can weigh 1000 pounds, while the interior grizzly averages two feet less in height, both formidable forces of nature for the occasional hunter, who doesn't care about braving the elements.

Earthquakes can originate at the island itself. If they originate from somewhere nearby, as is common, the island is subjected to occasional 100' high tsunamis and cyclonic storms. The daily high and low temperatures are relatively mild, until occasional cold fronts come down from Siberia to turn the entire Bering Strait into a solid sheet of ice.

Numerous volcanoes dot the land mass, at least one of which is active, because the Aleutians lie along the juncture of the Pacific Oceanic and the North American continental plates, with the heavier former subducting the latter. Just off the southern coast of Unimak, one can find one of the deepest ocean trenches on the planet situated at the boundary of the plate juncture that sweeps around the Alaskan peninsula.

Unimak is a wet and rainy place to live, that's why only and handful of people are clustered together in a "city" known as False Pass at the eastern end of the island that measuring some 59 by 72 miles. The population of False Pass totals 42. Eight of these are children with one teacher, which leaves a balance of 33. These are divided among the captains of ships, fishermen in the salmon and cod-catching industry, and administrators.

Groebels' surveyors and geologists kept their fingers crossed when they overflew Unimak, hoping that no ores of significance would be located on that rocky protrusion. Nobody wanted to get involved in mining operations in a place where no human in their right mind might want to work. Instead, with the assistance of deep-penetrating sonar and electronic signatures, they were shocked to find gold and the richest deposit of uranium ever discovered, never mind the plutonium that came along for the ride.

Subsequently, ecologists lamented their inability to use the open pit method for ore extraction. No bulldozing piles of ore deeper and deeper, loading them into trucks and taken to ships. Here, actual mines would have to be dug into the sides of volcanoes. This wasn't surface mining in Arizona, this was Unimak Island, for God's sake.

The venture would be costly, but could pay dividends many times over, if they played their cards right. Groebels needed to raise a half-billion dollars for their ante in the game, but stood to make 20 times that amount. This venture would tax their resources in every respect.

Still, if one could endure all that Mother Nature threw at you, untold riches were there for the taking, because ores typically befriend one another. The recoverable gold alone would pay for the venture.

Uranium is quite commonly found around the world in at least eight isotopes and daughters, as exemplified by U234, U235, U238, and radon. Its uses range from construction of nuclear reactors on land and sea to various medical devices. It's purification for use in nuclear weapons is an incredibly complex process and is no longer pursued in that regard by the bulk of nations. What's the point of getting killed 10 times over versus 100 times over? Interestingly, the presence of plutonium is critical for the making of nuclear weapons, a discovery that did not escape the attention of Groebels and their close contacts.

A number of nations would give anything to join the big boys club for purposes of threats and intimidation. This is a dangerous scenario professed by those who are not at all afraid to kill themselves or their entire populace for the sake of proving some kind of point.

Groebels had the money. The other players who wanted the uranium slipped the money to the company under a number of guises, simple stuff. The money originated from billions the United States gave under the table to the leaders of the two countries to shut up and play nice. The people never got any of it. They never do. Despite the cash, the countries never shut up or professed to play nice, especially now that they had some extra pocket change, which, to some, might have been the original point of those who ensured they got the money.

Good old international relations, like sending a 10,000 tons of rice to a country that didn't have any roads for purposes of distribution in trade for a UN vote in their favor. Much of the rice stays at the top of the food chain and what's left goes out on the black market.

It took Groebels 10 years to establish themselves on the island, painfully pay the highest wages ever, and spend money like a drunken sailor on shore leave. The harvested ore would be shipped to the smelter in Sitka, some 1200 miles away on the eastern seaboard of North America.

The powers to be were getting anxious. Making bombs and nuclear missiles takes time and investment dollars—along with two very critical elements, uranium 234, and especially, plutonium. Publicly reported as low-medium grade ore, the overall capture would be extremely rich; by far, the highest grade ever discovered. The real profit margin lay in the sales of the radioactive portions of the rock, once it is separated from the other valuable elements, most of which would be sold to a variety of buyers. Because of the radioactivity involved in the more purified products, extreme protective measures had to be exercised once the crude ore reached the Sitka crushers and smelters. This is where the processing stopped. Sitka didn't have what they needed for further refinement called for in the contract.

The buyers of the radioactive portions of the purified ore were Third-World countries that lacked the geniuses behind the Manhattan Project. They lacked Einstein, the Jew; Szilard, the Hungarian; Oppenheimer, the German; Bohr, the Dane; Enrico Fermi, the Italian; Richard Feynman, the eccentric bongo playing American, and the other naturalized or American-born scientists in a long list of geniuses and financiers. Supported by the UK and Canada, they all pulled together to be the first to accomplish a single goal that other nations, including Germany, pursued at the time.

That said, the nations slated to receive the goods had some pretty good people of their own. Like airflow and birds, neither stupidity nor intelligence stops at national boundaries.

As world tensions increased, the need for The Bomb became ever more pronounced. Groebels began to feel the heat. The top brass began to feel that they had overplayed a weak hand, having received billions so far with nothing to show for it. The ore grade they promised to deliver from the smelter was 20-30-fold better than standard. This would shave years off bomb development. Deliveries had to start immediately.

Unfortunately for Groebels, Mother Nature had been a bitch from the start on Unimak. She had other ideas. So did Draco Harwood.

One month after surgery, Alday's hair had grown back and the scar was barely visible. Both men were back at work, but to Harwood's way of thinking, things were going too smoothly. He began to plan.

Getting ready to set off a charge in a drift corridor, Harwood asked, "Say, Mate, that telephone man guy, what's his name, Franz Braun, gave me an idea. Do you want to go to Sitka?"

"Sitka, Alaska? No. I kind of like it here," Alday said, hunkering down behind a rail car and pushing the plunger.

The water mist kept down the dust and actually assisted in reducing the intensity of the echoing noise from the explosion, at least enough for Harwood to say, "No, not to move there, but to work for a short while. We both have vacation time saved up and your hospitalization didn't subtract from it. I've got an article in Mining News that will fill you in."

"What's the point in getting cold and wet? I'm getting to like it here," Alday complained.

Once Harwood told him his plan, Alday gave a show of approval and said, "I'm in for that hand. Have to check with Cheryl, see if she wants to go or stay. Wait, we'd probably need an inside man for a chance to make that work, don't you think?"

Harwood replied, smugly, "We already have one. I've been in contact with him. It's James Brooks."

Later the same day, the four sat in a local San Manuel pub at a corner table while the Alday boys played video games in a room set aside for children. In a small community, social norms belonging to a larger metropolis tend to be more lax.

Harwood pulled out the copy of Mining News he had folded in his back pocket and laid it on the table between two pitchers of beer, icy mugs, fries, beer nuts, and napkins.

Alday picked it up first and Cheryl read along with him. The national mining magazine contained the usual stories about new ore discoveries around the world, mine closures, proposed government legislations, available assistance from the unions, and who said what about whom. Want ads occupied the last page of the 10 page paper. One of them had particular appeal. It read:

Wanted, experienced mine blasters needed to assist in development of new gold mine outside of Sitka, Alaska. Only the most experienced need apply. Top wages. For further information call . . .

Cheryl handed the paper to Ally, pointing to the ad. She read it and said, Draco, talk to me. "

Unimak gave Groebels hell from the start. Although no tsunamis of note had occurred, an active volcano decided to become more active and inundate the mining area with pyroclastic gases to such an extent that everyone had to migrate miles upwind to avoid an unpleasant death, reminiscent of Pompeii. Bringing in heavy equipment just to begin operations required that an actual harbor be created large enough and deep enough to shelter a 20,000 ton ore hauler that would gross out at ten times that weight after loading.

Accustomed to working in hot mines, the highly paid crew of two hundred men were not accustomed to working in 120°F tunnels leading into a volcano. Special effort (and expense) dictated that numerous air conditioned rooms be created, over and above the number normally present in proper mining tunnels.

The workmen were limited in their ability to find alternate activities after working long days and would engage in frequent fights, sometimes causing injury to another, resulting in a loss of work days.

All told, the time required to complete a given task amounted to three times normal given the variables of cave-ins, floods, fires, freezing rain, injuries, poisonous gases, and marauding bears that enjoyed any food stores humans left around, not excluding humans who stood between the bears and their newly-found food sources.

Clueless as to the state of affairs in Unimak and world politics in general, the foursome found Harwood's plan risky, but feasible, especially when they found out that James had put in a transfer to the Sitka operation. The transfer was approved, in large part because of his high status in the hierarchy of the International Mine Workers Union along with unnamed connections he had at the top.

Ally felt great disappointment when she approved the plan, but found she lacked enough seniority on the job to be let go, even for a relatively short period of time, the length of which had to be defined. When Harwood explained that the company could find another deep pit driver, the company retorted 'yes', but her skills in the repair shop are vitally needed.

Ally snapped her fingers in revelation. She remember her old boss in Phoenix who had told her that if there was ever an opening in San Manuel, to call him and he could let his son handle things for a while, because his son was also his business partner.

2

Sitka is famous for its fishing, both commercial and recreational. The city has the 6th largest port by value of seafood in the U.S., where salmon, trout, char, grayling, halibut, and rockfish are abundant. The mining of gold, silver, and uranium serves to assist the local economy and, as such, crushers, smelters and refineries are present to process ore samples provided by local mines, or from shiploads of ore that may come in from elsewhere.

The mines are operated by a number of companies, one of which is Groebels. The small city has a population of only a few thousand, but it is lively with fishing trawlers and tourists. The high temperature is relatively moderate ranging from 37°F to 61°F, with rain falling at least half of each and every month. In comparison to Unimak, Sitka is a paradise.

Harwood had written ahead, once he had found out who ran the show at the Groebels mine, and more importantly, who wouldn't be

there, or, if he stood a chance of being recognized from so many years before. If so, the
plan had no chance of success. He and Alday
needed to get their hands on explosives, which
would include dynamite and preferably C-4. If
caught in their criminal act, they could spend
the rest of their lives in jail. If everything went
smoothly and they got away with it, nobody
would get hurt, but Groebels would suffer. He
already knew the smelting process, he needed
to see it.

As for Cheryl, she could have home-schooled
the boys. Instead, she and Josh opted to put them
in the public school while in Alaska, for the experience. She figured the new kids in town could
take care of themselves, if it came down to it.

The men presented résumés of their past experiences without any mention of having worked
in PNG. When questioned on the phone, they
proved to know more than the questioner and
were invited to make the move. There existed no
company housing, per se, which left the task of
finding a place to live to the women.

With minimal luggage and no furnishings,
Ally and Cheryl had no problem locating a bed
and breakfast more than happy to rent three
rooms to the boarders who would be with them
for perhaps a month or longer. The two boys
were delighted to learn that they would have
their own suite.

When Harwood called James upon their arrival, James made plans for them to have dinner that evening at a seafront restaurant, a short walking distance from their B&B.

James had arrived before them and when Ally saw her father, she ran ahead. James saw her and stood to receive a great bear hug. Except for his increasingly bald pate, James Brooks did not look his 47 years. Clean shaven, he had a square face without lines of age or serious worry, although his hands were nicely calloused. He was one of those people who never showed too much excitement or sorrow. He rolled with the punches, yet stood for no nonsense, having served as foreman for chute blasters, ore haulers, and general mine manager in charge of the welfare of all men under his charge.

Ally introduced Cheryl and her sons, and by 7:30 pm, the seven feasted on lobster tail, baked salmon, shrimp, cocktail sauce, rice, beer, soft drinks, and double fudge cake for desert. By 9:00, the boys were supercharged and wanting adventure. Their mother took them outside, rented a couple of poles along with a supply of bait and told them to see if they could catch any fish. The one who did would receive a prize. Returning to the restaurant, Cheryl kept a wary eye on the brothers through the double-paned picture windows of the restaurant.

Ally went into teaching mode, not inserting herself into a conversation unnecessarily, but still serving as their in-house librarian, who occasionally found it necessary to speak up, even when not spoken to. She began, "Dad, maybe you can help me with some of this. While Draco and Josh were playing hospital and occasionally doing actual physical labor, I've been conducting research on our problem. An article I read some time ago in one of my science magazines gave me the idea."

Ally glanced from Harwood to Alday and said, "Sorry, guys but you may not have to destroy even a tiny portion of the smelter to accomplish the same goal, not even on a time-delay device." She said this because Harwood had gotten that idea from Braun's use of such a device at the Alday household.

At a loss of what to say, the men remained silent, waiting for the next shoe to fall. They had no doubt Ally had already explained it to Cheryl.

"Does anybody here know about transporting uranium or plutonium?" Ally, inquired.

The men shook their heads, waiting, preparing to get schooled.

She continued, "Uranium emits gamma and beta rays that can penetrate skin. Plutonium emits heavier alpha particles that won't. Both are radioactive and shipped as oxides in powder form. They're packaged in parcels that weigh several kilograms each, which are loaded into larger lead-lined containers. The containers have the yellow and black circular RADIOACTIVE HAZARD sticker on them.

"Because they're in powder form, the particles are easily inhaled, that is, if they get loose. It's sort of like breathing in a pile of radioactive gunpowder after you have a fan on it. The guys who work on the final product at either end probably get serious hazardous duty pay."

Harwood injected, "My guess is that from here the powders will be loaded onto pallets and forklifted onto a truck where they will be taken to the shipyard for transport somewhere else."

James said, "Correct. They won't be purified enough at that point. They're going to a quality refinery in Massachusetts. Once the bad guys get it, they'll do the final purification, which, by the way, is a relative term because the bad guys still need to use centrifugation."

Harwood surmised, "I'm guessing the truck will not be a flatbed because letting the public see what is being carried is could be a stupid move, like a drug dealer with a carload of cocaine getting pulled over for a bad tail light."

James reported, "The crusher, smelter, and refinery are off a side track about five miles from our mine and about four miles from the airport. The area between the tracks and all three facilities is completely open for easy delivery of ore and shipping of finished products. There is a lot of activity for such a small community because of the cluster of mines in the area that they serve. Dump trucks and open box cars come and go frequently. They get their power from coal, so that's always being delivered. What else do you want to know?"

Cheryl held up a hand. "Back up. Even if we identify the vehicle in question and sabotage it, they'll repair it and get another. What's the rest you're not tell us?"

Four sets of eyes returned to the science teacher, who continued, "Suppose word gets out that there actually was a spill. Even though there wasn't, the press would go ballistic if the information is worded correctly, and the IAEA will get involved in a flash—sorry, the International Atomic Energy Agency. Not only will the investigation drag on for weeks, it could be months. And, from what I researched, the IAEA would want full disclosure specifics as to where the stuff was going. Groebels would be in the public eye, and the bad guys could get very pissed at them, especially if the IAEA confiscates the product while they try to verify the claim.

"Dad, if you can find out when the products are getting packaged and transported, that will give us time to set up our whistle-blower exposure game."

"Who's your source?" Alday asked.

James said, "You don't want to know his name. He likes the company in general, but there are aspects of this dirty work he has a problem with. This whole thing could come down within the month, possibly after you're slated to return home, so whatever we do together, it better be fast."

Cheryl returned, "You know, our whistle-blower could report that the spill occurred at the in-house packaging site itself," Alday contributed.

Harwood said, "Maybe, but they might have to shut down the entire refinery, then."

"And?" shot Cheryl, her favorite word

The four conspirators gave grave thought to what Ally had presented. Harwood sighed, "If we don't act, it could be a game changer for a lot of countries, and it won't be good."

Ally added, "Whatever we do, let's try not to leave our fingerprints all over it, eh?"

Disappointed at having traveled all this way and not being given the opportunity to destroy something belonging to Groebels, Harwood said, "It will be a tight window. I'll begin to work on that part of the plan immediately. We'll meet again same time here for dinner tomorrow and compare notes."

"I'm thinking Chinese," Cheryl inserted.

"There's a good place on the next street. They even have a game room," James said, as the others stood to leave.

"Hang on," James said, patiently. "There's more."

Four adults froze in place and regained their seats. James went on, "When I worked the uranium mines in Saskatchewan, I learned that uranium is used in conventional warfare in terms of making armor-piercing bullets and small missiles."

"You mean the radioactive U-235? How does that work?" Ally inquired, truly puzzled.

"No, the DU, or depleted U-238 that is left over after the U-235 is extracted from the ore. It's not very radioactive, but when combined with tungsten, it reshapes itself into a hardened needle point when it hits the side of a tank, the weak point of the machine, not the more heavily armored front. It penetrates the steel easily, and explodes inside. You can also shoot them down the turret. If costs of production are equal, you can get 1000 times more shots of this nature than the Javelin missile and do the same thing. Once either of them penetrate the tank and explode, it sets off anywhere up to 50 shells in the magazine. Tank warfare will soon be obsolete."

"What does that have to do with us, Dad?" Ally asked, not grasping the point.

"Because, my dear, a lot of the uranium that is being sent to Iran includes a goodly amount of DU, and that's upon their request. Millions of tons of all types of both raw and concentrated ores are shipped throughout the world on a regular basis. You can now include this stuff in the mix."

With perfect timing, both the children ran into restaurant, each clutching a small Sockeye Salmon, trying to keep the slithering fishes from escaping their grasps. The oldest, David, declared, "Look, mom, now we both get a present."

"Great, let's call the chef. Maybe we can eat them now," Alday offered, teasingly.

"Cool," cried both children in unison.

3

Although the previous day had been cold and clear, a freezing rain had taken its place, which promised to last for several days. No fishing this evening for the boys. They would have to settle for spending their parent's money in the game room.

Once everybody had a drink in front of them in their corner booth and the light chat over, Ally pulled out a sheet of paper and quietly passed it around, explaining, "I didn't want this on our laptop's memory, so I found an old word processor in a thrift store. Once we've settled on the final version, I'll toss the thing into the ocean."

"That's a little paranoid, isn't it?" her father asked.

"Dad, I don't know. I did that once when I was a teenager and wanted to frame another kid who stole my bike."

"So that's how it got returned, heh?" James smiled at his daughter's attempts to hide their activities. He gave her an "A" for effort. He and

Harwood read the letter together, then passed it to Alday who shared it with Cheryl. He gave her another "A" for her literary ability.

"Good letter."

"What happens to us?"

"Are you sure about this part?" were the comments that came forth.

"I made misspellings on purpose, because, in all honesty, something this heavy scares me to death," she owned.

The letter read:

    I would like to espress my deepest
    concern for a Grobel coverup in the
    ore refinry in sika, alaska, where
    spiling radoactive dust from uranum
    and plutonum ocured in the final pak-
    aging of the products. These purifed
    ores are supposed to go to iran and
    north korea for there nuclear pro-
    grams. I also sugest a portion of
    the refinry is contamminated.
    Grobel discovered a very rich ore
    body on Unmak Island. This ore body
    has gold, silver, zink, and magne-
    sum, along with the radoactive ele-
    ments. Everything got sent by ship
    to sika for more refinement once they
    came form the smelter. Anchrage was
    much closer and could have went by
    rail, but speed was of the esence.
    The refinery in sika is for the pro-
    cesing of the two ores and along

```
with the DU 238, would be shipped to
massachusuts with the DU 238 to go
to iran for guns and stuff.
```

"They'll know it was stupidly written on purpose," said Alday.

"And?" responded Cheryl. She had a point.

Ally asked, "Dad, how are we going to mail these copies, and to whom. We can't exactly put our return address on them?"

James smiled, again, "I have a good friend who flies freight from here to Vancouver once or twice a week. I'll ask him to mail them from Canada. That will put it some distance between us. The copies will have the Vancouver postal stamp. I'll feel better about that. As to whom, you tell me."

Harwood said, "Definitely not to Groebels. I want this to be a surprise with no chance for them to prepare for anything."

Ally contributed. "Definitely the IAEA. The agency is based in Vienna, but they have regional office around the world. You can express mail them to New York, Tokyo, Toronto, or Vienna, take your pick. We can also send copies to the United States Atomic Energy Commission, or AEC, based in Washington, D.C. I would also suggest we send a copy to the Anchorage Gazette, but not as a letter to the editor. He might dismiss it as a sour grapes complaint. We'll send it to their reporter who covers Mining News. If we're going to blow this thing up, let's do it right."

Alday offered, "You know that most whistle-blower complaints are from disgruntled former employees who are making up stories. They'd soon come to that conclusion."

Harwood said, "It doesn't matter. It will expose the operation here. We'll be out of it because we're slated to return home, as per prior contract agreement, and, from all appearances, James is in good standing with Groebels and the union with no ax to grind, so I really don't believe anything will be traced to us."

Cheryl looked concerned, "What if it does come back to us? Or they offer us protection and immunity from wrong doing if we promise to testify as to what we know?"

Harwood grunted, "We really don't know anything—no offence, James. And their promises don't mean dingo shit. Not with entire countries and multi-billion dollar corporations pissed-off at us, if they discover our involvement. Let's hope we do this right and plug all possible ways the water can get through the dike."

"What's going to happen to Groebels after this?" Cheryl questioned.

James said, "I can answer that. Their stock will plunge. They'll keep operating, although, if they do get accused of aiding and abetting an enemy, they may have to declare bankruptcy, or something akin to that, which means somebody will buy them out. Again, I don't think there will be any stoppage of work to any great extent."

Harwood confessed, "I'm getting nervous about the letter. Let's go over it again, sleep on it, and go over it tomorrow. I'm hoping we're not telling too much. Let the powers dig it out."

The Anchorage Gazette is published daily. It may take a week to arrive at various outposts in a state 2.5 times the size of Texas, but, what the heck, things are pretty laid back there, anyway. Consider it current events when the paper arrives and after it's read, it's saved for fire-starter.

That said, the Gazette is delivered daily to Sitka via air. Five days after the letters were mailed from Vancouver, British Columbia, the firestorm hit the same day a storm brought in freezing sleet sideways.

James had returned to being a foreman, the men were doing what they did best, the Alday boys were improving their fighting skills at school, while the women anxiously awaited delivery of the newspaper.

Suddenly, a number of copies of the newspaper showed up in the downstairs lobby of their B&B. The story appeared, not as some back page hide-all notation, but top of the fold front page headline: GROEBELS INVESTIGATED FOR TREASON written by John Waltrop, Mining News Reporter.

In typical newspaper fashion, the article

smacked of hyperbole, exaggeration, and un-substantiated statements, yet did its job. It read:

Anonymous out-of-country sources have accused Groebels Mining of aiding foreign powers in obtaining nuclear weapons, ostensibly to be used against the United States and possibly Alaska. Copies of a letter received by myself were also sent to . . . . (here he named the agencies listed at the bottom of the letter, who were copied).

This reporter was present when representatives of the above-named agencies descended upon the mine superintendent, Jerold Armstrong, apparently in a coordinated effort. He claimed absolutely no knowledge of anything they were talking about, but authorities refused to show him the letter. According to the agencies, the anonymous letter also claimed that serious radioactive contamination had affected virtually all of the refinery's operations, and perhaps the smelter, as well.

Federal agencies are preparing to insert inspectors in lead-lined hazmat suits armed with Geiger counters to ascertain whether there is any truth to either of the claims, while other investigators are trying to determine who wrote the letters,

where the shipments were directed
toward, and why the letter was sent
from Vancouver. Mr. Armstrong challenged them to find a refinery that
purifies radioisotopes that doesn't
have latent radioactivity.

Mr. Armstrong asserted that nobody has been fired in his operation
for over a year and, in fact, they
are hiring more workers. He doubts
if it is an angry former employee.
He referred any further questions to
his lawyer.

Watch this column for follow-ups
on this important story that is being picked up by mainland States,
and the international press.

James put on a serious look when he read the article in the kitchen of the B&B. He said, "I think it's time you left town. You had the option to stay until I didn't need you anymore and I'm telling you that now. Nordstrom is the big hon-cho for the corporation and he's a quick flight away. He could show up here any minute to deal with the situation and he doesn't need to see you guys. If he recognizes me, no big deal. Every-body gets around in this business and I never did him any wrong, at least not directly. No planes are going to come or go during this ice storm, so you have a few days to make plans."

Cheryl said, "Come on, Ally, let's make some phone calls."

"Damn, I hate to have fun from a distance," Harwood groused.

"It's a lot better than Nordstrom seeing us both and connecting the dots," Alday contributed.

Harwood said, "No argument there. Let's go help the girls. James, we'll be in touch."

The flight time from Sitka to Sky Harbor International in Phoenix was a quick 4 ½ hours. When they arrived, the temperature stood at a balmy 82°F. Another three hour drive brought them home again.

It seemed as though it had all been a dream they shared in common, a dream involving international conspiracies, atomic energy, endless seafood, oceans, freezing rain, and for the boys, adventures in school. The return brought them back to the basics of life, good Mexican food, lots of warmth, and desert sands.

Harwood could not let go of a sense of angst he had been feeling the entire trip back from Alaska. He wondered if this current of events they were all were swimming in might have an undertow that might suddenly yank them far out to sea.

The "family" took the day off after their arrival to settle in, unpack the meager belongings, make calls and prepare to return to a routine life. In the afternoon following their arrival, Bob Cargill, called Harwood at home and asked him to meet him the following morning. When Harwood arrived, Cargill didn't ask him to sit, but handed him a copy of the Mining News carrying the story. He looked piqued.

Showing the article to Harwood, Cargill cleared his throat and said, "Draco, you and Josh just got back from Sitka. This is crazy. Did you know anything about this? What the heck is going on over there?"

Draco speed-read the same story the reporter had written. His emotions roiled, but on the surface he showed a poker face. "Man, I don't know. Our foreman said that we had completed our contract and wrote us a letter of recommendation. We had already made reservations to come home when the story broke." Reaching into one of his many bib pockets, Harwood handed Cargill the letter James had written, who read it, said nothing, and handed it back.

Cargill, a former member of the Army Corps of Engineers, didn't believe in coincidences, not where Harwood was concerned. Looking his visitor in the eye, he said, "You were there, now you're here. That is a straight line between two points. I don't need anything to come back to bite us. First Josh's house is burned to the ground by an international criminal, no less, then you guys go over to a place where the fucking world is looking for blood over this whatever it is, then you come back here to work. Get my drift?"

"Yes, sir. Can I go back to work now?" asked

Harwood, with the innocence of a child.On the way to the door he stopped and turned to face his superior. "Almost forgot, poker game at my house on Friday night. Coming?"

"Wouldn't miss it," Cargill replied, almost cheerily. "Who's going to be there?"

"Usual crowd. Big Mac said he wants to come."

"Good, how about if you and I team up against him now that his foot's all better and we don't have to be nice to him anymore," Cargill suggested.

"See, Bob, that's why you're the brains of the outfit," Harwood uttered, turning to leave, pretending not to see the one finger salute Cargill gave him.

4

"I hear Big Mac's been coming over," Josh said, as he helped his friend secure the Jack Leg by spiking the telescoping legs into the ground, preparing for the task at hand.

Harwood began to hook up the pneumatic air hose and the water line to the drill while Alday marked the spots in the wall to be drilled for insertion of the dynamite sticks.

"Spot on. Ronnie's been coming over every Tuesday evening, which means tonight. Turns out the guy had nobody to talk to until Ally came to town. He's a big history and current events buff. Last week they talked about different types of energy used by various countries," Harwood said, without casting a value judgment, feeling pleased that she had somebody she could talk with on an equal footing.

"Sounds interesting. I wouldn't mind getting into that topic," Alday commented. The men paused in their conversation to drill several holes and clean them out. Harwood walked over to a train car and brought over the box of dynamite sticks.

Alday chuckled, "Some time ago, when I was talking with Jennings, he said that when Ronnie first started here years ago and they ran a background check on him, he found out the man is related to the Gambino family. Some distant cousin or some such."

"The crime syndicate bunch in New York? It got busted up over a half-century ago, didn't it? And him with a last name like Donald? Go figure."

"They ran a big organization with a lot of key players with different last names. Maybe one of the daughters came out west, broke tradition, and married a guy named Donald. No matter, I like the guy."

"I do too. He's my idol as far as blasting skills," Harwood countered. "Obviously, he's out of the old family game."

"Obviously. What do you do when they're having their conversation?" Alday inquired.

"Same thing I do most nights. I try to update the mine diagrams to scale while I listen and learn with one ear at the same time. By my calculations, in addition to the deep pit, we've got over 200 miles of shafts, levels, and drifts so far, half the area has tracks. I've got them marked to scale. They average nearly three miles in length. Why don't you come over and help me, say around 7:00. I might be able to find a beer for you," Harwood offered.

"Sure, I'll tell the boss to give me permission."

"By the way, I've been meaning to ask you, do you know anybody who drives a Camaro?" Harwood inquired.

"That's out of the blue. Not in this town, not unless Camaro makes pickups or SUVs," Alday replied. "Why?"

"There's one that's been cruising around here off and on the last couple of weeks, that's all. No big deal."

The two blasters hunched over a drawing on the kitchen table using a ruler and a protractor, penciling in lines, taking notes, while Ally and Ronnie conversed. The visitor had changed to cutoffs and a short-sleeve button down, which contrasted with his slicked-back gray hair and his is unkempt gray beard he maintained at a moderate length. After all, beards are flammable.

"Do you know that England and Germany get almost all their liquid natural gas from Norway?" Ally asked her visitor.

Ronnie answered, "I don't know about England. I do know Germany gets the bulk of their petroleum from Russia. They're also phasing back their coal. That could be problematic if Russia pulls back."

The sound of a deep-throated rumble came

from outside. Harwood went to the window to look through the blinds. He asked, "Do either of you know anybody who drives a Camaro?"

Ronnie said, "Around here? Nope."

"Not here. Doug's brother does up in Casa Grande," Ally said.

Harwood and Alday took a sudden interest in her statement. "How so? I mean, when did you see it? Is it black and jacked up with yellow pin-striping?" Harwood inquired.

"One and the same," she replied.

"This is the third time I've seen it. Do you think he's looking for us?"

"Why would he be looking for you?" Ronnie expressed a sudden interest in the vein of the conversation. They were all family. Secrets could be shared, which frequently evolved into common knowledge, or rumors at the least.

Harwood put his hand up to put Ronnie's question on hold. He asked Ally, "Tell me about it."

"Back when Doug and I were dating, we went out a few times with his older brother and some of his friends. Honestly, I didn't like any of them. They were always high on something. They all carried guns."

"Guns," exclaimed Alday.

Ronnie said, "This is Arizona, Josh, come on. I've got one in my car."

Ally continued, "His brother works as a mechanic and puts every cent he has into his car.

The guy is married to it. So is his girlfriend. I swear she goes out with him just to show off to her friends about how cool her boyfriend is. He said he saved up for it since forever and finally bought it last year. He had them put in the biggest engine they had, threw a couple thousand into the stereo system, took it down to Mexico to have the interior done, big tires, loud pipes, blower scoop, always spending time tuning it up. Last I heard, he trying to find an insurance company with rates he could afford, what with his age and number of speeding tickets and the nature of the car. He and his buddies were and probably still are into home break-ins, always showing up with new toys."

"Did you ever ride in the thing?" Alday asked, intrigued by the tale.

"Yes. Scary fast. Five on the floor, close to 500 horses. He bragged about the license COOL MARO."

Seeing Ronnie's interest in the tale, Harwood nonchalantly told him about her sad story with a happy ending. Alday ensured that his side of it got told too. They were all family. No big deal. People get beat up all the time.

The look on Ally's face told the two miners they had overstepped their bounds in that Harwood had only mentioned to her that Doug wouldn't be a problem anymore, not that they had kicked the living shit out of him.

Ronnie pondered, "Looks like maybe this

brother and his friends are looking for you two." A rhetorical statement at best, he said it as though it were an afterthought of little consequence.

Alday looked shocked, "Us? I can't imagine why. Doesn't matter. We can't take the time to go up to Casa Grande to search for this guy. We'll have to wait and see how it plays out."

Ronnie scratched his throat beneath his beard, conjecturing, "Be a shame if somebody checked his home for stolen property at the same time the cherry car got boosted, you know, if there was, say, an address associated with the license and the car maybe got borrowed by somebody and taken across the border on a one-way trip, or God forbid, got parted out right there in Phoenix. Just saying."

Ally tried to keep from laughing as she pictured, almost in cartoonish fashion, a too-embarrassed-to-ask-for-a-ride brother, riding a bicycle over 100 miles down to San Manuel to look for the men in order to exact retribution. Chances were pretty good that he might try looking for another project, if not another girlfriend.

She began the conversation anew. "In contrast to Norway, you look at Sri Lanka. They have almost zero fuel. Prices double each month."

The two miners returned to the drawings. They had work to do. Like twins they thought alike. Ronnie wasn't the inattentive, vulgar, cocky, obnoxious newbee, he was the real deal, more than happy to help a friend. Without saying another word about it, both men felt confident they would never see the Camaro again. In a short period of time, neither would Doug's brother.

Amusing as this might appear to play out, Harwood felt disappointed in a way. He had entertained thoughts of an alternate plan for the car and its owner. Those feeling would have to be redirected.

5

Harwood pushed the plunger. The end of the drift wall exploded. This particular drift showed larger than normal veins of copper, silver and gold within large bodies of quartz, veins that were getting heavier the deeper they went.

When the misters had settled the dust, the pair stood and stared into the distance. Their headlamps reflected off sparkling objects that covered a large area of the floor nearest the blast site. The objects were also strewn about, even as far back as where they were, taking shelter behind equipment. At first the men thought that the dynamite had blown out a large cavity of pure quartz. But the reflections were not white, or even off-white, but sparkled yellow.

The men walked slowly toward the sheet of glitter covering the floor, trying not to break a leg on the rocky debris strew about. The closer they got, the more curious the sight became. In a single instant, the men saw what few people had ever seen, perhaps had never seen. Before them lay a jagged rock of gold the size of a bowling ball with other rocks the size of baseballs, golf balls, and marbles, laying among golden nuggets numbering in the thousands. Their sizes varied down to particles as small as dust motes. Indeed, a golden haze suffused the air.

Wordlessly, Harwood tried to pick up the larger piece with one hand and failed. He squatted down and like a weightlifter, used two hands to lift it off the ground. Neither man spoke. Grunting, he lifted it off the ground a foot then set it down, trying to estimate its weight, and finally said to Alday, who was busy examining a roughened softball-size piece, "Mate, this must weigh close to maybe three ingots."

Alday knitted his brows at the statement. He set down the heavy piece he held weighing several pounds. It resembled a lopsided Rubik's Cube with irregular squares and points. He gave the big one a try. "You're right. Here, try mine." He gave Harwood the piece he had set down.

Both miners ran a mental calculation. Ingots vary from 27 to 32 pounds with an average of about 30 pounds. That would equal some 480 ounces of pure gold per ingot. As if to add highlight to the event, one jagged portion of the large piece had a silver tinge accent inside a small portion of quartz. The veins on the cavern wall appeared to be thinning. Apparently, they had hit the mother lode.

The men stood on a veritable sheet of gold

nuggets. Behind them lay more pieces of varying sizes. Harwood said, almost in a whisper, "This is fucking insane. Can you believe it?"

Alday, said, also speaking softly, "Everybody's already gone. It's past quitting time. We'll come back later. It's a good thing only a single shift is working this drift."

"And they'll collect this, I'm presuming," Harwood surmised. "For what it's worth, this isn't ours. It belongs to the company. I want to ensure that it goes to the right place," Harwood said, turning to leave.

"Right. You plan to leave it here so the crew can find it in the morning so you can lecture them about moral values. Got it. Want me to tell you what they're going to say to you tomorrow when you tell them that?" Alday lectured.

"You're right. Thinking it through, we need to collect as much as we can. If we leave it for them, we'll lose half the crew with their new-found riches. What would you rather do, cash in your gold and take off for the beach, or continue working here?"

"Continue working here," Alday confessed, in all seriousness.

"Okay, that's you and it's me. We'd be bored to tears after a couple of weeks on the beach. These guys are different. They're normal. Plus, we'd be inundated with new job applications and work slow-downs. The whole thing would fall on our heads. We have no choice."

Alday prompted, "Let's get our lunch buckets and load what we can. We'll leave them in the car for now so the girls won't see anything until we're ready to show and tell."

Three hours later the sun had set when the two men returned to the drift, Alday with a heavy backpack and a handbag, Harwood pushed a refrigerator dolly with two reinforced handbags and wore a backpack.

Each man went to work loading as many of the large pieces as they could carry, along with handfuls of nuggets. Harwood turned one satchel onto its side and rolled the big piece into it. With the assistance of flashlights, they swept the floor and collected the glittering dust, adding it to their carryalls. The floor still reflected the light from the headlamps with tiny nuggets and flakes. They went back to work and hand rubbed remaining loose golden and silver particles of varying sizes from the wall and ceiling.

Assessing what remained, Harwood said, "They'll be fine with what's left. At least we'll still have a working team."

"A happier working team," Alday added.

A quarter hour later, Harwood walked in the front door of his house to the smell of coffee. "You were gone for a while. Where'd you go, honey? What's that?" Ally asked, watching her man wheel in a dolly with two satchels stacked onto one another. He hunched over and slid the pack off his back onto the floor.

Ally put down her book, drawn to what looked to be a curious event.

"It's a surprise," he said. "Something we found."

"A silver dollar?"

"Better."

"A diamond ring?" she teased,

"Better." Harwood unzipped the first bag and spread it open.

Ally looked inside. It took a moment for her brain to register what she saw. She reached in and pulled out a number of the smaller rocks among a thick layer of nuggets, examining them beneath the light over the table. She tried to pick up a larger baseball size piece, but had difficulty with its weight. None of them were smooth like river rocks washed to roundness over the ages. They looked as though a dynamite blast had separated them from their brethren; all light reflective, terribly golden in color, and knobby with rough protrusions intermixed with occasional smooth patches.

Harwood stooped to the bag on the floor to turn it on its side, rolling out the granddaddy. Ally looked back and forth from the rock to him and asked, "Is it real?"

"Yep."

"It's not fool's gold?"

"Nope."

"It's ours?"

"Nope. It's the company's. I needed to show

you first before I gave it to them." At that, Harwood told her the story.

She took a closer look at the second bag. The base inside was filled with glittery dirt that clearly required sifting to isolate the gold. Silver and copper glittered in the mix. The backpack was half-filled with more clumps of ore, these mostly silver in color.

The landline phone rang. Harwood picked up.

"Cheryl wants to keep some of it," Alday said.

"Do what you want. It's your decision to make," Harwood replied, without judgment. He set down the receiver.

His gut told him to give it back. He'd heard as many stories about finders of treasures who either came to an ill-fated end, or could purchase everything from material goods to positions of power. On one hand, he possessed miner's superstitions, and to him, it would be bad karma to keep it. On the other hand, at some point in life, he could be down and out and would tear himself to shreds emotionally for not having this "investment" to fall back on. If the mine belonged to them, that would be a different story.

He had beaten men without remorse, he had killed one man with remorse, a man who had a wife and children, however he ran his business. He had taken it all from them. Had he learned anything from that bitter memory? Here he was years later, still angry at the world. No, this was different. This was cold business.

The pendulum kept swinging two ways. All he had to do was to adjust a mental screw and say, "fuck it" and keep the rocks in the bag. Nobody would know and what they didn't know wouldn't hurt them. What the fuck was right and what was wrong? He couldn't remember his head spinning so much as it had when he spoke with his parents, listening to their advice, choosing a path offered by the first crossroad of his life.

He could not help but recall the stories of superstitions relating to miners the world over. If Groebels were part of a lineage going back to the mid-1500s, fairies, gnomes, ghouls, demons, and goblins were part of the mining mystique. From Russia, to Norway, to Australia. PNG, Zambia, all miners fell prey to the netherworld who occupied the mines in wait for a man to make a misstep, to leave his lunchbox in a different place, to say words that might curse those at home.

When he told Ally about the short conversation with Alday, she put her hands on her hips, staring at him intently. "You can thank me for my power of positive thinking, Draco. You think I don't worry about you and wish the best for you, for us, hoping someday you'll make it to the top? Do you think the work crew in the morning will pick up the pieces and run right over to the

IRS to report a sudden source of income? Or, do you think you will be fired for being so stupid as to not keeping at least some of it?"

She reached into the first bag to pull out a handful of golden rocks from the two-inch-thick layer covering the bottom. She hefted one several times before dropping it back in, listening to the dull sound of solid piece of gold clunk against the others. Gold weighed a lot more than lead. She tried to pick up the first bag on the table bag containing the nuggets with two hands. By her estimation, it weighed 30-40 pounds.

"Now you're being sarcastic, baby" Harwood said, weakly, defensively. He found himself in uncharted territory.

"You're goddamn right I am," she shot. "It's called a crossroads in life. I presume you know about those." He had pushed one of her hot buttons, spending her energy wishing the best for somebody only to find them rejecting their successes.

Before he could speak, Ally physically forced him to sit down and confronted him. "Listen up, Mr. Draco, I know you for what you are and you're a decent person who has a passion. The trouble is, you don't know what it is. You work it out. I, too, have a passion, and it's you. I want to be bonded to you, to integrate, to laugh and cry, and, yes, marry.

"I'm trying to help you here, sweetheart. Everything will be fine. You, we, have been given a gift we can do good with. It's not about you striving for riches so you can piss away your money cars and boats, it's about making some kind tiny difference in the betterment of humanity, maybe neutralize evil to a tiny extent. This is a crossroads for you, for us. There is no replay in life, no redo. There's only fast forward. I could go on, but I'm done. I'll love you, whatever you decide."

Ally sought perfection of mind, body, and soul. Like Benjamin Franklin, one of her idols, she made a list of daily To Do items she tried to follow. She also recognized that most people did not share her view of life, in fact, more often than she preferred, she got pulled into theirs. This begat a quandary. She enjoyed crossing over into the realm of retribution, which did not at all relate to her life's goals. In a word, she enjoyed backsliding too much.

Not yet finished, she said, "Just a second." She walked into the bathroom to retrieve the digital scale which she placed on the floor next to the big rock. "Go for it, big boy," she said, standing there with hands on hips.

Chuckling at her melodrama, Harwood hefted the small boulder onto the scale. Both leaned in for a closer look. "I'm reading 95.4 pounds," she said.

They both ran mental calculations: 95.4 pounds and 16 ounces per pound equals over 1500 ounces times the going price of gold came to a lot of money, which would only increase as the price of gold increased. Both understood it wasn't infinite wealth and careless spending could quickly negate the period of momentary wealth.

"Still want to give it away? That's only one piece, my dear," she stated.

Harwood exhaled loudly and looked at this woman who had just ripped him to the core. He had no experience in how to fight this kind of attack. The vulture had picked his bones clean. Feeling hollow and exposed, he punched in a single number on his phone.

Harwood slept poorly that night. Dreams came and went about riches and Ally's excoriations and her protestations. His true feelings for her intermingled with a sense of helplessness as the primary theme of that which faded in and out. When he awoke for the nth time, he had made a decision. Allison Brooks was a good woman. He could find none better. She had gone the distance with him and would share his pain, pleasure, and sorrow. She loved him enough to beat on him and she had no qualms about letting him know about it. It's a crossroads, for you, for us. The words ran like an obsessive song that wouldn't go away, until it did.

At 8:00 the two men arrived at the super's office, Harwood carrying a small satchel. Cargill looked up from his paperwork and nodded a greeting. Alday carefully moved the papers on the desk to one side and Harwood set the satchel down on the desk without a word, opening it to expose the contents. Alday told the story of how they had come upon the contents.

Cargill stared into the satchel, then dumped the contents onto his desk. Gold gleamed in the light of the room and from the reflected light of the sun coming through the windows. He picked up a roughened chunk of pure gold the size of a golf ball that lay amidst a dozen gold and silver nuggets. He looked up at the two men who were staring at him more than at the rocks, and, as if they were puppets on the same string, both men shrugged in unison.

"They're not ours, they belong to you," Harwood said. The two men turned and calmly walked out. What Cargill did with his gift was his business. It was Ally's suggestion that they make Cargill a friend for life. Having a private talk with the sheriff at some point wouldn't hurt to bond them closer as well. The same was true for Ronnie. If the past had been any indication, they would need friends.

Compromise is a good thing.

Harwood started the vehicle and pulled out of the lot. Alday said, "Well, Mate, what say we go back to the drift. The first crew will be there by now. I wonder if they'll find anything interesting."

"Ay, maybe enough turquoise to make a

bracelet, eh?" Harwood grinned.

When the men walked back into the tunnel turning onto the drift, a commotion could be heard. A dozen men were on their knees, picking up small fragments of gold and silver, stuffing them into their bib pockets, some at the site of the explosion and others further back. One of them saw Harwood and said out loud, "It's Harwood."

Some men ignored the cry, others stood up not knowing what to expect.

Harwood raised his voice, "What's going on here?"

"Sir, did you blow this last night?" asked another man.

Alday answered, "Sure did. Blew it late and left it to settle out for you to haul today. Why?"

"There's gold here," said the man. Realizing he wasn't going to get chastised, returning to find more. Others worked on one of the walls with hand picks.

"Stop that or you will be fired immediately," Harwood bellowed. The echoes reverberated as though a stick of dynamite had exploded.

All activity ceased. All eyes turned to him. Harwood said, "This is company property. You are not to chip out to personally collect anything of this mine of value. You are stealing from the people who pay you."

"Now get back to work," Alday yelled, reinforcing the edict.

The men instantly grasped that they were not ordered to empty their pockets. Was that an oversight on Alday's part? Perhaps it might be best to accept it as such. Mining companies don't like employees stealing ore, however the word 'stealing' might be couched. The removal of 700 million tons of ore over the lifetime of this mine's operation is separate from theft of company property, which includes the dirt and chipping out pieces of value for personal gain. It was no different than the strict supervision that is maintained within diamond mines the world over to prevent theft.

What the two hypocritical leaders had done was to commit the greatest thefts in the history of the art of mining, excluding the numerous murders of mine owners, or their cheat, occurrences too numerous to count. In terms of overall crimes, it ranked very low on the list. Still, their act would make headlines around the world, akin to the pronouncement of war, should the truth be told when accompanied by colored photographs of the loot. On the other hand, the belief that one might not be caught and punished for their crime does tend to assuage any feelings of guilt arising from such an act.

Like school children trying to delay the handing over a test while adding last second answers when the teacher announces, "Time's up," the men slowly and reluctantly left what they were doing and returned to get their shovels to clear the area for the laying of track. Harwood grabbed one of the men and said, "Charlie, you're in charge. We're leaving for a while. Make sure nobody steals anything."

The men noted the lack of glitter on the floor, a far cry from what it had been only hours earlier. Alday picked up a nugget wedged beneath a rock, examined it, showed it to his partner, and tossed it back onto the floor, in case anybody might be watching to see what they did. After all, this was company property. Mysteriously, that nugget would vanish by the end of the shift.

6

"That's our goal," Harwood said, pointing to a copse of trees at the top of the hillside. With the sun just peaking over the mountains, he left the well-worn path and led Alley over gravel, stones and desert scrub.

Once among the length of alder, birch, and conifers that ran perhaps a half-mile south-to-north, they descended down a slight embankment between the trees to the edge of the stream. It originated from the side of the mountain to their left and ran a good half-mile before reentering the ground at a shallow depth before diving back downward.

He found a sandy patch in the shade that measured a good ten degrees cooler than the desert outside the copse. Harwood dropped his pack containing a few meager supplies and Ally followed suit.

The stream might be designated a babbling brook. It ranged some two-to-six feet in width and up to eight inches in depth in places, running a casual three mile per hour. The air felt clean and fresh, an idyllic day for placer mining for gold.

"Do you think we'll find any?" she inquired.

"Nah. Hundreds of people come up here all the time to give it a try, but so far no go. We're here to teach you how to pan, not to find anything. In case you haven't noticed, we don't need gold," he chuckled.

"Still, you never know," she said, enthusiastically. "Maybe we'll find it and become even greater zillionaires like Sutter did back in, what, 1848."

Harwood laughed out loud and shook his head, without saying anything. He pulled out a pair of trowels and two pans. Lightweight stuff. Play toys. Nothing serious. No diesel operated dredgers, sifters, shakers, or water pumps. No vials to take back their flakes.

"What did I say that struck you funny?" Ally demanded, hands on hips, as was her wont, turning to face him.

"Honey, John Sutter started out a pauper and ended up a pauper. From what my father told me, he was a German who left his family in Switzerland. He was bankrupt and destitute at the time. Somehow, he made it all the way to northern California in 1839 to the Sacramento area where he persuaded the Mexican Governor to grant him lands. Once he had the lands, he attempted to construct a water-powered sawmill until his carpenter found flakes of gold in the stream bed of the Sacramento River where they were located. The two swore to secrecy in their new partnership.

Somebody talked. The word got out like greased lightning on ice skates and next thing you know, by 1849, the place was overrun and the name of Forty-niners came into existence. People poured into the area like a magnet attracting iron filings. Two years later, a quarter-million people could be counted thereabouts, some of whom hit it big, most of whom went bust. He claimed the land and the gold belonged to him and his partner, but the U.S. courts denied his Mexican title and by 1852, he was still destitute. Slam bam thank you ma'am."

"Loose lips sink ships," she summarized, philosophically, staring at this man who possessed these nuggets of knowledge.

Preparing to begin panning the stream, the couple heard a shout from behind them. They turned to see two men, one about Harwood's size, but not as broad, craggy faced, bearded; the other clean shaven of average height like a tag along. Behind the men lay an abundance of digging equipment, a tent, large drink cooler, two shovels, several pans, a screen-sifter with a battery-powered electric shaker, a stack of empty Mason jars, and a new Jeep Cherokee 4 x 4 Off-Roader partially hidden behind a boulder.

"Hey, this is our spot. We were here first. Get

out," yelled the big man.

Harwood replied, innocently, "There's no reason to get rude. This is our first time. Give us a break."

"I guess you didn't hear me," the man repeated, ominously,, stepping forward. The second man followed by his side. Completely clueless weekend warriors living a century in the past.

"No, worries. You do know, this is public land. Ball's in your court, Mate."

"Move," ordered larger man.

"Or?"

"Or we'll make you move." The man smoothly pulled out his man toy, a nasty USMC full-tang serrated-edge knife from a worn sheath at the left side of his belt, the blade a full eight inches in length. He did it deftly, smoothly.

Harwood threw his hands in the air, showing fear at the sight of the weapon, and sighed in apparent exasperation. "All right. You don't have to get rude about it. We'll got upstream in that case," he teased, knowing that if there were gold or silver, the chances of finding them would be improved by doing that. Their lack of reaction to his statement and the amount of equipment the men had brought told him all he needed to know. These guys were playing at mining, overspending, ignorant of the basics, rushing to judgment, and not having researched the area properly. In short, is what you spent the money on going to be cost effective, not in term of wishes, hopes, dreams, and fantasies, but in terms of reality?

Ally grabbed his arm. She didn't like where this was going.

In a moment the couple moved 50 yards upstream around a slight curve. Harwood glanced at the men now partially out of sight, laboriously setting up their large sifting screen engaged in a detailed discussion about where to exactly place it.

Harwood said, "Be right back."

He circled around into the copse and returned within two minutes.

"Where did you go?" she asked.

"Mining is a tough business," he replied in a brief statement of fact and began to pass on the early teachings of his father on the proper way to pan.

For his 10th birthday, Mason had showed his son how to pan for gold. "The pan I used has sloping sides and with the middle lower than the rest of the bottom," he had explained.

"The reason gold is so expensive is that it is hard to find. Millions have tried and millions have failed. When you wash it properly, the heavier elements will settle toward the middle. You can tell what the others are by their color and amount as they circle the center like a target. The angle of the pan should be thus (he showed to boy how to hold the pan properly). You want to wash out the finest and lightest particles without losing any gold flakes. You want them all. You move to opposite sides of the river, or rivers, back and forth, logging, tracking. Panning is a practiced art that takes many hours to get right, even when working with an experienced teacher," he instructed.

After Harwood concluded the explanation, he revealed an idea he had been formulating, which, despite herself, caused Ally to giggle. There was no shortage of surprises from this man. He could serve as a point man for a comedy show that specialized in dark humor. Despite his plan, she saw it as good karma. At that point, the two went to work in their pretended quest for riches.

An hour of instruction later, Harwood reached into this pocket and pulled out a roughened gold nugget the size of a BB and placed it in Ally's pan of silt. He let her sluice off the water to eventually isolate the heavy golden piece amidst the remaining silt, a no-brainier at this point.

A BB is not a flake. The latter can easily float off with the wash. Still, he had her practice numerous times, with and without the BB. Finally, he glanced downstream to see the men loading dirt onto their sifter. He walked about 10 feet from her to work his own pan for some time. Finally, he muttered in a low enough voice that only she could hear, "Okay, now."

This was too much fun. Ally squealed loudly. Harwood looked over at her and shouted, "What!"

She squealed again. They had drawn the attention of the two men. Ignoring them completely, Harwood carefully examined her pan and exchanged excited words with her. He took her pan of silt and walked down to where the other men stood, while she continued to work the second pan.

The men stood frozen in place watching Harwood approach. One taller man pulled out his knife again. Harwood came up to them in all innocence and asked, "Is that real gold or fool's gold?"

The smaller man picked up the piece and consulted a small picture book he carried in his back pocket. In a moment he declared, "Why, that is gold."

Ally squealed again. "I guess she found another one. I better get back," Harwood said. He grabbed the gold piece to quickly return to her. A moment later, he pulled out a larger nugget. He held it up in the sunlight for a too obvious look, then gave her a big hug.

Again, ignoring the watching men, Ally held up her watch and tapped on it. She and Harwood engaged in a lengthy heated discussion with him gesturing wildly, occasionally pointing at the water, one time pointing downstream to the men to inform her that they had verified the find as gold, until he reluctantly gave in to her demands.

Their loud argumentative words could be heard at some distance. Angrily, he threw their pans and trowels into his pack and a minute later, the two disappeared down the hillside.

Descending the hill took them half the time it took ascending it. When they were safely inside the car and on their way back, Harwood said, "I wanted to make it a longer learning session for you. Sorry it didn't work out that way."

"Hey, for me, it's the experience, not the end result that counts. I learned a lot. By the way, where did you disappear to when we first moved upstream?"

"Nothing complicated. I stuck my own knife into all four of their car's tires. I don't like rude people or threats when there's no call for it."

"Couldn't you have done just one tire?"

"Naw, they had a spare on the back. The jerks would have had it changed in a flash. Where's the fun in that? I stuck that one too."

"Honey, you're not only vengeful, you're vindictive," she observed, beginning to understand him a little more, all the while enjoying the sing song of his accented English, almost a lilt.

"I know," he confessed. "It's a driving force that's been there as long as I can remember. There's a thrill in it I can't shake. It makes me want to hound some people till the end."

"The end of what?"

"The end of time."

She shook her head. Glad it's not me. The man has patience to a point. He's protective and family oriented. It would be nice if he understood art or science a little better. And then what? Would she be happier? "Do you want to talk about it?" she asked.

"Now is not a good time."

"When is?"

He shrugged quickly, then withdrew into himself.

"All right. Two can play that game," Ally commented, feeling greatly relieved that she wouldn't have to confess to her own sins, at least not until he confessed to his.

Shifting gears, she began laughing, "Those guys will probably be digging and sifting the shit out of our part of the stream till sundown and not find a thing. I can see them up to their knees in the hole they dug, then, when they get ready to go home and discover what happened to their car, they'll put the whole thing together and want to shoot themselves for being duped. They're miles from nowhere without any transportation."

"Welcome to my world. Like I said before, mining is a tough business," Harwood declared.

He thought for a moment, grinned, and suggested, "How about on the way back, we role play? You're the big tough guy, let's call him Mugs, and I'm the tag along, let's call him Pugs. What kind of conversation would they have when they start to figure it out, then pack up and discover the car?"

"I'm calling Cheryl, first. We're all eating at our house tonight. We have a new story. I get to tell it first," Ally announced, excitedly, punching in the numbers. She halted for an instant to ask, "Do you think the boys might be influenced by our behavior?"

"With Josh as their father, I doubt it. This will be lightweight stuff for them. Invite them too," he said.

The entire drive home the couple laughed so hard role playing that tears came to their eyes, and they bonded.

After he stopped laughing, Harwood reflected upon what she said about him. He openly admitted to being vindictive, even to excess. He didn't have to ruin their tires, the joke about the fake find in itself would have been sufficient. He had wrestled with the problem for so long that he was concerned about how he would handle another issue of pay back. In the end, Harwood settled on the fact that he would resolve his personal problems after he and Alday resolved the matter of Groebels. This was no time to soul search and detune, not when the bad guys are trying to kill you and yours.

7

While Ally drove the dozer at work, Harwood went home during lunch break to call any assayers who might be in Tucson. Knowing the price of gold, he was ahead of the game. That weekend, he invited Ally to drive into town with him to find an assayer's office. He wanted to sell a couple of gold pieces for cash. She suggested, "Let's go downtown. The world's biggest gem and mineral show is in progress. Everybody who is anybody will be there."

"That sound like fun. I must tell you, though, I don't know anything about gems, not really," he protested

"We don't need the cash. Can I ask why you're doing it?" she inquired.

"Because I want to buy you an engagement ring," he replied, simply.

Ally scratched her butch haircut and said, "Oh. Sweetheart, that's backwards. Aren't you supposed to asked me to marry you first and see if I say 'yea' or 'nay'?"

"You're right," he answered, without elaboration. She did not appear to be surprised by his response, nor did she reject his offer.

The downtown area of Tucson was awash with tents and signage. Buses drove people by the hundreds to drop them off at hotels, street venues, and the community center. Not only downtown, but virtually every hotel on the drive there posted gem exhibits, some highlighting gems and minerals from a particular area such as country such as Fire Agate from Sedona, Opals from Mexico, rubies from Cambodia and Thailand, or diamonds from South Africa.

"This is where you need to be," she told him. "I've been reading all about the show."

"No doubt," Harwood responded.

The couple paid for parking at the community center and walked indoors to see a quarter million square feet of exhibitors showing rocks from around the world on different levels, the booths like stubby stalagmites within a giant cave.

Taking his arm, she informed him, "From what I found out, people from everywhere come here every year to rent houses, to take their rocks out of local storage, sell what they need, and return to Bolivia or Nigeria. Million dollar thefts make the news each year when careless dealers lock their goods in the car.

"Plus, particular this state has eight different kinds of gem stones. Let's look a while to get a feel for the place, then you can see what you can get for what you brought.

Thousands crowded the walkways, stopping to look at every type of handcrafted gem set in every kind of setting; amethyst, tourmaline, fire opals, blue diamonds, turquoise, Apache Tears, 100 pound geodes, chrysotile, hematite, beads; every kind of ore, all were intermixed with hot dog and hamburger stands that were as popular as gems unto themselves. Rock Hounds sold whatever one required from trowels to gold sifting screens. Need something more serious, just ask. It didn't get any better than this.

Neither had seen anything of this magnitude. A miner for decades, Harwood felt ignorant of this gemstone world, a hobby in which tens of millions engaged worldwide. Even Julian, Alday's youngest son, collected. Videos played in one room showing everything from polishing rocks to panning for gold.

Ninety minutes later, Harwood approached the end booth where a row of gold merchants displayed their wares. Unless somebody wanted to pay for two or more spaces, the business on the end paid the highest booth price, and likely had the most money for cash flow. This particular business card proclaimed them to represent Crawford Gems out of Denver.

"What'll you give me for this?" he asked the lady behind the counter.

A man seated in a folding chair behind her

stood to join her when he saw the size of the golden rock the customer displayed. He appeared to be middle aged, not wearing Western, as were many of the sellers, but dressed smartly with tassel loafers, tan slacks and white shirt open at the collar. No wedding ring. He had a full head of dark brown hair, handsome, well balanced facial features. Harwood immediately suspected the two had more than a casual business relationship. The man introduced himself as John Crawford, owner and introduced his assistant Mary.

"Can I ask where you got this?" Mary asked. She, too, was dressed smartly, as befitting a seller and buyer of expensive items.

"My grandfather gave it to me. He said I could sell it if I ever needed money," Harwood smiled in his response.

"So you need money?" inquired Crawford, all too quickly.

Harwood laughed and ignored Ally, who perused the items in the showcase. He said, "No, I don't. I only want to find out what this is worth to you, or perhaps, to any one of the people in this row, if it's not to your liking."

"Mind if I take a close look at it?" Crawford asked.

"That's what I'm here for," Harwood told him.

While the woman pulled out golden items for Ally to try on, the man stepped five feet to the rear of the booth. He pulled out a small chemical test kit and a gram scale. He verified the authenticity and weight of the agate-size piece, nodded, punched some numbers into a hand calculator, and returned to Harwood to make him an offer.

Knowing today's price of gold, he asked Crawford what it weighed, ran the numbers in his head, and shook it. "Too low. Up it another 25 percent and I'll show you something else."

"Show me first," Crawford said, deadly serious. This kind of deal didn't come along very often. Both women turned to watch the negotiations. Ally had all the confidence her man would win the hand.

Harwood pulled out a second nugget three times the size of the first. Crawford's eyes got large, as did those of his assistant. He tried to look casual as he looked around, hoping no competition would be watching him trying to buy a pure gold nugget nearly the size of a golf ball.

At the conclusion of the negotiations for the two items, Crawford said, "I don't have that kind of money with me here. Can you give me a few minutes to go across the street to the bank?. Will you wait?"

"Sure, we'll be over in the diamond section over there," Harwood replied, so casually, he might have been ordering a hot dog with fixings.

"Draco Harwood, what are you up to?" Ally prodded.

"I told you before."

Without a word, he led her two aisles over to the end booth. It might as well have been a jewelry story. Armed guards and a plethora of private security personnel, both men and women, probably made up a sizable portion of the attendees.

Stopping in front of a jewelry counter, Harwood shrugged, "Not much. I'm going to buy you an engagement ring and a wedding ring."

All activity stopped when Harwood said, "I am asking you to marry me."

Ally's sense of propriety dictated that the man should go down on one knee to propose when he knows it is proper to do so, but this was Draco Harwood. His gentlemanliness only went so far. "Yes, I will marry you," she replied, to deep-kiss her man. Everyone in the nearby surrounds applauded.

Some 20 minutes later, Crawford found Harwood. He pulled him back to his own booth to reassess the quality of the nuggets, lest a scam be in the offing. Satisfied, the men concluded the deal. "One favor, sir. Can we do this without me writing you a receipt?" Crawford implored.

"Absolutely," Harwood agreed. Crawford handed him an envelope with cash. Harwood counted it, then returned to the diamond dealer to make arrangements for the rings Ally had chosen to be sized, while Crawford returned to his booth to play with his new toys.

Their joy was short lived. Arm and arm the happy pair left the convention center preparing to return home when Ally's eye caught the headline of local paper in a box. She halted. Fishing around in her purse, she said, "Got any change?"

Harwood reached into his jeans pocket gave her what he had. She plugged it into the box to grab a paper. The headline read, MINING CEO INDICTED FOR TREASON.

A car horn blared in the street, tires screeched. Two cars crashed in a fender-bender. Ignoring the scene in front of them, the couple stood paralyzed for an instant, until Harwood led them to a bench set outside the west entrance to the building.

Their hearts stopped. A heavy wave of history sloshed forward in time, the past rushing to meet the present—Doppler in reverse. The moment they had dreaded had finally occurred. It wasn't that the nefarious affairs of the company had been exposed, or that one or two bad guys were going down. Somebody would probe deeply enough to find out how it had occurred— exactly how it had occurred.

Federal grand juries weren't convened unless prosecutors believed they had enough evidence to convict. The story itself only repeated the same rumored information since it first broke by John Waltrop in Miner's News. His story wasn't another flap blowing over in light of another distraction, now there existed actual substance to the claims.

Ally grabbed his arm and said, "What now, babe?"

Harwood rubbed his head and scratched his neck in an effort to reason it out. A moment later, he suggested, "The other side probably doesn't care about us. Groebels screwed up. The bad guys don't care how they did it. Notice our Mikael Nordstrom's name didn't get mentioned, only the name of his father and the site supervisor in Sitka. My gut tells me the father is into this thing up to his eyeballs and he's the mover behind the retribution."

Ally was in no mood for cloak and dagger intrigue. She had just left a jewelry store where Harwood had proposed to her. Trying to cast light on the moment, she kept it simple by agreeing with her future husband—date of marriage to be determined—"If you say so. Let's take the paper with us and go home. I want to talk about us and make plans for our wedding."

Unfortunately for her, Harwood had lost the romantic mood. He had contrary thoughts on his mind.

8

Nordstrom was sick of freezing his ass off in Anchorage during one winter and in Nome another. He'd much rather freeze his ass off back in Germany. He presently suffered because his attorney advised him to lay low after his short stint behind bars, you know, to show the public you're just a simple working stiff. Even that didn't work. Out of the blue, the Feds wanted him to fly down to Sitka for a chit chat.

On top of it all, a Siberian cold front had dropped the temperature in the entire Bering Strait down to 30 below. This included operations on Unimak Island. Nobody was going anywhere.

Which bought Nordstrom a lot of time to reflect on the matter at hand. Okay, anti-Semites ran Groebels. Specifically, anti-Jews. Let the Persians build nuclear missiles and Israel would be gone in a flash. It came with the territory. Iran would then escalate terrorist activity in Saudi Arabia. Although Saudi Arabia controls about one-third of OPECs oil reserves, Iran, Kuwait, Algeria, Nigeria, Libya, and a few other nations control the rest. In general, Iran would play a more dominant role in control of the oil. At that point, it didn't matter what the United States did. Once that happened, Iran would control the major flow of oil for a big portion of the world. This would likely open up a can of political worms. The Russians were courting Iran and were allied with the Saudis at the same time. Russia had its own oil. Everybody got Russian guns. Diplomatic realignments would occur. The bully on the block usually got what he wanted.

The Americans already lacked enough fuel for their ships and planes, let alone their domestic vehicles, thanks to their current policy of cutting their own throat; this would put an exclamation point on it. Even if they wanted to, it would take them years to gear up. Iran would further their relationship with China because China needed oil and Iran needed money. Iran would own the Middle East while simultaneously expanding their brand of terrorism.

Although Russia had plenty of oil with which they could supply satellite countries and Europe, the supply was unreliable. If one looked up the word "corruption" in the dictionary, the definition would be "The Russian government." On the other hand, America had enough oil to last for centuries. The country could be oil independent. As it stood now, even if they wanted to, it would take years for them to get up to speed. Now they seem to be siding with Iran to bring down their own nation, which they seemed to have a bent toward. Even more unstable than the Russians, the Americans were too unreliable, changing presidents every time you turned around with their own back door corruption rampant throughout their higher government. Their wars were won and lost by political decision. For them, "winning" was a word with unbridled flexibility.

One thing about the States that absolutely fascinated Nordstrom was that no matter how much a politician stole or violated the laws foisted upon the public at large, no glaringly corrupt politician ever went to prison. Perhaps once every ten years a single man might get sent to a resort to play tennis and smoke a joint or two, but he'd be out in a short time, write a book, and get his money back.

The objective observer might wonder why Nordstrom Sr. had made a side deal with North Korea. From the Chinese standpoint, the country was a loose cannon, but at least the cannon rolled loose on its own ship. Once that country had nukes, all bets were off. The Chinese could always overrun the country, but who wanted to feed another 26 million starving people with nothing to show for it.

If conflict did come to the Korean peninsula again, a very like scenario, China could be ruined economically. They would have to gear up their military, redirect badly needed resources into the conflict, and could find themselves sitting on a power keg with some 20 million people in Beijing at risk only 600 miles from North Korea. Plus, China had a half-dozen nuclear reactors along its Eastern seacoast with another 20 under construction. Anything at all nuclear going off in the area would wash back and forth between the peninsula and Eastern China, contaminate fishing waters, and would likely blow into mainland China. The reactors could flood and it would be bye-bye eastern China along with the entire Korean Peninsula. Economies around the world would go into a deep recession lasting for years.

For those in the know, like the Nordstroms, North Korea had its own share of geologists. Just as Groebels had discovered Unimak and its riches, so had the geologists of North Korea discovered a monster load of lithium and gallium in the heart of the country. The extraction of these elements would complement their years-old mining of iron and coal. Equipment stood ready to be diverted at a moment's notice, plus steel manufacturing plants were directed to create the needed heavy equipment for accelerated removal and separation of these elements from ever present contaminants. These trace elements were absolutely critical for the upcoming technological era already enveloping electronics, energy, space, communications, transportation, and weapons. The value of these elements would skyrocket, which didn't leave a lot left for the little guy.

There's always a tradeoff. The north was slated to receive enough ore to speed up their own nuclear capabilities in trade for Groebels to have the rights to construct all the mining infrastructure necessary to harvest the elements for a percentage of the profits. Receiving missile technology from China was one thing, Groebels giving the hermit kingdom quality uranium and plutonium was quite another.

And who might be this whistle-blower who had exposed the operation, Nordstrom queried himself. His people could not come up with any answers other than to agree with authorities. The letters had originated from someplace other than Vancouver. To his mind, somebody in the hierarchy had leaked the information. It wasn't him or Ernst, his father. It wasn't Francois Gervais, his Director of Transportation in charge of ore shipping, whether by rail or sea, because Gervais had been appointed by his father.

Gervais' family owned the largest shipping company in France and the third largest shipping fleet in the world. Years ago, Groebels used a number of companies to freight their ore. This became complicated when, unpredictably, companies would become insolvent, or work stoppages occurred more than they should.

Sometimes too many questions were asked. If anybody understood how to mask cargo, fly different flags, even make transfers of cargo on the open seas, it was Francois Gervais.

Under directions from his uncle, Gervais stepped forward to make the company an offer: Hire me as Director of Transportation in exchange for our company to be your exclusive carrier. We'll set a stable rate without fluctuations and no questions asked. This met with the full approval of Groebels' BoD and both sides inked the deal.

Regarding the leak, one possibility remained, the junior vice president of the company, Khaled Al-Yamani, a Palestinian and long-time trusted friend of the family, although he knew virtually nothing of Al-Yamani's personal life. Groebels likes to hire managers from foreign countries. It was good for optics.

Al-Yamani had already been in administration when Gervais joined the company. Gervais held no ethnic prejudices, per se, but he had a distrust of those who were highly educated. He appreciated what they had accomplished, but his resentment ran deep. He had been forced to work onboard ship the day after he had graduated high school. As such, he had been deprived of an education to pursue whatever future he might choose for himself. So there was that bit of personal division between the two men.

Al-Yamani would be the last person to protect Israel and hates anything Jewish with a passion. Each month his bank sent an automatic payment to his parents, who still lived in Gaza.

As Nordstrom saw it, there was a flaw in the man's reasoning. If Israel dies from an Iranian nuclear attack, so do the Palestinians. A man-made border separating Gaza from Israel proper will not protect against nuclear blasts or radio-activity. Iran would get another bonus: Virtually all their own population follows the Shia branch of Islam while most Palestinians were of the Sunni sect. The two mix like water and oil.

Depending on the number and type of bombs used against Israel and the way the wind blew, other cities could also be affected, including Amman, Jordan; Beirut, Lebanon; and Damascus, Syria. Egypt might also receive fallout. Millions, if not tens of millions, would die outright or suffer a slow painful death. If you want to play on the world stage, then you must be willing to bet the farm to win the hand. Therefore, it might be a good idea to check on Al-Yamani's personal contacts.

Nordstrom picked up the phone. At least something worked for now until the ice brought down the phone lines. It wouldn't hurt for somebody to install a cell phone tower in Nome, either.

Three hours later, Nordstrom flopped down in his easy chair preparing to read from a sheet of paper he had printed from his computer. He looked out the window at icicles hanging from anything they could hang from and tried not to listen to his wife complain about why they had all the money in the world and had to live like goddamn Eskimos in an igloo. She had a point. To make matters worse, the TV was out, so she was reduced to reading scandal magazines and romance novels.

Most names on the list he read from were corporate businessmen whom Nordstrom was familiar with, others he presumed were people with whom he associated on the golf course, although he might have heard one of their names mentioned on occasion. One name on the list did stand out: James Brooks, who presently work for him down in Sitka.

Everything seemed to come back to the PNG days when he had gotten off the phone with his then wife who wanted more shopping money and, stupidly, angry at her, he threatened the Kiwis, instead of her, when he really wanted her to disappear. Yes, Harwood had taken it out on his man, to put it politely. This led him to wonder how Brooks, who worked in Germany, coincidentally got transferred to Sitka, of all places.

He began to make associations: Al-Yamani to Brooks, to Harwood and Alday, to an anonymous letter mailed to the Feds, to Sitka, and back to Groebels and himself. He needed to have a talk to Brooks before he spoke with Al-Yamani. Depending on what he found out, well, accidents in bad weather happen all the time.

Nordstrom was going stir crazy in this damnable apartment, not as bad as it was in prison, though, so he shouldn't complain. Sitting on this powder keg situation did not help his disposition. He also needed information. The site super in Sitka had been replaced. The assistant ran the show, both men ignorant of the current circumstances.

Once he talked with Brooks, he hoped to learn more than he knew at the moment, which was basically nothing. If Brooks were innocent, he would have no trouble speaking. If he were guilty, he would be guarded and looking over his shoulder all the time and probably expecting the call. Doubtless, the Feds had already spoken with him, so calling could only help.

Nordstrom checked his watch and placed a call to the assistant super in Sitka who answered immediately. The connection sucked. Nordstrom identified himself and said he'd be down, once the storms let up. He had to repeat himself several times with nearly every other word garbled. One time the connection cut off and he had to reconnect. After 10 minutes of interrogation, he had learned absolutely nothing and wanted to know if James Brooks might be on shift, and if so, could he please come to the phone. Not trusting to a recall, he doodled for 20 minutes while holding the phone to his ear, until, at last,

Brooks came on the line.

"This is James Brooks. Is that you, Mr. Nordstrom?" he said, his voice crackled and garbled, while checking to ensure the site superintendent had gone into another room.

"James, hello, yes, this is Mike Nordstrom."

The two exchanged cordialities until Nordstrom got to the point. "James, the reason I'm speaking with you is that I trust you. I remember we worked together back in, what was it, New Zealand . . . ?

"PNG, I believe, sir," Brooks replied, with open honesty.

"Yes , correct. I always liked your work and tried to help you get the transfers you requested."

"Thank you. I really appreciate what you did for me," Brooks came back, knowing a set-up when he saw one. He also knew that Nordstrom was not the one who had arranged his transfers.

Nordstrom could have taken his response two ways, but let it go. "Jim, I'm looking for site superintendents for two new silver mines we're opening up, one's in Anchorage, the other is back in New Zealand. I believe you've worked in both countries for us. You can take your pick of either. It will mean a serious pay increase, as I'm sure you know."

It took a several minutes before Brooks understood the entire message, piecing together broken words and sentences. He replied, "Thank you, sir. I'll consider it and get back with you."

Nordstrom continued, fearing the line would go dead at any instant. "Before I forget, I'm trying to get down there, but I can't find out hardly anything what with communications so bad. What's going on with the Feds there and all the press talking about South Korea and Iran and radiation?"

That was a long communique for a time when short sentences needed to be spoken. Finally, Brooks replied, slowly, word-by-word, "Nobody tells me anything, sir. All I know is what's in the local papers. By the way, while I have you on the phone, I'm slated to go on vacation once the weather clears. My wife is giving me grief about this place, to be honest."

"Of course, Jim, I completely understand. By the way, how's your old crew doing? Do you ever see any of them?"

Nordstrom treated this discussion like a lie detector test. Ask somebody their name and address and their favorite TV show, then ask them if they ran over somebody on purpose while simultaneously checking their vital signs.

Brooks rubbed the speaker of the phone against his pant leg while talking mumbo jumbo at the same time, then gently hung up the phone. Connection lost.

Five days later, James Brooks and Ally's mother, Lorraine, warmed up in Arizona. They rented a car and checked into a B&B in Oracle.

Two hours later, they joined family and friends at the steak house, a two minute drive from their residence.

Time differences notwithstanding, this was the same date Nordstrom arrived in Sitka, Alaska, to meet with a room-full of federal agents who had cabin fever, salivating at the opportunity to rip the throat out of anybody of authority they could get their fangs into.

For the moment, Brooks was enjoying himself more. The party consisted of family only, with few miners at the other tables during this Wednesday evening. Lorraine had decided to take a leading role in the conversation.

If there is any truth to the saying, "If you want to know what your future wife will look like, look at her mother," then Harwood had a lot to look forward to. Lorraine could have been Ally's older sister. They were of the same height, weight, and body proportions. Admittedly, Lorraine spent a lot more time styling her long hair than did her short-haired mechanic-diesel-driving daughter, but their hazel eyes and auburn hair were the same color. She had spent the last quarter-century by her husband's side and believed herself to be up-to-speed on his adventures, although some information remained on a need-to-know basis. Now she needed to know.

Light banter and toasts were over. Lorraine broke the ice. "Cheryl, Josh, I'm surprised they caught the guy who torched your house. Did you ever figure out who ordered him to do it? Did he say?"

"Yes and no," Alday replied. "He had received money from Groebels, but he wouldn't say for what; and no, because he worked for a lot of people. In short, he freelanced. This made it difficult for Interpol to nail a single employer of his. In our case, it must have been somebody at Groebels who paid him to go after us."

Harwood added, "This Braun guy did admit to working for Groebels to keep an eye on possible troublemakers among the crews—no offence, guys—when the PNG workers were killed. Some of it he did on his own, believing the company wouldn't care, after all, he does have principles. The guy is scary ruthless—tortured animals as a kid, that kind of scary. The men know he worked there at the time, but think he's taking the fall for the Nordstroms."

Ally raised her eyebrows. "It's a moot point now, isn't it?"

"Not at all, it might be a sign of problems down the road," Harwood said, in all seriousness. "The question on my mind is, what are you going to do, James? You can't dodge Nordstrom forever. At some point you're going to have deal with him."

"Unless dad retires," Ally said.

Lorraine looked aghast. "What, retire? Wash your mouth out with soap, Allison. He's not 47 yet."

The others laughed. Harwood offered, "It's not what James does, it's what Nordstrom does."

Cheryl added, "Don't count out the investigators. Who know, maybe they'll come up with something."

"Don't count on it," Harwood told her. "These are world class manipulators, wired to the top of the food chain."

James glanced around. There were relatively few people in the large room and most of those were watching TV sports. He leaned forward to speak more privately. "My source tells me that, although the shipments were to be divided onboard the ship after it set sail, it hadn't been done so up to this point. But he doesn't know when it will happen. A lot of different ships carrying different flags could be involved, although one investigator must have had serious authority because he ordered the harbormaster to lock down the freighter. If he hadn't, it could have opened a can of worms regarding its cargo and public safety. At the present time, neither the ores nor the ship are going anywhere. How much will go to whom is the big question and nobody on the ship knows anything, which does not surprise me."

Ally contributed, "It's a commercial vessel. As such, it is registered with the IMO or International Maritime Organization and must have an operational GPS homing device on it, so its position can be tracked. In some cases, it comes in handy, such as with illicit oil shipments. But not in this case. Like Draco said, these guys are ahead of the game."

Harwood asked, "How do you know all this?"

"I read a lot, sweetheart," Ally responded. "Besides, I like sea stories."

"Back to you, James," Alday said. "What are your plans?"

James looked at his wife and replied, "We're not going back to Sitka. I'll keep working for them and take Nordstrom up on his offer for the job in New Zealand. If he's after any of us, I guess it doesn't matter where we go."

Lorraine squeezed his arm, with a look that said it all. For better or worse, we're all in this together.

9

Upper level management typically doesn't get involved in day-to-day problems with employees or various incidences that occur on a particular job. Those tasks belong to others who have more experience in such matters. Upper level management is concerned with the greater picture, such as landing new contracts, cutting loose ventures no longer profitable, fighting off those who want to take what they have, and growing the company.

Now back in the sanity of his plush office in Cologne and with his wife happily ensconced in the hair dressing salon gossiping with her friends, Nordstrom found himself acting CEO.

With his father laid up with a heart attack and out of the picture, he quickly found out that the responsibility at the highest level differed significantly from the duties of Executive Vice President. The years he had spent in training and understanding the roots of the mining industry and rising to the rank of being a site superintendent were over. Next in line behind him was Khaled Al-Yamani. He couldn't let him rise any further. For the moment, he had appointed no one to fill his vacated position. As acting CEO, he'd have to check with their attorneys about the legalities of leap-frogging someone over Al-Yamani, perhaps moving Francois Gervais into the position.

He had faced the interrogations in Sitka. In the end, the great powers could prove nothing. He wanted proof of their accusations and they could only provide theories and possibilities. Even the legally binding Bill of Lading for the ore slated further refinement at one of their upgraded facilities in Massachusetts. "Feel free to ask them about it over there."

The final destinations? Both the uranium and plutonium had been requested by the German government for use in their new generation of reactors. People need energy and we supply it. Feel free to contact the German Chancellor. He's the one who signed the Atomic Energy Act." Never mind Groebels' contribution of millions of Deutche Marks each year for the betterment of the German people, or at least to some of them.

To Nordstrom, there were two types of people in the world. There were law abiding citizens who occasionally forayed into the illegal—with its endless shades of gray—and the people with criminal minds who occasionally forayed into the realm of the straight and narrow. He considered himself to belong to the former group.

Standing up from his seat behind the desk, he walked to the picture window to look over the Rhine River and its numerous castles lining the river banks. The notoriously romantic area once served as the European center of the Holy Roman Empire and a central point for European shipping. Today, it is renowned for its quality Riesling wines and haven for artists worldwide.

It is the confounding nature of the human to have morbid thoughts in the face of extreme beauty. Elements of the past nagged at the man. He felt out of the loop. He began to pace. A moment later he exclaimed out loud, "Damn it. I'm CEO, for God's sake."

Returning to his phone, he made a call to one of the numerous attorneys the company maintained on retainer and spoke with the senior attorney on staff. He wanted them to find out about Brooks, Harwood, Alday, and whomever else they were associated with, including where they're and what they're up to. He told them to start working on it yesterday and related what little he knew of the bunch. Wait. Braun had tried to burn out Alday in San Manuel, Arizona. We can find them there, he thought. The fuse was lit.

In the evening, he and his wife attended a business meeting thrown by a shareholder who had purchased a million shares of Groebels and had lost a small fortune in stock value thus far. The Nordstroms had been invited weeks before the flap occurred and since they had not received non-invitation notices, the couple attended the gathering. It did not go well. Getting glowered at for much of the evening, both Mr. and Mrs. Nordstrom drank a little too much, left early, and went straight for the bottle when they got home.

Loyal to the cause, early the next morning, after a sleepless night and feeling like shit, Nordstrom sat at his office desk when the phone rang. The caller ID noted an incoming call from the legal team. Nordstrom dismissed Marta, his slightly overweight, but highly efficient secretary, who had entered to go over the day's schedule.

Marta had worked at secretarial positions all her adult life. She received high praises for her accuracy in taking dictation, typing skills, and loyalties to those who had employed her. She had enjoyed her present job for nearly 20 years, but had only received a pay raise once several years ago. Her husband of 30 years worked as a manager of a supermarket. Together, they barely earned enough to survive, with inflation on the rise and the need to take care of her aging parents, who lived in a retirement home only minutes from their own small residence near the outskirts of the city.

Intrigued by what the attorneys might have

to say and hoping for the best, Nordstrom listened for several minutes, before hanging up the phone. He reached down to a lower desk drawer where he kept a fifth of Jack Daniels and a shot glass built into the cap, took a drink, thought a second, and took another. Then he poured a half glass of ice water from a cold pitcher atop his desk atop a large coaster, rinsed his mouth, swallowed and finished the glass of water. Good to go for the day, he thought.

One thing irked him. He had to find out third hand about Braun getting picked up by Interpol in Austria. The man had a laundry list of charges against him and trying to burn out Alday would prove to be lightweight stuff. He already knew this Braun had claimed responsibility for a number of deaths in PNG, which had gotten Nordstrom released. Apparently, Braun had several families, some of them quite extended. The man did get around. Apparently, he cared for one or more of them enough to do somebody's bidding.

He buzzed Marta and asked her to have Mrs. Peggy Steward, their American-German media director, come to his office for a conversation. Then he checked his calendar for the rest of the day. He had a scheduled meeting with a Mr. Kim in an hour, then he and his wife needed to attend a political fundraising dinner where he would be expected to make a significant contribution.

Marta buzzed and told him that Mrs. Steward had gone to Paris at his direction in order to lobby for their company to open several mines in France. He thanked Marta and told her he had forgotten because of all the ongoing events. She completely understood.

He then decided to make some calls of his own to check online about weather in Unimak and the status of operations there only to find communications impossible, either by phone or on-line.

Time passed quickly. An hour later, to the minute, the phone buzzed. "It's a Mr. Kim to see you, sir."

"Please show him in," he requested. Another beggar.

The door opened wide, Marta stepped to the side to give way to a man who entered the plush office at her motion. Preparing to close the door and enter with the guest to take shorthand notes, Nordstrom took one look at the man and gave her a quick shake of the head. She departed and closed the door gently behind her.

Mr. Kim looked as though he might be able to sell a ten billion dollar airline contract and make a $400 million dollar commission from the deal. Clearly Asian in facial appearance, the handsome man stood an athletically solid six-feet in height, his black suit costing easily two thousand dollars. His razor-cut black hair was cut short and combed without a single hair out of place. With a perfect complexion, Kim looked very comfortable in these surrounds. He wore no glasses, nor did he possess a paunch. A wedding ring adorned a finger. Nordstrom instantly knew world-class when he saw it.

The man carried no briefcase or loose documents. This was no beggar. Still, Nordstrom had been in the presence of presidents and heads of state. Why would this guy be any different? "Please have a seat, sir. How can I help you today?" he managed to say, reaching out his hand for a shake. The visitor accepted the hand and Nordstrom detected no calluses or dampness, only a firm grasp.

Kim began speaking in almost flawless British English. Perhaps he had grown in up Britain and attended Oxford or Cambridge. "Mr. Nordstrom, I know you are a busy man, so I won't take much of your time. In the interest of time you won't need to respond, only listen.

"I represent the Democratic People's Republic of Korea, or DPRK, as you know it. Our Supreme Leader asked me to send you his best wishes for a happy and prosperous life. He is wishing this because we have a business arrangement of which I have no knowledge. He also asked me to remind you that in business, as in everyday life, there is a certain element of trust. When there is no trust, there can be no relationship. Some relationships even end badly."

Kim was about to say something else, when he stopped speaking, seeing Nordstrom raise a halting hand to stare at the visitor with a stone cold look. Anger crossed his face. Nobody bullied him. If anybody did the bullying, it would be he. "Mr. Kim, we are both secure in our positions. I am in full control of mine. Are you? Please tell your leader this. Sometimes major steps forward incur minor steps backward. Any present problems will be resolved shortly."

With those words, Nordstrom stood to indicate the conversation had ended.

Kim remained seated. Looking up at the standing man, he grinned broadly, showing perfect teeth, as though he just understand the punch line to a joke and said, "Quite, Mr. Nordstrom. You didn't let me finish. I started to say that relationships can also end well. Clearly, you misunderstood me. I am not here to threaten you. I am here to offer my assistance, and that of my country's assets, to resolve any problems you may have."

Nordstrom regained his seat, trying to calm his racing heart. An entire country offering support? This is too good to be true, he thought. "Is there a time limit here?" he asked.

"A reasonable amount," came the calm polite response.

"Which is?"

"Sorry, that's not up to me." Kim stood, reached into a breast pocket to pull out a gold embossed card, handing it across the desk. "Call me whenever you like," he said. Within seconds, Kim had exited the room, closing the door gently behind him.

Less than a minute later, Nordstrom exited is office. Approaching his secretary he asked, "Marta, when is Mrs. Steward coming back?"

"In four days, why?" she answered.

"Please get her on the phone now," he requested, then returned to his office to reflect on the previous few minutes. For all he knew, the ambassador to Iran would walk through the door with a camel without making an appointment speaking in Arabic, or whatever they spoke over there.

A moment later, the phone buzzed. He picked up. "She's unavailable until tomorrow, sir. I left a message," Marta told him.

He'd deal with it later. No big deal. After two more calls, he felt good about the day. Checking the clock, he grabbed his overcoat to leave the office at an early hour, having recovered from his morning fatigue. Feeling secure in his game plan, he mentally prepared himself to party, patting the pocket with Kim's card in it.

10

In the late morning, the extended family met at Harwood's house to say goodbye to James and Lorraine. Cargill had given them the morning off for the occasion having befriended James and sharing mining stories with him. During the gathering, Cargill made a quick stop to show off his new truck and wish the couple well.

The flight home would leave in a little over three hours. From Tucson, the couple would fly to Los Angeles and take a nearly nine hour flight to Tahiti for a three day vacation followed by a nearly seven hour flight to Wellington.

Harwood had purchased first class tickets for the Brooks' and gave them few gold nuggets out of love. The story told by Draco and Josh about the great gold strike delighted and thrilled the couple who couldn't hear enough details, while Ally and Cheryl threw in their perspectives.

Cheryl effused, "Josh walks in the door all hunched over with this backpack and carrying a satchel like he's got lead weights in it. He says,

"Sorry I had to rush out. Thought I'd go shopping.

"Me and the kids are eyeballing each other and he drops both bags on the floor. 'Damn, that's shit's heavy', he says, rubbing his shoulders. He opens the pack and the bag. Me and the kids go over to have a look-see. For all I knew, it could have been ice packs on a dozen steaks. Two seconds later we're going nuts. Josh already has two beers in this hand and hands me one while we rifle thought the stash. He tells us all the story, then looks David and Julian in the eye and gets serious. He says that if they ever tell anybody about how they got this everybody could lose it all. He made the kids swear an oath that they would take the secret to the grave, or at least, until after he and their mother were dead. Of course, Julian didn't understand much about gold—I hope he's not retarded—but David had a knack for such things. The kids swore. Josh made David responsible for his younger brother for keeping his word."

Ally followed with her own monologue, describing her encounter with her own nether world, one consisting of a strange stew mix. The ingredients included a stupidly large hunk of everybody's future, a man she didn't know what to do with, untold riches interfaced with right vs. wrong, a history of bad luck when gold is involved, conscience, self-examination, corporate need, personal needs, family needs, perceived needs, and overall confusion. Add a dash of temporary insanity. By the time she had finished, everybody was beginning to nod off.

Before James and Lorraine drove to the airport, Nordstrom needed to be telephoned in Germany. Even with a six-hour time delay, he should still be in his office. Using the land line and putting it on speaker, James punched in the numbers. Marta said, "Groebels. Mr. Nordstrom's office."

"This is James Brooks. I'd like to speak with Mr. Nordstrom, please," James said, pushing the speaker button.

A moment's pause, then, "James, where the heck have you been. Look, it's not my doing. The board made the decision."

"What are you talking about, sir?" James asked, looking at the others who were frowning in wonder. "I called to tell you that I'm returning to New Zealand to take you up on your offer."

"No, no, wait. The offer is off. It's not my doing. Don't you read the papers? The board of directors insisted on filing charges against you and some friends of yours for defamation and conspiracy."

"Again, I ask, what are you talking about?" James asserted.

With a quick change in the tone of his voice, the CEO said without apology or apparent whining this time, "I think you know very well what I'm talking about."

On hearing the tone of Nordstrom's voice, a flush came over Harwood. He motioned for James to hand him the receiver, which he did. Harwood put on the hardest face he could and said, "Well, Mike, I guess we're just going to have to blow this thing up, aren't we? Even more than we have. Everyone will have you to thank."

"Who the hell are you?" Nordstrom spat.

"My name is Draco Harwood. I'm looking forward to meeting you," he replied, gently hanging up the phone.

A continent away, Nordstrom sat back in his chair, thought for a moment, and pulled out the business card Kim had handed him. He initially planned to tell the Korean that the problem had been resolved. Now, after that conversation, he wasn't so sure. He returned the card to the breast pocket of his suit. He needed to think, perhaps to talk with Al-Yamani and try to read through his lies. At least he knew that James and the other criminals had been the ones plotting against him.

When he placed the call, he found the man to be in Egypt. Doesn't anybody tell him anything?

A new thought occurred to him, one that had nothing to do with the rest of it. Coal mining for energy. Coal existed on every continent and on many, if not most, islands. It ran smelters, provided steam for electric power, served as the backbone for the steel, cement and paper industries and served as a source of carbon fiber for the production of airplanes and automobiles—it wasn't going anywhere. His father had shunned underground recovery and always treated it like a jilted lover. He had spent some early years underground and swore he would never get involved with it again.

Despite entreaties by staff to deep mine coal, Ernst refused to invest in this aspect of the industry that was so active in scores of countries. Open pit mining was used in some 40% of coal operations worldwide. Therefore, 60% was lost to Groebels because of the old man's policy. When the two methods of mining intermeshed, he sub-contracted the deep mining operation to other agencies and got little in return.

Once Nordstrom could be certain of his permanent position as CEO and his father out of the picture, he could expand the company's reach and begin deep coal mining operations. He knew Al-Yamani felt the same way he did and because the man could speak several languages, his exceptional skills extended to international relationships, not one of his own strengths. He salivated at the thought of a company growth spurt under his direction.

At least one problem remained. Al-Yamani knew most of the details of the uranium-plutonium operation, details the authorities had been unable to unravel. If Al-Yamani had talked, Nordstrom could hazard a fair guess as to whom he had spoken to. Things could become complicated. Fortunately, time was on his side, and so was a Mr. Kim.

Ally followed her parents out of San Manuel until they drove south on 77 toward Tucson. Once she saw they were on their way, she turned left onto the back road leading into Oracle. Stopping at the local convenience store, she grabbed a Tucson newspaper to find the article in question on page 3. She purchased a second paper. Twenty minutes later, she handed one paper to the Aldays. Returning home, she spread out the other on the table to read with Harwood.

```
UPI
(The following story is a reprint
of a previous article that appeared
in The New York Times)
Groebels, arguably, the world's
largest mining company, has filed suit
for defamation against several indi-
viduals whom they claim besmirched
their reputation. Peggy Steward, me-
dia spokesperson for the company,
stated that the persons in question
either work for, or did work for the
company at one time. They provided
false claims to the government of
the United States and assert that
Groebels was implicated in the ship-
ment of enriched ores to foreign na-
tions sanctioned by the U.S. They
further assert that Groebels' pro-
```

duction facilities are contaminated with radioactivity.

The individuals named in the suit are James Brooks, Draco Harwood, and Joshua Alday. The latter two are currently residing and working in the State of Arizona for Copper Mining, Inc.

Everybody eyeballed everybody else. "What the fuck!" spat Cheryl.

On a hunch, Harwood went to the computer and dialed in 90 DAY STOCK SHARE VALUE FOR GrB.

A graph appeared to show the initial value at $83.22 followed by a steep plunge to $43.57 and a further decrease to $22.18. However, within the last 48 hours the value had increased back to mid-range and suggested a further climb.

"Looks like we're a little late reading the paper. This story broke a couple of days ago."

"I guess we know Nordstrom's game," Alday said.

"They can't prove Jack," Cheryl said.

"It's not about proof. It's about image and earnings," Harwood replied.

"What now, honey?" Ally asked.

"I say we put part of our newfound money to good use and hire an attorney familiar with the case. Do you know of any?" Harwood prodded.

Alday checked his cell phone for the number, picked up the landline, and dialed the number for Wilhelm Schmidt and Associates, Munich, Germany. He handed the phone over to Harwood, who put it up to his ear. Because of Josh's deformity, most would say he sounded a little mush-mouthed when he talked. In a moment, Harwood identified himself and asked for Mr. Schmidt. A couple of clicks later, the German said, "Yes, good day, Mr. Harwood."

Harwood began, "Mr. Schmidt, we have a situation we'd like you to handle. Money is not an issue. I will be wiring you a retainer for $25,000 to get you started."

By the time he hung up, Cheryl had four cold beers ready with the caps off, despite the early hour.

Ally pulled out her cell phone. "Who are you calling?" Harwood asked.

"My folks to let them know," she replied.

Harwood gently placed his large hand over hers and said, "Let them enjoy the next few days. They'll find out soon enough and call us when they do."

Harwood returned to the computer screen, then pulled out his phone. Ally asked, "Who are you calling?"

"I changed my mind. We need to talk to your dad now. He kept talking about his source. Suppose his source has been compromised and Nordstrom is starting to put things together. We need to know who it is and so does Schmidt."

"It's Khaled Al-Yamani, Junior Vice President of the company," James told him on speaker phone.

"You two are close?" Harwood asked.

"Yes, I saved two of his kids' lives years ago in a boating accident, if you can believe that. We've been like close brothers ever since," James replied.

"I never heard about any of that, dad," Ally declared, feeling a little cheated out of not knowing about a big part of her parents' lives she never knew about.

James reported, grimly, "Remember about 10 years ago when you went to Canada to visit your cousins and your mom and I went to Egypt to see the pyramids?

Well, we took a couple of days to go boating on one of the lakes in the Cairo area.

"The second morning, we saw two boats collide and some people got thrown overboard. A couple of adults got hauled up by their friends, but the boats had drifted and nobody could reach two young boys. Few people know how to swim over there, but I did. I dove in to pull them both to safety. Their father was Khaled, who had just been hired by Groebels at the time. He and his wife invited Lorraine and I to dinner. I told him my background in mining, and he told me his. We had great fun sharing adventures.

"Both of them had a little trouble understanding your mother at first what with her deep South Carolina drawl. As a matter of pride, he asked me never to mention what happened on the lake.. I never did till now. Even you didn't know, Ally. By the way, none of you ever heard this story."

"Mate, if you have any private way to get hold of him, it might be a good idea to do so. His life may be in danger," Harwood advised. It went without saying that the statement included all of them.

Khaled Al-Yamani knew his way around Cairo like nowhere else. After his uncle and aunt had brought him to Egypt as a youth and raised him, he learned the true value of loyalty and trust. He also knew the opposite. His uncle had been a man of means, even back in the day. He had obtained his parent's consent to take the boy out of Gaza to begin a new life under his tutelage.

Al-Yamani helped his uncle in his tobacco shop after school while his mother helped him with his lessons, until he got accepted to Cairo University where he discovered his niche. He excelled in mining engineering and geological sciences. After getting his Master's Degree from MIT, he applied to Groebels, who made no secret of looking for people with exactly his skill sets. Thanks to his ability to befriend people, along with his discovery of new ore bodies and linguistic abilities, he moved up the ranks into higher administration.

Although his uncle and aunt had never visited the States, or had never traveled outside of Egypt since the early years, Al-Yamani had visited them many times and they spoke regularly on the phone.

Now he needed his uncle's advice and assistance. He was in trouble.

The dark-eyed Palestinian was not a tall man, nor was he handsome. But he exuded a relaxed charm that gave off a feel-good energy. He kept his personal prejudices well hidden, had married a college-educated wife, also from Egypt, whom he had met at MIT. She gave birth to three children who still lived with them.

The uncle led his nephew into the back of the store letting his assistant mind the front while they conversed.

At the completion of his story, his uncle asked in Egyptian, "Are you sure you can trust this Brooks?" He took a deep drag off an opium-laced cigarette and handed it to his nephew, who followed suit, then handed it back.

"With my life, uncle," Al-Yamani replied.

"Tell me about these others," the uncle requested, after reading the newspaper articles his nephew had brought.

Al-Yamani told him what he knew and could find out. He had his own sources who had made him aware of the present story about them confirming what had recently made the press.

The uncle knew of the Nordstroms after

years of discussion with Al-Yamani and did not short them for their business acumen. He didn't care two cents whether North Korea lived or died. However, it immediately became evident that many of his friends and family could be in deep quicksand once Iran became nuclear independent.

His uncle did not become extremely wealthy selling tobacco out the front door of his numerous stores throughout the country. He had inherited his own father's and grandfather's business of selling opium out the back door.

The two began to hatch a plan. One phone call and a half-hour later, two dark-haired hatless men wearing loose-fitting slacks, T-shirts, and sandals, entered the store. Nodding to the assistant, they walked to the rear of the store and closed the door behind them.

Quantas Airlines Flight 0623 touched down at Wellington International Airport at 2:30 pm. Passengers departed the plane en route to the baggage claim, when Lorraine noticed a man holding a sign that read: JAMES BROOKS.

James walked over the man, not surprised at all, and identified himself. The man checked a photograph in his possession and said, "Sir, I am authorized to present you with these papers."

James nodded and said, "Right. Have a nice day, Mate," and received the envelope. He already knew the contents.

On another continent, Draco Harwood and Joshua Alday got called off the job to the site supers office. With bibs covered with dust and hardhats in hand, the pair entered the room to see a man overly dressed for the climate of the day.

Cargill explained, "Gentlemen, this is a legal matter, one that excludes me. He asked me to summon you."

Whereupon the man said, "Under legal authority, I am presenting you with these documents."

Alday took the packet and presented a semblance of a bow. "At your pleasure," he said, knowing the man was likely a minimum wage earner doing his job. Why give him grief?

"What kind of trouble are you two into this time?" Cargill asked. He couldn't keep the grin off his face, surmising the matter had everything to do with the newspaper scandal.

Harwood answered, "It's a civil matter, not criminal. We've got it under control."

"Let me know if there is anything I can do, all right?" Cargill asked. He owed them.

11

UPI

Ernst Nordstrom, longtime CEO of Groebels Mining Conglomerate suffered a stroke while his home in Berlin, yesterday. This followed an earlier heart attack. He is 87 years old and his right side is immobilized. Now wheelchair bound, medical reports indicate the man is cognizant and very coherent. He was recently cleared of wrongdoing regarding his alleged shipment of elements necessary for the making of nuclear weapons to foreign nations. He announced his immediate relinquish of the company to his son, Mikael Nordstrom, who was also cleared of the same charges.

The Atomic Energy Commission of the United States, or AEC, which had authorized seizure of the ship containing the cargo in question, is expected to release the ship to resume its passage to the east coast of the U.S. where further refinement of the ore is expected to occur.

Ernst Nordstrom's son has expressed heartfelt grief regarding the deteriorating condition of his father, and pledges to expand the company well beyond its present status, whatever it takes.

The new head of a 50 billion dollar corporation had no time for reflection on personal matters. He found himself wined and dined by the U.S. Department of Interior Bureau of Mines, the German Mineral Resource Agency, labor unions, environmental groups, and endless suck fish from left field. He reflected on how he had been caught up in the minutiae involving men such as Harwood and Brooks in light of the bigger picture. Still, at night, when his brain sorted through the myriad of events in his life, as is the wont of man, Nordstrom schemed to contrive a method of retribution against them and Al-Yamani, whom he knew could not publically reveal the plot. If he did so, he would look the fool sinking his own ship.

At the moment, he only knew in general that Brooks had gone to New Zealand or Australia, where he could easily find employment. He also knew exactly where the others were located, which gave him pause. After the conversation, he had come away with fresh ideas along with the names of a couple of contacts, should he desire to continue the game.

With the freighter making its way to Massachusetts, Nordstrom informed Kim to tell his Supreme Leader to finalize arrangements for the mining of lithium and gallium. He also informed his Iranian contact that their shipment should be received within short weeks.

Al-Yamani returned home and after a number of days had not yet received word of a promotion. He had his doubts. But he also had his own agenda and continued to stay in touch with his old friend, James Brooks.

The lawsuit against the three troublemakers appeared to be languishing in light of a seemingly endless barrage of challenges, counter-suits and new accusations issued by Schmidt and Associates, who, like a bad relative, refused to move out of the house.

Early Sunday afternoon, Ally answered a knock on the door. She opened it to find a young man dressed in casual wear with a large plastic bag in one hand. A magnetic sign on the door of the old Chevy behind him read: CASA GARCIA MEXICAN FOOD, ORACLE, AZ, PH. 520-326-4777.

"Is this the Harwood residence," the youth asked, checking a slip of paper in his other hand.

"Yes. What's this?" she asked.

The youth replied, "Delivery, courtesy of the Aldays."

Ally beamed, "Really. How nice." She fished in her pocket and found some money for a tip and handed it to the boy, who politely thanked her, turned, and walked back to his car. She thought of taking his picture like Cheryl had done, but by the time she retrieved her phone, he had driven off.

She closed the door and brought the food to the kitchen table. The smell of the Mexican food mingled with the smell of stew slow-cooking on the stove.

Ally pulled out the Styrofoam cartons to find burritos, tacos, enchiladas, rice, beans, and chips in ample supply. Opening another container, she found salsa. She loved their homemade salsa. Everybody did. Dipping a finger into it, she sucked on it, nodding her approval.

Harwood had been watering a bed of flowers Ally had planted in the backyard. He had to admit she had a creative talent. She had constructed a small greenhouse to grow a variety of fruits and vegetables, including tomatoes, squash, okra, and cucumbers. For his part, if he purchased a vase of plastic flowers, the plastic would have wilted by the time he got them home. There's true balance in this relationship. Like I told her the first day we met, she creates, I destroy.

Entering the house through the rear kitchen door, he saw the boxes. Recognizing the smell of Mexican food, he beamed, "Where'd ya get the food? I thought we were doing stew."

Ally didn't answer. She flushed, began shaking, tried to sit, and almost missed the chair. "I can't breathe, scared, heart pounding, delivery from Cheryl and Josh. Bad salsa," she managed to say, bending over grasping her stomach.

Harwood picked up the phone and called 911. Then he called the Aldays. Cheryl picked up. "Did you order Mexican food for us?"

"No. Why?" she replied.

Harwood told her.

She said, "A young man from Garcia's just pulled up. He's getting out with a bag in his hand."

"Stop him. Ally's sick. Call Josh. Do it. I'll be over when I can," Harwood said. In his profession, he tried to remain calm while dealing with emergencies. This differed from directing others or foreseeing danger. This was another personal attack.

Next, he reported the incident to Jennings. "Meet you over at Josh's," the sheriff responded with a curt reply.

Within short minutes the ambulance arrived to pick up Ally and to take the food for analysis. Harwood needed to be with her, but knew she was in good hands. He could do nothing at the moment. He'd be at the hospital soon enough.

Sixty seconds after the ambulance's departure, he screeched to a halt in front of Ally's old home and where Josh and Cheryl's now lived. Harwood arrived to find the youth encircled by the sheriff, Cheryl and Josh. The young man was clearly frightened, but intact. Cheryl had resisted the urge to kick the kid straight away using her specialty technique. Instead she let her husband hold onto him until help arrived.

Harwood joined the group. The sheriff reported, "Draco, he said he does the deliveries for the restaurant. Some man with sunglasses came in and placed the two orders, then took them out to his truck. A couple minutes later, he came back in with the bags and said he just received a call about a family emergency and couldn't bring them himself like he wanted to. He gave the kid $100 to do it. He doesn't know any more."

Jennings wrote down the description of the man who had placed the order and the vehicle he drove. He went to the car radio and contacted Mammoth, Oracle, and Catalina police, thought for a second, then contacted the Florence police department in case the guy decided to branch off at the junction and head 45 minutes further north in their direction. In Florence, the industry revolved around money generated from employment at a state prison. Harwood had met some of the guards who worked there and thought they should be the ones behind bars to be guarded by the current inmates.

Returning to the hospital, Harwood found the

attending physician, who told him, "We're treating her for strychnine poisoning. I've never actually seen a case, but it's textbook. There might be something else in there, as well. She's fortunate in that she only took a taste. Otherwise, you both would have never made it to the phone."

"Doc, can I see her?" Harwood implored, showing deep concern. He loved Ally. He knew it. Losing her might be too much to bear. He considered himself to be a passionate and compassionate person, yet he hated himself for his inability to tell the woman he loved how much she meant to him. He couldn't even propose properly to her.

The doctor did his best to calm the visitor. Clearly, the miner felt deeply for the patient. "You'll have to wait. She's on IV and we're bringing down her temperature. I also put her on anti-convulsive medication. The poison hasn't reached her colon, so there won't be any significant absorption. Check back in an hour or so."

Harwood needed to rip somebody's face off. He did his best not to get into a one car accident on the fast drive over to see his friends. Jennings had taken the frightened boy's information and followed him back into Oracle to interview anybody else at the small, but popular, restaurant, who might have seen the person who had purchased the food. After the youth shyly asked if he could keep the $100, the sheriff responded in the affirmative.

A quarter hour later, Oracle police reported the apprehension of the suspect after a high speed chase. He had taken the turnoff to Florence on a two lane road at speeds in excess of 110 miles per hour. Florence police came down from the other end to block the road. He was still in the jurisdiction of Oro Valley, which included Catalina and Oracle, at which time the Oracle police took custody of him and impounded his truck. The small community lacked a jail, but maintained a detention center for the occasional drunk and miscreant.

"I'd invite you over for stew tonight, but I'd better go stay with Ally, Harwood told Cheryl.

Cheryl announced in no uncertain terms, "We're all going, I'll have a neighbor watch the kids while they watch their new TV. They'll enjoy their new toy more than a hospital visit, even if it is Aunt Ally."

Shortly, the trio arrived at the hospital to find that Ally's muscle spasms had ceased, save for an occasional flutter. A heart monitor showed a normal beat. An IV needle penetrated her arm.

Ally had spent a fitful period, as though in a surreal trance. Like a train racing toward you, reaching you, and speeding past, she soundlessly perceived the Doppler shift of future becoming the past, leaving in its wake a suction of litter being dragged into the partial vacuum. In the wake of time, motion pulled along the memories of lost loves, unattained goals, words spoken deeply regretted, heartaches accumulated, opportunities missed, wrong paths taken, unbridled promiscuity, and an accomplishment or two. They were all gone, save in the memory banks, accelerating the farther away they got, like a galaxy expanding, with the stars the farthest away moving at a faster rate.

In a way they were the mirror images of the distant future that is comprised of hopes, dreams, aspirations, fantasies—a future accelerating the closer it approached, goals speeding into view waiting to be grasped, until the future and the past collide for a brief instant called the undefinable present and the opportunities speed away.

"Some people will do anything for attention," Cheryl chirped, shaking her head.

Ally opened her eyes, gathered herself out of her psychedelic mist, smiled, and managed a wink at Harwood, "That's me. Not enough loving." She added, "The doctor wants to keep me here overnight for observation. I should be able to go home in the morning."

Alday said, "Ally, that's great. You dodged a bullet. I doubt they'll ever get anything out of the man. He's probably way down on the pecking order."

Cheryl shook her head, "Don't be too sure. If the lab finds strychnine in the food, or in his truck, he's up on several counts of attempted murder. His life is over no matter what. He might plea bargain to see if he can get out of prison in 20 years instead of 50 years, that is, if he has anything to offer."

Alday agreed, "True. You don't take orders to kill people from somebody who gets up off a park bench."

Harwood grunted, "Doesn't matter. We know who's behind this. When we get back, we'll see if we can reach James. He is going to go ballistic when he finds out his daughter got attacked. It's time to gear things up. Enough with the lovey-dovey shit. I've got an idea." Looking around to ensure the absence of medical staff, he discussed what he had in mind with the other three. Ally, too, paid attention. Whatever the scheme, she wanted in.

The ship had departed Massachusetts, ostensibly to deliver ore to Germany. For the moment, in Nordstrom's view, it appeared as though he might be caught in a cross-fire. First, that damnable Harwood wouldn't die and doubtless had deduced himself to be a designated would-be target. This fact applied to his trollop and the two friends of his.

Furthermore, the suit against him wasn't going anywhere and probably never would, thanks to Wilhelm Schmidt, who seemed to have endless funding. The attorney had petitioned various energy commissions to present their evidence of clearance, wanting to know why the ship had been released, why Harwood, Alday, and Brooks had been sued, demanding to see recordings of emissions from the radioactivity tests, along with another boxful of requests.

On second thought, the suit didn't have to go anywhere. Fighting back served to stabilize the stock value, which was the whole point to the exercise.

Third, the link of Al-Yamani to Brooks disturbed him to the extent that he had come to distrust his own vice president.

Endless funding carries a lot of weight, especially when one desires to tap into the GPS tied to the International Maritime Association's satellite link in order to follow the ship in question. It would be up to Gervais to ensure the ship(s) reached safe harbor. Onboard, monster rolls of copper wire came as finished products from the refinery. The cores of many consisted of lead-lined boxes so thick they were radiation proof and easier to hide or disguise, while other rolls lacked the core and were all accounted for.

No worries. Similar to the projects he had managed throughout his career, he likened this one to a Pachinko game where the steel ball bounces from side to side, hitting different pins, always making forward progress, inevitably reaching its goal.

12

The oceans of the world consist of a network of busy highways and byways. At any one time, some 10,000 oil tankers plow the high seas. They are joined by twice that number of cargo ships, cruise ships, military craft, and another million or so privately owned pleasure boats. Intermixed within the conglomeration is the North Star, the flagship of the Gervais Shipping Company, a 20,000 ton container vessel measuring some 1200 feet in length by 200 feet in width. It can carry up to 20,000 standard steel containers, each measuring either 20 or 40 feet in length, coded as to location and contents with the rows and tiers numbered. Mistakes in numbering can happen.

There are approximately 500 million shipping containers, either in port, or in transit on the seas. They carry absolutely everything imaginable and some items unimaginable.

After he left Egypt, Al-Yamani went north

to visit his aging parents in Gaza. He had given up trying to convince them to live with him and his family. They were where they wanted to be when they died.

Returning back to work in Germany, he had decided to confront the new CEO about his own position in the company. He checked with Marta to ensure the man would be in his office and asked her to announce his presence.

Al-Yamani entered the familiar office to be welcomed by Nordstrom and took a seat. After cordialities were exchanged about his travels abroad, the visitor expressed his concerns to which Nordstrom responded, "Khaled, I expected your question. To let you know, I gave the matter great thought about appointing you as the new Executive Vice President, really I did. Your international connections and new contracts abroad have brought us great success. However, after having our accountants go over the figures and presenting them to the board of directors, it is our opinion that Francois Gervais has brought greater wealth to us from a number of standpoints, although I don't see any reason why you can't get a significant increase in salary."

Al-Yamani smiled and took it like a man, despite the insult levied against him; as though he needed a pay raise like a common laborer. He wanted to make the company profitable, that is, within the extremely broad definition of legitimacy and decency, without clandestine and nefarious side deals going on with world super-powers to be.

Forced into making a hard decision, he stopped at a hardware store to have some keys made. Three days later, Marta called in sick with a bad cold.

Al-Yamani knew that Gervais liked to play with fire. When the ore-carrying ship left Unimak Island, it passed through the Panama Canal on the way to Massachusetts, a distance of some 4000 miles, where the processing was highly efficient. Because time had become a critical component of the equation, the ship retained the flag of the United States where it went to an American refinery and reloaded onto another American vessel named the North Star. Thus, the ore fell under American authority, which basically included the entire suspected vessel or group of vessels tied to the enterprise. In so doing, he had put his entire shipping line at risk.

Gervais knew the Americans could seize whatever ships they deemed to be problematic once they left international waters. He also knew that, unlike the Americans, not all countries had partial or full embargoes against Iran and North Korea. By flying different colors using a good half-dozen ships in an advanced version of the old cups and balls shell game, Gervais hoped to get around the problem. And only Gervais knew the vessels in question.

"Time is of the essence," James cautioned. "Never mind the computer. Nobody is going to suspect us, and if they do, so what. We're not party to a crime, we're trying to stop one. Besides, I've got my friend's okay on this."

He sent Ally an email of what Al-Yamani had told him of the project. She composed the letter, which she polished and emailed back to him, ironing out details on the phone. Finally, she sent him several copies with different headings. Again, James made arrangements to have them mailed from Vancouver the same day.

By the time the atomic energy agencies received a second express letter sent from Canada, the North Star had already stopped in Mauritania on her way to Portugal, where she would drop off more cargo, then transfer some cargo to another ship while loading more for herself, each time flying different flags on different ships, some of which even lacked a seaport. Contracting with countries and companies lacking a port is a common practice.

Scores of ships a day enter and exit the Strait of Hormuz in the Gulf of Oman, most of which are oil tankers. Some deliver a variety of commodities including machinery and grains. Approximately one-quarter of the world's oil flows through the strait. Delivery of the ore requested by Iran should go smoothly given the mass of traffic. No problem there.

As for North Korea, Gervais didn't know much about flying goods around the world. To him, shipping to the hermit nation was the preferred method of delivery. Of the 17 seaports belonging to the country, he had been directed to stop at the port of Nampo. The port was not only deep, it was proximal to Pyongyang, the capital city, where rail lines and roadways branched outward. Nampo serves as a fishing hub and manufacturing center for steel, ship construction, and auto making—a perfect drop-off point.

Based on the second letter, once again, the IAEA descended on Gervais, who pleaded innocent of all charges, especially to that of treason. Almost with the attitude of "Please, you're beginning to bore me," a nervous Gervais dismissed their accusations, at the same time avoiding calls from his father.

Nordstrom, too, expressed outrage at yet another intrusion into his company's affairs. More hearsay. It had to be Al-Yamani who had cooked up the scheme, probably yucking it up with Brooks and a bunch of miners who didn't know how to play hardball. He tried to locate Al-Yamani, only to find out the man had disappeared.

On a second tip from a person supposedly in the know, the German Drug Interdiction Agency recovered a substantial amount of opium in Gervais' office, so much that charges were leveled against him for trafficking. The same tip led to a similar find in Nordstrom's office, as well as a major stash in his home duct-taped in plastic bags to the bottom of his bed. Both men were found to have a large collection of child pornography pictures on their home computers. Surprisingly, authorities found Nordstrom's current wife to have male porno on her personal laptop. No charges were leveled against her.

Prisons were filled with cop killers, murderers, butchers, bank robbers, and sadists galore. They shared one thing in common: the hatred of those who engaged in child pornography and sexual abuse of children.

The value of Groebels stock plunged again.

At that point, the Americans called Gervais Shipping Lines HQ sending the same message via Fax, strongly informing the company of a single fact: All their ships around the world would be sanctioned and not be permitted to dock until the items in question were recovered in full. Obviously, the Americans had no authority to order other countries what to do, but the message held weight. The company stood to lose billions.

Both Gervais and Nordstrom knew their lives were over. It was only a matter of who would do the job on them and when. It was a lot for a father to ask his son to admit to treason, which would cast a shadow on the company. Still, his parents implored him to do the right thing. This was bigger than all of them. Gervais had not only sunk his own ship, he could bring down the entire fleet. Gervais pointed the finger at Mikael Nordstrom, who ordered him to do it, who then pointed a finger at his father, presently wheel-chair bound and trying to figure out what had gone wrong.

In Nordstrom's case, opium and pornography charges aside, he could only be accused of the minor matter of treason, which was still a rumor. But the Groebels Board of Director had heard enough and ousted both men forthwith, moving Khaled Al-Yamani to the position of CEO and stripping Nordstrom of all pensions and further income from the company. In his haste to move into the top position, he had neglected to create a golden parachute. He would be fortunate to have enough money to trade Top Ramen packages in prison, should he survive for any length of time.

Marta had recovered from her illness. She took great delight in a substantial increase in her salary by the new CEO, ostensibly to account for inflation, along with a large swelling of her bank account, not necessarily in that order. The stock in the company quickly increased in value.

The nefarious ores had been recovered. This required international cooperation to seize nu-merous ships belonging to the Gervais Shipping Lines, to the great discomfort of two nations in particular. These two would have to find another way to reach stardom on the world stage.

James and Lorraine Brooks were tempted to move down to Arizona to be with their soon-to-be married daughter, until James got invited to be site supervisor at his choice of any of Groebels mine anywhere in the world. They chose to live in an upscale neighborhood in Morocco, not far from where a new discovery of phosphorous had been made.

Draco and Allison made plans—at least Allison did—to be married on a Sunday two weeks hence.

At least, that was her intention.

PART III

1

At 3:25 am, an explosion rocked the community of San Manuel. It could be heard as far away as Mammoth and Oracle. The occasional sound of dull, muffled booms were part of mining life when daily explosions echoed throughout the tunnels and drifts. Not so, this time. It was as though a magnitude 6.0 earthquake had originated with San Manuel as ground zero, which, in fact, it was. A thousand lights in the township went on within seconds.

The first thought of most was that, somehow, the storage area containing the many cases of dynamite, C-4, blasting caps, and det cord had exploded. Others thought an airplane had crashed. Still others believed an earthquake did, indeed, occur in a part of the country not normally associated with such events. The shock wave of the explosion rattled windows and set off car alarms adding to the chaos. A long low rumble after the blast served as a long exclamation point.

Mining operations maintained high explosives stored in a skirted brick or concrete shelter with a substantial foundation under lock and key distant from traffic. A truckload of dynamite cases is brought in on a regular basis, ordered from a manufacturing plant, actually constructed within an old mine, some 200 miles from their location. From this storage area is drawn cases of 60 dynamite sticks per case, for daily use. Their usage is so common that cases of dynamite are maintained on each level, as it is worked, with caps stored in a different location. These are ordered the day before by blasters with a particular need. Anybody who needs explosives can get them from their respective levels; at this point.

With the general alarm blaring, Harwood, Alday, and Ronnie converged at the main storage area to find it intact beneath the glare of nighttime spotlights. Puzzled, the men looked around them, finding it difficult to breathe. Something about the landscape had changed.

The dust cloud became obvious. It originated from one area of the mountain where mining was in progress to the southeast, including the level on which the mine tour had occurred. The excavation had since expanded into miles within the mountain to follow the rich ore body.

The mountain had collapsed around the hollows, as though rejecting the intrusion of man. Somebody had blown the levels that now numbered 10, including at least 40 of their drifts, destroying ore-carrying trains and millions of dollars of equipment within them.

This kind of destruction doesn't happen. Back in the old days, if you wanted somebody's mine, you shot them, called it a hunting accident, and took over from there. Absent that, hostile corporate takeovers, agitation by union members to call a strike, and forming environmental groups to cause closures, were more modern methods used to slow the growth of competition.

Ignorant of the past activities relating to Groebels, Ronnie speculated that only a competitor would go to such lengths. "In that regard, we have lot of possibilities," he said, watching the emergency response team try to find a way up the roadway leading to the vertical shaft and the upper levels, only to back off when they ran into a pile of dirt several stories high with dust in the air like a heavy fog. Light morning breezes stirred the air to blow the cloud toward the population center, laced with uncountable micro-fragments of trace minerals and heavy metals.

Under Al-Yamani, Groebels had been restructured. At first thought, his company should be eliminated from consideration. Like any new CEO, he would ensure that those around him were loyalists. The event was too structured and smooth to be brought about by nut jobs from the outside. Somebody would have to check the fence for a breach.

Or it could have been one of their own collection of blasters. Perhaps he had chosen to bury himself in the rubble. A head count would have to be made. At least he or she had enough consideration to do it when 1000 people weren't working at once. Evidently, world-wide coverage was not to their liking. Why not? Why didn't they want to bring Copper Mining, Inc. to its knees with mass murder charges against them?

Who stood to gain the most from their down time and where did the company go from here? The answer to the first blared noisily: Every copper company would gain. As for the second, hard corporate decisions would have to be made regarding the physical direction of their operations. The government would get involved. The next weeks promised to be long.

The community center had been built by the mining company when it constructed the entire township. At 8:00 am, the center played host to more than a score of people including Cargill, Sheriff Jennings, Scott, Harwood, Alday, a half-dozen other men with blasting skills, as many geologists they could round up on short notice, Ally and Cheryl, and a few miscellaneous miners who had heard about the meeting. The two women had already volunteered to assist in making phone calls to tally the head count. If anybody wasn't home last night, where were they?

A low murmur of voices filled the empty

room, each telling their side of how they had been awakened and what thoughts had first crossed their minds. No person had slept since the blast.

The room held 650 when all the folding chairs were carted in hooked together in rows. This morning, less than thirty chairs faced the front with Cargill standing behind the podium. No speaker system was in play. Cargill could be heard easily by using a slightly raised voice. A screen behind him had been pulled down, connected to a video recorder on the podium. He and a very tired three man work crew had spent the last two hours setting up the presentation.

Cargill had obtained and reviewed the recordings from the security cameras surrounding the perimeter of the fenced acres enclosing the mining activity. In their years of operation, aside from the entrance of a stray skunk or coyote that may have crawled beneath the barrier, no previous breach by humans had been recorded, or, if it had occurred, not reported. Security was only present during shift work. Here, only a single shift was in operation at the time. Thus, during the shift, security was present in the lunch room, shower room, and parking lot. The latter practice was employed around the world to check lunch pails in the event a miner decided to take home a stick of dynamite or a solid piece of valuable ore. The rest of the time, no security walked the perimeter, either inside or outside the grounds, and nobody looked at monitor screens inside an office for evidence of an incursion that would never occur.

Cargill played one recording on-screen to reveal a black late model Toyota 4-Runner slowly driving up to the south gate entrance of the work area at 1:15 am. Two relatively small hooded men wearing black clothing, hoodies, and ski masks, emerged. Each reached behind him to pull a large backpack from the vehicle. Both wore black gloves. No interior light of the vehicle went on when the doors opened. The pair slowly closed the doors to the car and walked to the chain link at the side of the gate. Pulling wire cutters from the pack, one man cut the 8' high fence enough to slide the pack through and enter afterward. The second man followed, perhaps thinking that if the lock on the fence were cut, an alarm would be set off. They would be correct in that thought.

The men walked effortlessly up the drive to the top level to enter the mouth of the cavern. One hour and 43 minutes later, at 2:58 am, the pair emerged together without their backpacks, slid through the fence, and drove away. A license plate number was clearly observable, a curious occurrence for a clandestine operation.

The simultaneous explosions occurred five minutes after their departure. Either one or both returned home or were on their way out of town when the alarms sounded.

A second recording from a different camera showed the actual explosion. Horizontal shafts above ground and below ground blew simultaneously, with dust billowing up the vertical shaft that led to tunnels as far down as 1500' in depth and from the above ground horizontal levels, as though they were part of a creature of many lungs, exhaling dark contents at once, like cartoons depicting coal miners of old who had contracted black lung disease. Then the mountain immediately above the mining operation collapsed to drop hundreds of feet, filling the voids created by man. The view became obscured when the great cloud measuring a half-mile in height and breadth filled the screen. Doubtless, watchers of satellite images might have thought a volcano had erupted in the middle of the Arizona desert.

The video didn't show the animals. Those that hadn't been buried ran or flew by the thousands in all direction. Coyotes, squirrels, field mice, Saguaro wren, woodpeckers, jays, quail, owls, vultures to feed on the dead, another dozen bird taxa, bats and insects, lizards, horned toads, Gila monsters—the town might soon be overrun. The audience gasped and stared wordlessly, in awe at the magnitude of what had just occurred and might still occur.

Jennings stepped to the side and made calls to Tucson International Airport and Sky Harbor in Phoenix, and to the bus stations. This hour of the morning one or both of these men should stand out like a sore thumb. He also alerted other law enforcement noting the approximate height and weight of the men, a description of the vehicle and the license plate number. Finding them would be a longshot. The men might have had one or two other cars waiting, or got picked up by a third party, probably anticipating, in all likelihood, that commercial carriers would be alerted.

The services of the two women would still be needed to find out if somebody's husband had found a different occupation during the early morning hours.

Harwood doubted the criminals had any idea of the magnitude of what they had done. You might sit around and plan to blow up mine drifts and tunnels, but you don't have conversations about the realms of local ecology and scenic wonders, or the removal of skylines. Once this unexpected side event hit the news, their employers could be sweating bullets, perhaps even making plans for a quick escape to a secret location where they could hide for the rest of their lives.

Alday said, "I don't get it. We set the cage at the top with the power off, like we always do after the last man has left. How did they get to the lower levels, and, after their handiwork, how did they get back to the upper level to get out?"

"Can't check the position of the lift now. It's

gone along with the rest of it," Cargill frowned.

"I can think of a couple of ways," offered Harwood. "They'd have to be skilled at rappelling down open raises and going down the central shaft below the cage. They'd set their charges to go off by radio control, not chance using a delay-timer without knowing exactly how long they'd be down there. They probably brought pounds of Semtex in their backpacks, which they tied into the exiting cases of dynamite or used separately. The explosive is stable enough to haul around like that. That's what I'd do if I were small enough. Personally, I'd be lucky to climb up 10 feet of rope."

"Which means they had lengths of rope with hooks attached, and were small enough, like we saw in the video," threw in Alday.

"It's a possibility," Cargill admitted, shaking his head. "This is very well coordinated and very well planned.

Jennings put down his phone to report, "We found the vehicle on a side pull-out on the road to 77. We're towing it in for prints. The plate was stolen from another vehicle. Apparently the owner lives in Oracle and reported his car stolen when he got up his morning. It's the same Toyota 4-Runner. Oracle police are at his home now."

Knowing the answer, Harwood had to ask "Where do we go from here, Bob?"

Cargill gave his signature cough before replying, "I want you all to go home. If you haven't eaten yet, then do so. I'll meet you back here in exactly one hour. Plan to spend the rest of the day here. We'll have sub sandwiches delivered."

He lifted the screen to reveal a white board behind it with colored markers in a tray. At the top of the board he began to write the headings: WHO, WHY, HOW.

The women were the first out the door to tend to their own tasks.

2

Three days passed. Animal and pest control personnel were called in from Tucson at descend upon the beleaguered community. Local facilities couldn't come close to dealing with the aftermath of the explosive number of creatures that invaded the small township, both outdoors and indoors. In addition, a myriad of mining experts and various authorities took refuge in Tucson to be bused to San Manuel due to the lack of housing and eating facilities in the nearby communities. At least they were doing land office business. Hot dog and hamburger stands sprung up like weeds after a hard rain. News satellite dishes flowered like large gray antennae probing the skies for signs of alien life.

The community center remained active. Fifty-three men and five women sat in groups, discussing geology, film footages, logistics, mining operations, economics, and who had inside information about whom. The video tape of the attackers played on a loop, the white board filled with as many details as experts could discern, or even hypothesize.

Not sitting around in the groups were members of the FBI and National Terrorism Task Force. These men and women took center stage for their occasional presentations.

Heights of the men were fairly accurate, guessed to be at 5'4" for one and 5'6" for the second, based on their relative size next to the vehicle's top. Weights were approximate, tending toward the leaner side, based on agility and strength factors. They were both white in skin color, based on the reflective nature of skin around the eyes beneath their ski masks. For the men to survive their feats of athleticism, the masks would have to be removed for breathing purposes during their operation. No help there. Neither of them appeared to engage the other in speech. The men were likely fed information by somebody inside the mining operation who has intimate knowledge of the status of raises and lack of security. Neither had a limp or outstanding personal feature that could be discerned except they both were somewhat hunched when returning to the car, suggesting upper body fatigue. Both were robotic in nature, obviously having rehearsed the in-fill and ex-fill, including their actions within the mines.

Some personnel reviewed photographs of the mining area prior to the explosion, others walked the grounds. A light rainfall the night before managed to reduce the amount of airborne dust with the side effect of liberating countless insects from unspecified locations related to the former low mountain, now reduced to a tall hillock. If the press could be considered noisome insects, they too were in abundance, buzzing, reporting, photographing, recording, interviewing, spinning tales and theories, conjecturing, rumoring, reproducing, knowing as little of the real truth as anybody in attendance. TV Prime time for talking heads.

Cargill released Harwood, Alday, and other foremen from bondage, charging them with the mission of opening up other levels that had been discontinued in lieu of the newer portions occupying their time. By the end of the week, the crew examined several levels to clear them for further traditional mining procedures. This was to the great relief of the miners, who found a solid week of home life too demanding for their skill level.

This part went smoothly, until the FBI called in Harwood for questioning.

The digital clock on the small living room stereo read 7:48 pm. "You were gone an awfully long time, honey. What did they want with you," Ally inquired, concern clouding her face.

"I'm what they call a person of interest in this case." Draco spat. He was so pissed off he couldn't see straight. He had been interrogated by agents from three kinds of hell; not interviewed as to what he thought might have happened, but approached as a criminal who could face a lifetime in prison. This was a new experience for him. An attack on his personal integrity was uncalled for, whatever the guise.

"You mean they suspect you?" Ally displayed honest confusion.

"I'm one of the few skilled enough to play all the half-dozen types of blasting roles. Why? Because I'm the one who has the most certificates from blasting schools. I asked them if I look like I'm 5'4" tall like the bad guys. Scott got beat up, too. Josh is another story. He called them enough names to start a pornographic dictionary. He's lucky he didn't get arrested. At least he didn't threaten them. They're looking at somebody who fed somebody else inside information. I wanted to tell them to go fuck themselves, but I didn't have an alternate explanation at the time.

"Look, whenever an extra hand is needed for blasting, either Scott or I normally fill in. Josh is under me and also knows pretty much what I know. I can visit any level I have to reach in order to perform my job. They're also looking at present and past employees. Normal investigation. It's a lot of work. Don't accuse me, that's all."

Having a hard time trying to appear emotionless, Harwood flopped down on the sofa to remove his boots. He explained, "Personally, I think somebody inside might be feeding our present status to somebody on the outside. Cargill and I can provide a list of people who know our overall status, including the various foremen.

Ally sat next to him and placed a hand on his leg. "Draco, sweetheart, there's no way anybody can find a link between you and the terrorists. Don't worry about yourself," she told him in reassurance, as much for herself as for him.

Harwood offered, "Oh, I'm not worried about anything happening to myself. I'm worried about the others. In fact, I'm starting to get some ideas along those lines."

"Which are?"

"For one thing, it doesn't have to be an inside job. Hell, anybody can see what we're doing by reading. I mean, you're not running the largest copper mining operation in the world without making the print news."

He grabbed a stack of Mining News issues on the end table next to him. Ally sat up straight to see what he was up to. He paged through the latest issue to read a report on the progress of mining operations in select areas around the world. Like a stone skipping on water, small sections dealt with everything from major outputs of virtually all ores major and minor.

Harwood poked his finger into the air in front of him, reflecting, "They didn't need the raises to be empty. They're flexible and take what they get. They could have descended down the main shaft, too, like we talked about at the start.

"How many thousands of people run marathons each year around the world?" he asked rhetorically. "Well, these guys trained for their own type of marathon, one that required them to be fleet of foot, have endurance, roping, climbing and descending abilities; I mean, they traversed miles of tunnels and drifts in a short period of time.

"I'm also thinking they didn't need to blow every single level. Most of the dynamite is in the production level drifts, where the real ore removal occurs. It's only occasionally that the raises have to be cleared from the ceilings of the haulage levels. If every other level collapses, it should do the trick. But what do I know? I've never done it, or heard of anyone doing it."

"Did you tell all that to the Feds?" Ally inquired.

"Like I said, 'no', I just thought of it. They tried to keep me off balance the whole time so I couldn't think straight. Besides, when I get pissed off, I don't give a shit about a whole lot."

Ally expressed great concern by asking, "What if it's like the movies where they come to our house. They might take my laptop. Worse, they might find all the gold you found. Is it still in the closet?"

Harwood replied, "No. Josh and I didn't need

some housebreaker coming in to steal it so we took our stashes out."

"What did you do, hide it in an abandoned mine somewhere?" She wondered what a person does do with pounds of pure gold they want to hide. She couldn't think of a thing that made sense.

"No and yes. I got to talking to one of the geologists who I already knew when we were looking at the core samples. We had a pleasant chat about how he makes small ingots of various elements to give away, or to make a profit from. He's got a setup at home out in the country where he melts down just about anything you can think of and turns metal into ingots of different sizes. He can even make you a miniature horse made of pure nickel or copper. I asked him if he does gold. The guy looks at me slyly and nods real slow, so I tell him that if he wants to make some real money, maybe we can make a deal.

"Afterward, I brought over some nuggets. We weighed them precisely and a few days later he gives them back to me in the form of these little golden ingots. He weighs them again in front of me and it's almost the same. There's always going to be a little loss from volatilization and other factors. I pay him our agreed percentage and we're off and running.

"Next time I show him a couple of the bigger rocks and thought he was going to pass out. After we settled up on those, Josh brought him his stuff. Finally, we showed him the granddaddy. I told him sit down before I rolled it out of the bag. Neither of us cared if he had a heart attack, we just didn't want to have to give him mouth-to-mouth to bring him around."

Ally laughed long and hard. Finally, she caught her breath and asked, "How did you deal with all the dust mixed into a lot of it?" She was totally fascinated by the tale, a fitting tag to the original discovery.

"Simple acid wash removed the carbonates and sulfates, which is what most of the dust is anyway," Harwood replied. "The geologist took an extended leave of absence from work to spend full time on our project. He told Copper Coring he had family issues. He's working on the big boy now.

Josh and I took half the pile of small ingots and opened a few safe deposit boxes at the bank. The other half we buried in metal boxes in an abandoned 100 year-old mine near Mammoth. Only scorpions and rattlesnakes visit the place. It's probably best to go there in the winter when both critters aren't looking to protect their property."

Ally had no more questions for this man who seemed to be one step ahead of her, not on everything, but enough to keep her endlessly impressed. She gently took the Mining News issues out of his hand and began leafing through the issues, while Harwood returned to his beer.

A minute later, she reported, "You know, honey, something you said got me thinking. These guys had to train for the marathon. Right?"

"Without question."

"That's the easy part. There are endless mines around the world where you can practice your gymnastics for the big event. However . . . "

Harwood exclaimed, "However, you don't know if the levels will collapse without experimenting."

"Exactomundo," Ally declared, as though he were a class student correctly answering the pop question of the day..

He grabbed another stack of the newsletters and both began to scour them looking for the same thing. "We need to go back maybe five years," he thought out loud.

"I see the News is published out of Cleveland, Ohio. We can contact them for back issues, or, how about, if we go to the San Manuel Times office. They might have archives. Better yet," she exclaimed, "Let's start on line and see what we can find."

Ally got to her feet and walked over to the computer desk. She Googled: Mine Explosions. A variety of topics popped up including: Methane in Coal Mines, Coal Mine Safety Procedures, Advances in Gas Measurements in Mines, Technology of Gas Detection Devices for use in Mines, World's Biggest Coal Mine Disasters, Mine Blasts, and other non-relevant information.

Reflecting on the content, she said, "You have to put in exactly what you want." She Googled: Tunnel Collapses in Mines. This time she got articles on removal of gas and water pockets, earth subsidence, improper shoring techniques, and endless articles relating to worker training.

Ally stood up and waved her hands about. "If you want quality sunglasses, you don't go to a drug store, you go to store that specializes in sunglasses. Let's go." She grabbed her purse and marched out the door with Harwood following like a dog on a lease trailing its master.

She drove them to the headquarters of Copper Coring, Inc., only to find the office closed and a posted note explaining that all the geologists were out in the field.

Unperturbed, she marched to the newspaper office, two buildings over.

The vacant small front office smelled of ink. Walking through an open doorway leading to the rear, a quiet printing press stood in clear view. The press measured some four feet in width by eight feet in length. Two employees worked at computers who sent their stories to the editor, who had his own office clearly in view. He would edit the stories and format them to fit into the paper. It published on Mondays, Wednesdays, and Fridays. A separate room contained hard copies of back issues. One window-mounted exhaust fan made noise, a turbine fan set in the ceiling remained silent in its rotation.

A man seated behind a computer disk littered with paper saw the couple enter and recognized Ally. One of his reporters had written a story about the do-it-all woman who befriended everyone, to Ally's great embarrassment.

The editor stood. A short, overweight man wearing loose fitting jeans and a large western press-button long-sleeve shirt, he had lost all his hair years before. President of the local Kiwanis Club, he maintained a jovial attitude toward everyone he met, especially those who appreciated his approach to life in general, a good man to know when you're feeling down.

"Yes, Mrs. Harwood, is it?"

"Ally will be fine," she corrected, painfully reminded of her condition. She introduced Harwood as her fiancée and introduced to Harwood the editor by the name of Clarence Darrow.

"No relation," he said, for the thousandth time, in reference to the early 20th Century Chicago politician, who made headlines covering famous cases, such as the Scopes Monkey Trial.

Harwood had never heard of him. "Some people are what their names are," Darrow would say on occasion. "I might have led a different life with the name of John Paul Jones or Wyatt Earp. Terrible thing, what happened," Darrow shook his head in sorrow.

"We're trying to look into why it happened, Clarence," Ally said. "Do you carry old copies of Mining News, by any chance?"

"Heavens, yes," Darrow proclaimed. "I'm the one who submits local mining news to them. Have done so thirty years. I've got every issue going back to when the newsletter began publishing nearly half-a-century ago. I worked the mining desk out of Tucson back then."

"Sir, would you mind terribly if we looked through some back issues?" Harwood requested.

"Not at all," Darrow replied, jovially. Dwarfed by Harwood's size, he was accustomed to being around big miners. He led them to the archives room where file cabinets lined the walls. In the center of the room, two chairs were pulled beneath a table. Darrow pointed out the stacks of Mining News piled on the floor, with the latest issue on top. "They're in order, so if you don't mind, please put them back in place when you're finished," he requested.

Harwood thanked Darrow profusely and told him, "Clarence, we might need your help, if we find something we have questions about."

"Draco, I'm at your behest," chirped Darrow, obviously pleased to have the young couple peruse the stacks in the interest of finding their own brand of treasure. He turned to leave them to their own devices.

Ally pulled out her cell phone in lieu of using a copy machine. She reached into her purse to pull out a notepad while Harwood grabbed three years-worth of issues. The couple went to work.

Several articles drew their attention, which

had to be evaluated for misinformation. One tried to blame a coal mine explosion in Botswana on an earthquake, another related to a mine collapse due to faulty geological data where the amount of soft earth exceeded the amount of granite, another due to poor shoring, which may have been the source of the Google hit Ally had found.

Time passed quickly. At last Ally mumbled, "Did you ever hear of EuroCo?"

"No."

"About two years ago. It says authorities believe an explosion brought down four levels thanks to improperly trained men who set off their charge near other crates of dynamite. This occurred in Austria. The EuroCo bunch says they think the men had been drinking and had been warned about it. Interestingly, they were the only ones to die."

Ally photographed the article, then using her phone, she began researching the name EuroCo. In a moment she reported, "EuroCo is a newly founded mining company based in Germany. The parent company is General Mines, which is on the New York Stock Exchange. The stock symbol is GMG, which appears to be growing in value very nicely."

"So?"

"So nothing. Let's keep looking. We're done with this stack. Let's go back another couple of years."

Harwood reflected on his own experiences. He and Alday had blown a wall after everyone had left. Were they to make some dumb mistake, they could have been killed. Maybe that's what happened with the EuroCo situation on a grander scale. Mistakes are a human condition brought about by wrong thinking, He wondered if a bird flying into a window might think it made a mistake. Something else to ponder.

Which gave him further pause. It still didn't seem right. Original dynamite used enclosed gun powder plugged with a tube of wood, set off with a fuse running down the center of the wood. New stuff, invented in in 1867 by the Swede, Alfred Nobel, used nitroglycerin and diatomaceous earth, or even sawdust, to provide it with much more stability, making it pliable enough to insert it into the tubes.

Old dynamite sticks containing nitro did tend to sweat or leach out the explosive at the ends of the stick to crystallize, or pool. This caused them to become ighly unstable again, sensitive to vibration, even touch. Not modern day stuff, guaranteed fresh.

The bad guys knew a lot more than the basics. They probably set off boxes of sticks already stored for the next day's use by using a remote signal set on a stick they capped, or set off with a small amount of plastic explosive. Stable goes to unstable in an instant. Major league explosion in confined spaces, multiplied several-fold, all going off simultaneously, like uranium/titanium bullets going off inside a loaded tank. The walls come tumbling down. If it happened there, it could have happened here.

As history would have it, some 75 years later, several men would receive a prize named after Nobel for inventing the atomic bomb.

By the time the couple finished scanning each issue, no big leads emerged. At least a hundred multi-level mines were in operation around the world, many of them working three shifts, 24/7. Too many people. No chance to do dirty work.

"Want to go back further?" Ally asked.

"Nah, I'm done." Harwood stretched, stacking the issues, making a diligent effort to keep them in order, returning them to their previous location.

Leaving the room, Darrow waved at them and called out, cheerily, "Find anything interesting?"

"Sorry, no, Clarence. Only this EuroCo disaster a couple of years ago. Nothing there," Harwood returned.

Darrow stood. Leaving his office, he walked over to them and chuckled, "Thanks for reading the story. I wrote it like I did a lot of the others. The title to the story should be 'he said she said'." He was one of those people who chuckled at almost every sentence they spoke, like a single hearty laugh spread out over a conversation.

Desperately trying to catch a fish using bad bait, Ally said, "This EuroCo is a subsidiary of General Mines, from what I could find out. Who are they?"

Darrow agreed. "Right. And General Mines is owned by South African Mining, or the stock designation SafMG. Like General Mines, or GMG, the G at the end stands for Groebels. They own both of them. I thought you knew."

3

The couple sat in silence on the three minute drive to their home. Pulling into the driveway, Harwood suggested, "No doubt your parents are aware of the situation here. Maybe you should give them an update."

Ally said, "I spoke with mom a couple of days ago. I've been playing phone tag with my dad ever since the explosion. It's his turn."

Psychic precognitive intuition notwithstanding, Ally's phone rang. Her father's name came up. Following Harwood into the house, Ally held the phone in small talk, after which she caught her father up to date.

Ten minutes later she handed the phone to Harwood who flopped onto the sofa who spoke in technical man-talk miner jargon, explaining what he thought might be a winding trail leading back to a certain mining company they all had concerns about. James promised to see what he could find out.

Next, Harwood called Alday and Ally called

Cheryl. A meeting of the minds required serious dinner plans.

"Are you sure you can afford it? We can loan you the money," Cheryl offered, after Harwood ordered drinks, appetizers and steak all around.

"If I run low, I'll borrow it from Ally, no worries," Harwood quipped.

"Don't hold your breath," Ally grunted.

"Isn't love wonderful?" Alday inserted. "Okay, out with it, big buddy," he prompted.

After hearing the tale, Alday offered, "Maybe someone is so loyal to Al-Yamani they might take it upon themselves to slow down the competition, because I can't believe someone as smart as he is would stoop so low."

"Maybe the presence of Al-Yamani doesn't matter. Maybe somebody is part of the company, a person who has his own agenda," Harwood hypothesized.

Three evenings later the landline rang. Only a handful of people knew the number. Harwood picked up to find Brooks on the other end. "I spoke with Khaled, sorry, Al-Yamani. He heard about what happened like everybody else. He sends his condolences for your loss. He said to tell you he hopes to meet you and yours someday.

"He already anticipated our contacting him and he's got several new hires at corporate there in Germany. Those, and new hires in other countries are being questioned. It's a work in progress. He doesn't think any of them are the problem because they get screened quite thoroughly, but he'll do his best to put out feelers of his own around the mining world to see if any rumors are floating around. He does find it curious you think the EuroCo incident might be linked to yours, but he agrees it may have served as a trial run. He's on it and will let us know what he finds out."

"Thanks, Mate. Tell Khaled we really appreciate his assistance. If we can return a favor someday, all he needs to do is to call."

"Will do. Thanks for watching out for my daughter," Brooks offered.

"It's more like the other way around. She's too sharp for me. She's a work in progress too. I'm sure she'll say the same about me. Ciao."

The authorities, the press, and most of the critters had departed San Manuel, leaving the populace on their own to regroup. Guards were posted on roadways leading to the old mining operation. It still had a lot of life left in her. There existed enough equipment for hundreds of workers to return to their love, but equipment such as rails, ore cars, double jacks, air compressors, small pumps, and conveyer belts had to be ordered. In the meantime, the men would have to sweat in the old mines. There was no easy out. At least lunch rooms and hot showers were available within the tunnels. They were family.

Those miners who had worked in third world countries felt as though they had returned to the old days, without the conditions of slave labor and the hard whip of management domination to accompany poor wages. Here, the management did its best. They had a lot of ground to make up.

Bob Cargill asked Ally, Scott, and union representatives to hold weekly meetings in the community center to report on status of equipment arrival and to hear complaints. One newer recruit asked whether the collapsed mountain could still be mined. Cargill told him it couldn't be mined as such, because the ore body had been randomized in the dirt, therefore, the percentage yield would be minimal, plus the earth would likely be too to be workable. However, some recoveries of materials were possible through blading.

The meeting did not promise to offer Harwood any gain in knowledge, so he opted instead to make his regular run to the company market for their weekly food supply. Situated on the main street, the medium-size store carried a wide selection of fresh goods and non-food items, including a small clothing area. Typically, an 18-wheeler stood off-loading at a side entrance.

This evening a good twenty people shopped the store. Pushing his cart toward the checkout section, Harwood came up fourth in line, standing behind a man he recognized. The man carried a large bottle of Maker's Mark Bourbon Whiskey in one hand. He still wore the large knife. He was left handed. Turning to see Harwood, his eyes lit in recognition. "Say, you're the asshole who cut my tires," he declared. "Do you know how long it took us to get home?"

All eyes turned in their direction. The cashier rolled her eyes as if to say, "Here we go."

"No, how long did it take you? Oh, I'm sure you bought some new tires. They must have cost a lot," Harwood returned, genuinely interested in finding out.

"I should have cut you when I had the chance," came the quiet reply.

Harwood believed the man would have drawn the knife if he hadn't been holding the bottle, based on the look of fury in his eyes. "You didn't answer my question, which was your question to me. How long did it take you to get home?" Harwood asked, as innocently as a child asking the price of a candy bar.

"Outside," the man snarled, under his breath.

"Okay, let me put my groceries in the car, first," Harwood requested, calmly, as though he were helping a senior citizen walk across the street.

Keeping a wary eye on the man, who had checked out and waited for him, Harwood pushed his cart to the car. Taking his time, he casually unloaded his bags in the trunk and slowly returned the cart to its proper place at the front of the store, while the man still stood holding his bottle, watching.

Harwood dismissed the thought of simply driving home. He didn't need the guy to find out where he lived. He also didn't need a confrontation in the parking lot. Cars came and went and a security camera might be in play. This was a private matter. No witnesses required.

He returned to the car and motioned for the man to follow him. The man drove the same Jeep Cherokee 4 x 4 he had taken to the stream. This time, four new tires adorned the vehicle along with a new spare on the back. Not cheap.

Within thirty seconds, Harwood pulled into an unlit side street where several businesses stood in the darkness, their lights out for the night. He stopped the car and stepped out. The man parked behind him, got out, and approached Harwood to within a couple of feet, confronting him, almost in his face, backlit by the lights surrounding the mining area and the moon. Harwood watched him closely to see him slide the knife from its sheath with his left hand as he approached, holding it backwards hilt down, blade up behind the wrist, preparing to make a slashing motion followed by a back thrust, a move borne of practice.

The two rugged men stood of equal height, now face-to-face, Harwood much broader at the shoulder. He spoke first, "You jerk-offs were dummies. You can't fix stupid. Why did you have to pull a knife on me because you coveted sand and gravel in a stream? You really are a dumb son of a bitch. To top it all off, you bastards fell for the trick with the gold. You can't make it up." Harwood began to laugh.

The man appeared perplexed at Harwood's conversational tone. Before his adversary could make a move and playing the timing, Harwood raised his left hand slowly. When the man's eyes went to his right to follow the hand, Harwood grasped the man's left hand holding the knife with his right. He squeezed hard. The knife fell to the ground. The man yelped. Harwood applied hard pressure, crushing the hand, feeling bones break, then twisted his own wrist to twist his opponent's wrist back, still squeezing to break more bones. He tripped the man to the ground, picked up the knife, stuck it into all four tires of the Jeep, finished with the spare, opened the front door, and took the bag containing the bottle of whiskey from the front seat. Keeping the knife, in the other hand he closed the car door with his hip, preparing to return to his own car only a few steps away when he caught a flash of movement in the dark.

The man had gotten to his feet and ran at full charge, left hand dangling. Harwood's reflexes were instant and automatic. The player on the opposing team carrying the ball had nobody to lateral to. He needed to be tackled.

Hundreds of hours of training took over. With no space to maneuver and both hands occupied, he bent over double, firmed his stance, exhaled, and head-butted the runner in the solar plexus. At that, he stepped away from the car to let the man fall with his face hitting the side of his car, grasping his midsection, vomiting at the same time. Harwood finished by affair by reminding the downed opponent, "You can't fix stupid."

Receiving no penalty for a flagrant foul, the miner retained his new toys and with groceries in the car, left for home. This time, he felt no concern about being followed.

Ally returned from the meeting not long after Harwood had put away his purchases. When she walked in, he inquired, a little too casually, "Hi, babe. How'd the meeting go?"

Sensing something was up, she answered slyly, "Oh, fine. Bob told me to tell everyone that the misters will be arriving in a couple of days. Everyone will be looking forward to cooling off. He also wants to divert me over to working the collapsed area. He thinks we might be able to recover some of the ore cars and rails from the above-ground shafts."

Looking in the refrigerator and freezer for a snack, she said, "I see you went shopping." She pulled out a jar of peanut butter and tore off a stalk of celery. She looked at the side table next to the stove and called, "How did this expensive bottle of whiskey get here?" She always practiced frugality, despite their hidden riches. "One way to save money is to not buy what you don't need," she would lecture.

"Got it on sale," Harwood replied.

"I'll bet. How much?" she asked.

"Free," he grinned, smiling too sweetly.

Ally knew this man. You can't fool an old warhorse like me, she thought and walked over to the armchair where he sat. "Let me see your hands." She took both of them in hers for a close examination. Seeing no knuckle bruises or cuts, she leaned over to kiss him on the cheek, and said, "I don't want to know. "

4

The landline rang. The Caller ID read BROOKS. Harwood said, "It's your dad." He placed the phone on speaker. Wiping her hands on a dish towel, Ally came over to the computer/ phone table.

Harwood picked up. "James, good evening, at least for us it's evening."

"Draco, I have some news for you. Have a seat. Ally will want to hear this," Brooks began.

Harwood offered the chair to Ally, who took it. He stood. "We're listening."

"We, I should say, they, caught the two guys. Khaled looked into this EuroCo mine collapse. All these top level execs travel a lot. They don't really pay much attention to what the other guy is doing, so he started digging. It turns out old man Ernst Nordstrom hired his son-in-law to be his director of marketing. He goes by the last name of Jefferson, Ernst's son in law who's an American living in Germany. That was before the Stewards recently came on board—sorry, you don't know them.

"Jefferson was in Austria the same time the explosion and collapse occurred. Right after that Ernst found another job for Jefferson and got Steward hired to cover his tracks. Khaled confronted Jefferson on a suspicion. He told Jefferson he had direct evidence the guy was involved in the Austrian disaster, in addition to what happened to you, even though there wasn't any actual link, to see how he would react.

He made sure Jefferson understood his situation. After the Germans and Austrians had a go at him, the Americans would want their turn. If he confessed, Khaled would do his best to keep the jail sentence down to two lifetimes in prison instead of five lifetimes.

"In short, the son-in-law got scared enough to partially confess. He said he did contact someone to make arrangements for both mine explosions at the behest of Ernst Nordstrom. Franky, right now, Jefferson could deny everything as soon as he lawyers up. Khaled had nothing solid."

Harwood shook his head. He looked down at Ally, who shrugged. She didn't get it either. "James, it's illogical. EuroCo is owned by Groebels. Why would Ernst Nordstrom want to blow up his own company's investment?"

Brooks replied, "For the bigger picture."

"Which is?"

"The Austrian venture was small potatoes. It

served nicely for a practice run before the two guys blew up your operation in Arizona. With a diminished supply of copper on the market, their share value would increase because copper would be worth more. Multiplier effect would bring in tens of millions from a couple of simple acts."

Harwood scratched his never ending stubble and said, "It can't make too much of a difference, can it? I mean, between Austria and us causing the price to rise? There are ups and downs in the copper industry all the time for a dozen reasons in countries too numerous to count."

James went on, "Not as it stands at the present time. But apparently there's a second team out there whom Jefferson's contact also hired. They're also athletic and they're explosives experts. Once the biggest copper mine in the world shuts down, one that's not controlled by Groebels, the price of copper shoots up. I work for them, so I'm all right. You and Josh don't. You need to watch your asses, because both of you are sitting on a powder keg and the fuse is burning. For them, it's killing three birds with one stone."

Harwood thanked James and hung up. Getting ready to make another call, he saw Ally had already punched in a single number to speed dial Cheryl. Time for another meeting.

Several mornings later Harwood climbed

into Alday's car for a ride to work. Buckling his seat belt he said, "Bob's making everybody the same offer. Work hard labor until new equipment comes in while getting paid, or not work at all."

"I didn't know there was anything other than hard work, "Alday grunted, driving down the hill toward the mine.

"Ally will agree. It took her and two other drivers three 12-hour days just to clear the road leading to the site. She said they're running into a lot of mud where ground water seeped up."

"Good overtime pay," Alday contributed.

"Yeah, we can use it."

Alday laughed. "Did James say anything about Al-Yamani? Did he hang this Jefferson by the privates or what?"

Harwood laughed in turn. "James said he sent Jefferson to Unimak Island to assist their 'marketing department', which is the equivalent of a population explosion for them.

"This whole affair will make world news when it breaks and he doesn't want to scare away the latest couple of bad guys. He wants them caught."

Alday agreed. "Which leads to only one option. Leave a gap in our night security."

Harwood completed the thought. "Correct, but instead of them creating a distraction to pull us away, we'll create our own to see if we can suck them in."

"Given there is a lot of ground to cover and given there really is an imminent attack, maybe we can overfly some of these hills with a drone. Maybe we can spot an encampment where they set up to observe us," Alday suggested.

"Great idea. Do you know anybody who knows how to operate one?" Harwood inquired. "I don't think I've ever seen one in person."

"Sure. David has one. I bought it for him on his last birthday. But we're going to need something bigger than the toy he has. How about if we spend company money and take him to Tucson where we can buy something with real capabilities. I hear they even have drone flying clubs there. He can show us how to fly it, or let him have some fun on a big scary job working with us. He'd love it."

The following afternoon, David, his father, and Harwood unboxed the drone on a well-maintained lawn on one of the baseball fields the company had constructed. The trio had purchased a Ruko F11 quadcopter. The machine possessed a camera transmission range of nearly two miles with zoom capabilities, video stabilization technology, level 6 wind resistance, and nearly an hour of flying time, along with a spare battery. They weren't concerned with its speed or whether or not it could drop bombs. Both batteries had been fully charged and by the time they reached San Manuel, David had memorized the instruction booklet.

Teaching the two adults how to operate the drone, David used the words "yes, sir" and "no sir." None of this "bro" or "right on" verbiage. His mother would definitely take a hand to him if she heard those words. Perhaps she already had.

"What does the book say about this thing's altitude, David?" his father asked.

"It's not so much about altitude as it is about battery life," the boy told him. "We bought the one with the lighter motor, therefore the weight is less, which means less speed. Not an issue with us. With less weight we get longer battery life. Wet and humid weather makes it harder to fly and adds weight, not an issue with our dry weather today. Also, we need a time-safety cushion. You don't want the thing to die when you're at altitude, or far from home base. Get her home early to be safe. It also says to expect wind to increase with altitude. Trying to fight head winds will shorten your observation time."

The men looked at each other with mouths downturned, impressed. They were in the hands of an expert.

Harwood didn't want to set up near the mine. He assumed it to be under observation. The trio could operate quite well where they were on a cool lawn beneath the shade of a large cottonwood with a cooler of beer, soda, and ample chips to ease their pain and suffering. Cargill had given their venture the green light. He didn't need another disaster.

The men calculated. The drone didn't need to overfly every inch of a mountain chain. Any observers would have to be in line-of-sight of the vertical shaft leading down to the various levels. The entrance would have to be accessed by road, which meant their adversary might or might not drive in. If they themselves were doing it, they wouldn't be at the top of a freaking mountain, but part way up for convenience and speed.

There was only one way up the nearest mountain, which was the road he and Ally had taken when they went over the top to visit the geologists. This road ran up the mountain before the collapsed area. The shaft could be observed from any point from 100' up to the top of the hill some 4000' in elevation. David needed to find an encampment somewhere off the road.

The men weren't concerned about the noise of the drone. It would be drowned out by the three dozers cleaning off mountain debris nearby. Besides, the camera could pick up good-size images from some distance away.

After instructing David on what they wanted him to do, he lifted the quadcopter into the air, raised it to 500 feet, and, fighting wind currents, expertly flew it in the direction of the road. If their hunch was right, a small encampment and vehicle would be found, probably camouflaged.

The three watched the screen, David received instructions to move in closer or farther, while they zoomed on the monitor screen. At times, wind gusts of 20 mph or more caused the images to sway harshly, first in one direction, then another. Gusts were stronger nearer the mountains. Even with the stabilization qualities of the drone, David found it challenging to manage the steering from the remote toggle on the controller. The smaller unit his father had given him for his last birthday would likely have crashed.

Keeping track of the time, Alday requested David to return to home base for a new battery. Everyone had put their foot the water. The time had come to swim. Alday replaced the first battery, putting the first one on the car charger. David went back to work.

Thirty minutes later, they struck gold. With David continuing to fly and watching the monitor at the same time, all three saw what they had been looking for.

About a quarter-mile from the end of the deep copper pit, the road to the other side beckoned. Up 1000 feet and some 100 yards on the near side of the road, the terrain was broken by large boulders interspersed with stands of prickly pear cactus several feet in height. Over the cactus a camouflaged tarp had been stretched to encompass an area large enough to house a vehicle.

"We'll come back later and check it out after dark," Harwood instructed. Pleased with their find, the overexcited boy and two extremely pleased men packed up and went home.

According to Aunt Ally, if anybody planned to look for men at night, the drone should be outfitted with infrared capabilities. Armed with the knowledge the enemy had camped within range, the plan could be put into action.

Nearing midnight, it took an ambitious David some time to get his navigational bearing without the even lighting of the day. Tall overhead night lights from the mining compound cast shadows out to the area he needed to survey. He trusted the infrared sensor his father had purchased would work for them. Happy to stay up this late, David discovered two objects emitting heat from beneath the tarp. Suspicions confirmed.

Late the following afternoon, two miners carried numerous cases of dynamite into a couple of the shafts, ostensibly to be used the following day. During the work, a large utility truck arrived from San Manuel Electric Company. The driver emerged, moving away from the truck into the clear, to explain to the men why the entire grid would have to be shut down during the early morning hours for the purpose of repairs. This meant no lights on at home, either. Nobody should be too inconvenienced at that time. He pulled out his phone while talking, pointing to the broad glaring spotlights. The lights went off for several seconds, flickered again, then went on.

Like a replay of an old movie, Harwood began gesturing at the lights and pointing to the open mine shafts above and behind them. The power company man threw his hands outward to suggest he had no choice. Alday entered the fray. The power company man shook his head vigorously. The miners marched away in anger, turning once to glare at the man, who ignored the angry men and drove away.

At 2:30 am, the outer spotlights lights flickered before going off. No guard was posted, in the hopes any observers wouldn't think a trap might be in the offing.

Only one way existed to enter the spider-like network of tunnels and that was the same place Harwood and Alday waited. They personally wanted to meet an enemy who came to destroy 200 miles of cross-cuts, stopes, raises, production levels, haulage levels, breakrooms, showers, pillards, careers, and anything else man had labored hard to create. The artists were not about to let someone walk in to burn down their art studio.

From 100 yards back in the top production level, the two men entering could be seen back-lit by the moonlight. The miners slid back into the first drift out of sight, watching, waiting. Doubtless, the attackers had their own devices of destruction, but probably considered the extra cases of dynamite brought in that afternoon to be a bonus.

A short time later the intruders reached the first drift where the miners crouched near a wall, one on either side. Tracks ran alongside the raises. Using small flashlights focused ahead of them, the intruders failed to notice the figures clad in black with black soot covering their faces. One intruder pointed the light farther ahead toward the boxes and said, "There they are."

Suddenly, a 1,000,000 candle-power spotlight came on directly in front of the intruders. Both men shielded their eyes instantly, but the leading man still took a couple of steps forward. He stepped onto the partially sawed through planks covering the raise to serve as a walkway and fell through. He grasped outward to save himself, but the other half-sawed through planks gave way as well. He yelled as he fell through the empty hole in the ground into an ore car far below. The muffled thud of impact echoed upward.

The watching miners were not concerned about an explosion. Dynamite is stable on impact, as is plastic explosives. The second man would be needed for questioning.

Alday ordered, "Get on the ground." Had they possessed any skill at operating David's toy drone inside the near pitch blackness of the cave, they might have had more entertainment.

Harwood assisted the man by striking him from behind in the kidney with a fist. Alday joined him to tear off his backpack, and, in an instant, the intruder's arms were tied behind his back and a gag put in his mouth in the event others might be following. Alday sat on his back, with the man's face in the dirt.

Harwood opened the pack to find rolls of hundreds of feet of thin, but extremely strong, nylon cord, wires, pounds of plastic explosives, and timing devices.

The miners waited some time to ensure no others would follow. Finally, feeling confident these men acted alone, Harwood called San Manuel Electric and told them to turn on the lights again. Next, he next called Jennings. The sheriff would be upset for about five seconds to be awakened at this early hour. Five seconds later he would be delighted to find out he would be the one to turn in the bad guy.

Hauling the prisoner outside, Alday remained with him while Harwood powered the lift in the re-energized compound, descended to the haulage level and using a hand spotlight, found the drift and ore cars where the broken man had crashed onto. The invader's pack carried over 60' of knotted rope, presumably to descend and ascend through the raise. Six stories is a long way to climb up a rope, knotted or not. Still, the pair needed to carefully rope themselves to and from the level down in order to access the vertical shaft. The dead man had taken the faster route.

Once Harwood saw the rope, their plan became evident. A large number of dynamite sticks would be bundled, along with a large amount of plastic explosive in the absence of dynamite. A single member of the cluster would have a blasting cap. The package would be lowered down the shaft to the entrances of various levels with the thin nylon cord. The simultaneous explosion of those, along with the blown levels they were presently in, would not only collapse the vertical shaft, now some 4000' in depth, it would cause enough total damage to severely cripple the company's mining operation for months, if not years. Groebels would be the winner.

Searching the dead man's pockets, Harwood found a small notebook. On the first page were written two addresses: his and Alday's. He surmised the men had weapons in their vehicle, but doubtless, they had instructions to take care of business before pleasure.

He returned to the surface where he showed the notebook to Alday, who didn't take kindly to what he saw. He approached the prisoner, who stood tight lipped, glaring at him with whipcord muscles, defiant, an experienced professional. With the man's hands still tied behind him, Alday rammed a fist in his stomach with the first punch. "We know who hired you. You are one dumb son of a bitch." Straightening him out, Alday repeated the blow.

Harwood took over. "You are one dumb shit. We saw you in the hills. We wanted you to see us bring the cases of dynamite inside. We planned the blackout." At that, he showed the notebook to the prisoner. "You came to hurt our families, didn't you."

The man's eyes widened. Alday propped him up gain, then Harwood slammed his rock hard fist into the man's ribs, first on the left, then on the right, taking care not to send broken bones into the lungs. Howling with pain, the man's knees buckled. Harwood propped him up and Alday slammed him in the groin, leaving his face intact. He needed to talk.

"I don't know, sheriff," Harwood rehearsed his speech for the other two to hear." It must have happened when he fell on the rails on the way back, or maybe when he resisted capture. The man should avoid laughing for several months and only engage in taking shallow breaths to avoid severe pain during his extended recovery period."

When Jennings did receive the prisoner, he completely understood the explanation regarding the terrorist's injuries. "Those things can happen. Mining is a dangerous business," he said, and made the necessary calls to collect the dead body.

Harwood wondered whether this event would be the end of life-long anger issues. On second thought, he concluded that this was not a good time to make an assessment of such magnitude.

The friends were simple people who didn't want to make the news, only to be left alone. Jennings did his best to keep their names out of it by giving credit to alert employees who had caught the man without elaboration.

Like vultures pecking bones clean, the press needed more meat, trying to peck into the marrow. When the rabbit hole finally led to the two miners, Harwood and Alday had disappeared.

In truth, the two were giving statements in Phoenix to the FBI, ATF, and whatever agency wanted to stick their nose into the investigation. Cargill allowed for an extra week off until the dust settled. Unfortunately, the dust stays airborne when a story this big remains close to the ground. Wrapped in a cocoon of their own making, the two found themselves in bondage with the press sucking the juice out their bodies.

Because the men possessed no state secrets or sensitive information, they received permission from federal and local agencies to tell their side of the story. This tended to clear the air with only tailings remaining. Like weakening ripples in smooth water, the farther they spread from the initial rock toss, they resembled a fading Doppler effect defined by the passage of time.

The Anchorage bureau of the FBI sent two men to pick up Jefferson on Unimak Island. This first necessitated a four-hour flight to Cold Bay Harbor on one of the small islands in the chain, flying in a Boeing 727 Turboprop. The special agents luxuriated in their usage of an infinite amount of government cash.

This, however, quickly became neutralized by a ride to Unimak, an expensive ride costing brown bear hunters up to $1800 each way per person. The two agents suffered a very bumpy 2 ½ hour ride to the forlorn island on a much smaller plane in bad weather. Neither the flight from Cold Harbor, nor the cold overnight stay on the island, nor the return flight to Cold Harbor, served as entertainment for the two career agents—a journey they deemed cruel and unusual punishment, a stand-alone story not in need of excessive embellishment.

Finally back in Anchorage, Jefferson, the son-in-law, refused to talk unless represented by a Groebels' attorney. The attorney plea bargained. His client could get out in 10-20 years in a slightly better prison than a super max. This would serve as the German portion of the sentence. Two more countries awaited their turn. Again, he did not know the men who did the field work, however he did identify the contact Ernst Nordstrom had given him, who happened to be the site superintendent before Cargill came on board.

"He was the one who had made all the arrangements. Even the Feds can make a mistake. Imagine that. Apparently, somebody didn't look deep enough into his off-shore accounts to flag him as a suspect," Harwood explained, on the short drive to his wedding. "Both he and Ernst Nordstrom were arrested at the same time with Ernst seated in his wheelchair protesting all the way to the jail."

"Breaks my heart," Cheryl gleefully sang from the back seat.

Harwood's parents expressed their well wishes; unfortunately, flu-like symptoms prevented them from attending the small ceremony held in one of the San Manuel chapels.

Allison's parents couldn't make it either. They were ensconced in the North African country of Morocco, a country reported to produce 75% of the world's phosphates. Al-Yamani had found them a cliff-side villa overlooking the Atlantic Ocean in the capitol city of Rabat. In need of a quality site supervisor he could trust, Al-Yamani appointed James Brooks to the position to head a mega-operation for a new phosphate mine Groebels was opening.

Brooks, in turn, was tasked with finding quality foremen, drivers, and repair personnel he could trust. He tapped the newlyweds, along with Josh Alday, to be part of his team. Within six months all were reunited in villas in proximity to one another.

The Alday boys would have to learn a new language. Even though the brothers would be attending an English speaking private school, it might come in handy to learn standard Arabic.

They already knew how to fight.

Money posed no problem for anyone, especially since Groebels paid their rent, although living with some sense of frugality might be advised. After all, this was Morocco, home of the rich and famous.

Allison might have to take some time off work to ensure the twin girls she carried would be well cared for during her workday. She already had plans for their education.